JACOB'S CLOAK

Arthur G. Nelson

PublishAmerica
Baltimore

First printing

ISBN: 1-59286-487-2
PUBLISHED BY PUBLISHAMERICA BOOK PUBLISHERS
www.publishamerica.com
Baltimore

Printed in the United States of America

~

*Dedicated to my parents who
planted my roots so firmly and to
Connie who tolerated many months
of neglect during the writing.*

~

Introduction

I first met Jacob Svendahl in 1963. It was on a Sunday night and I had Emergency Room duty at Baylor Hospital covering for the regular physician who had a hot date with a SMU sorority beauty. He was a Times Herald sports reporter checking on the injury of a Cowboy football player.

It was early in the evening, too early for the drunks and car wrecks, so we went to the lounge and shared a cup of stale coffee. When we discovered our Scandinavian roots were similar, we became lifelong friends.

Over the ensuing years, we kept in contact; occasional phone calls, Christmas and Birthday cards, and about once a month we shared breakfast at the Waffle Shop near where we lived. We even double dated a time or two before I married and for the last several years we visited by email.

Over the years I came to know him as a lonely man with unresolved grief and a troubled soul who never spoke of his family and kept his feelings strictly to himself. I never tried to pry; I knew if I did, it would ruin a wonderful friendship. Once I invited him to accompany me on a visit to the town of my birth but he declined and I never knew the reason. And when he wrote that he was in a Hospice facility, I visited him often. Being retired with time on my hands I felt it my duty and obligation to comfort him.

On the days that I visited, in spite of his frail condition, I always found him pounding away on his laptop computer. Knowing he was a published author, I assumed he was trying to finish another novel. But when I inquired about the story, he said "You'll know in due course" and I did, but not until I read this manuscript... his manuscript.

JACOB'S CLOAK
J.K. Svendahl
The Reunion

June 1, 1992

It isn't possible I said to myself when the invitation arrived. It can't have been fifty years since I walked across the stage of the Arendal High School, shook Mr. Roberts's hand and received my diploma.

I had ignored all previous reunion invitation without giving it a second thought. But for some reason, this one seemed different. This was number fifty and would probably be the last opportunity to see some of my old classmates, not that I had any particular interest in seeing any of them.

I'm not going, I decided. Why would I want to spend a miserable half-day with a bunch of frumpy old women and bald headed farmers who would probably talk of nothing but their problems? It's been so long I didn't think I would remember a soul, and I doubted any would remember me.

Cousin Esther, my closest friend with whom I had shared so many hopes and dreams would not be there and neither would Cousin Joseph. Perhaps one or two members of the football team that lost the district championship in 1941 would attend. Maybe a few members of the band that marched in the Fourth of July parade and played at half time during football season would be there. If anyone remembered me, they would probably resent my success in breaking away from the drudgery of farming and I had no desire to hear their snide remarks.

I knew there were other reasons for my reluctance, reasons only I could understand. I did not wish to revisit memories of events that had caused me to renounce my religious beliefs and distance myself from the Norwegian community into which I was born. I did not want to go down that road again, it would be too painful. However, after a few sleepless nights, I changed my mind and decided to attend.

So, on the morning of the reunion, I stored away my apprehensions, found the Waco highway and after about an hour, I turned off on the country road that wound its way among the farms until it descended into the familiar valley and crossed the Arendal River. I passed the deserted depot, the stockyard, the Corner Drug Store, the theater, the new Post Office, the new hospital and the Norwegian Lutheran Church. I drove on to the Retirement Center where the reunion would be held and parked in the shade of an old live oak tree. Anxiety building, I walked up the steps and stood for many moments outside the door trying to decide if I should enter or gather my emotions and leave.

In the end I went in and much to my surprise, I actually enjoyed it. Even with nametags, I recognized few of those present. Most seemed to remember me and accept me as I am, a retired moderately successful writer of mystery novels with three published books to my credit. I could not detect any animosity or hidden jealousy at my success. Several brought copies of my most recent book seeking autographs. One classmate even brought a hand written manuscript she begged me to review and maybe help with its publication.

She didn't know it, but one of the things I detested most about being a published author was reviewing someone else's writing, especially that of an unpublished writer scrawled in longhand. I knew at a glance it would never be published, it was senseless drivel. But, for some reason I accepted the manuscript, praised her efforts and promised a critique within a reasonable time.

They insisted on calling me Jake though I hadn't used that name since high school. I much preferred Jacob, the name Momma and Cousin Esther called me, or J.K., the name my publisher used.

We discussed others of our class, and there were many, who had escaped the farming community and had succeeded in the outside world. We even discussed a few of the classmates including Cousin Joseph whose blue star on the flag in the church sanctuary had turned to gold during the Great War.

The Invocation delivered by Rev. Olson, Chaplin of the retirement center, was very down to earth, not preachy like I expected and the Eulogy for the departed class mates was even better. My vision clouded when he read Cousin Joseph's name followed by a summary of the honors he had won. And when he came to Cousin Esther's name, tears filled my eyes and silent sobs shook my body, the memories were just too painful. I knew then I should have stayed at home.

I had not planned to do it, but, after the catered meal and after the closing prayer, I decided to visit the old home place that I had abandoned forty-nine years ago. I found the country road, now a highway that climbed over the mountain west of Arendal. I stopped at the summit and looked out at the area known as Buffalo Flat, a five thousand acre fertile prairie surrounded on all sides by hills and small mountains whose name is buried in Indian myth.

Comanche legend speaks of a time many moons ago when the Spirits were pleased and the rains were plentiful and green grass grew as high as your knee and a big white buffalo lead his flock to the valley. Knowing this to be a sign from the Ancient Ones, the Comanche followed them to a place they named Buffalo Flat.

The legend also speaks of a time when the Spirits were displeased and the rain didn't come and the grass turned as brown as the earth and a white man they called Long Hair rode into the valley on a big black stallion, black as the palm of your hand at midnight, and killed all the buffalo and left them to rot in the boiling mid-summer sun. The legend also tells that when the Braves, who were on a hunting trip at the time, returned and the Elders told them what Long Hair had done, they hunted him down and burned him at the stake, the ultimate punishment for the most grievous crimes.

Few people and none of the settlers believed the story because they never found any bones or buffalo chips in the area and there were no buffalo trails leading down to the river. Besides buffalo were not native to the area. However, Comanche legend states that one dark night, when the moon hung low over the hills and the Spirit of the buffalo was troubled, the Comanche gathered the bones and buried and them in a Sacred Place far, far to the west.

Looking out over the valley, I could envision a pastoral scene with buffalo grazing on the tall grass and Indians in full costume riding their painted ponies among them. But the vision soon faded. Instead of the buffalo, I saw maybe twenty farms spread out before me like a giant jigsaw puzzle, some covered with maturing wheat, some covered in native grass. Looking closer, I thought I could see our old farm also covered with native grass with many cows that, from this distance looked like Black Angus.

Driving down the hill, I searched in vain for Grandma Svendahl's old house. Then I remembered someone at the reunion told me that, several years ago, the house burned to the ground and was never rebuilt. This saddened me because I loved that old house and its absence brought many fond memories to my mind.

I continued across the Flat until I came to the gate in front of our old farm. Overcome with nostalgia, I sat for many moments surveying the area.

I was right. The entire farm was covered with range grass and the cows were definitely Black Angus. I also saw many calves of various ages, some guarded by their mothers, others scattered here and there across the field. I watched a swarm of black birds swoop down and land among the cows. Cowbirds followed and landed on the cows and began to search for insects.

When I closed the squeaky gate, the cattle stopped eating and watched and a few started walking in my direction. But in a moment they stopped and resumed collecting grass.

Under a cloudless sky, I walked toward where the two-story white house had stood, the house that held so many memories. In my minds eye I envisioned the corrugated metal roof that turned my room into an oven during the summer and created a deafening racket when a hailstorm thundered across the Flat.

A Killdee, protecting her nest, fluttered across the trail feinting injury. A scissortail swooped to catch a dragonfly. A horny toad, feasting in a red ant bed, ignored my passing. Several baby calves approached, curious and unafraid, but when I said "Boo," they ran back to their mothers and began to nurse.

The far end of the land extended up to the mountains and we had used it to raise sheep. I wondered if Crazy Clem's shack was still there. How about the rattlesnake den, was it still inhabited by those vile creatures? I chose not to investigate.

My stomach tightened when I realized how much the farm had changed. Nothing remained of the house, not even a trace of the foundation or sidewalks or the flowerbeds Momma had so carefully tended. Where was the beautiful oak tree that towered over the back yard and provided so much comfort and pleasure in my youth? Where was the chinaberry tree that attracted so many birds when the berries matured? And where was the cedar tree Poppa planted in 1930 celebration of my recovery from near fatal pneumonia? I looked at the windmill that now seemed so much smaller than I remembered. Even though six of its fifteen blades were either broken or missing, it still squeaked and groaned in the wind, just as it did when I was a child. A buzzard perched atop the power pole next to the windmill eyed me with suspicion. Lacking a pumper rod, a submersible pump apparently pushed a steady stream of water into the adjacent tank indicating that the old well, after all these years, still contained water.

The milk barn with its four stalls still stood but badly needed painting and repairs. I opened the door and found it filled with round hay bales that extended to the corrugated tin roof. Many mud dauber nests still spotted the rafters and a huge long tailed rat watched, motionless and unafraid. A medium sized rattlesnake slithered across the floor and hid in one of the hay bales.

All the other structures on the farm had been removed; the garage, the silo, the hayloft, the hen house, the sheep shed, the birthing stalls for the pigs, the tackle room and the horse corral. Even the hog wallow now contained someone's watermelon patch. Where was the brooder house where we raised baby chicks? Where was the clothesline where Momma hung our clothes and sheets and towels to dry? Where was the giant black pot Momma used to boil our dirtiest clothes in a sometimes-vain attempt to render them clean? Where was the smokehouse where we cured our meat and stored our potatoes?

I noticed a few rusted tools and implement parts lying on the ground where the tool shed had stood. Several broken sickle blades from the mower, a rusted disc from the triple disc plow, a broken axle from the Model A truck, parts of an electric motor and several other items I could not identify. I picked up a rusted crescent wrench and took it with me as a reminder of my roots.

A corrugated metal tank replaced the concrete water trough that had furnished so much pleasure in my youth. Several cows, sleek, fat, pregnant and contented, ignored me as they drank from the trough.

The old pecan tree that had supported my favorite swing still spread its limbs near where the garage had stood. Ignoring the three cows standing in its shade, I walked closer and saw the rusted remnants of the steel cable that had supported my swing embedded in the lowest limb.

Someone had apparently removed the orchard where Momma sent us children to collect switches for disciplinary purposes. If the switches were too small, she would send us back for more substantial ones, the size somewhat dependent on the crime. If the infractions were minor, Momma administered the punishment. If the infractions were serious like running away from home, skipping school, talking back, cussing or telling lies, Poppa, with the aid of a razor strop, was the sole judge, jury, and executioner.

After about an hour, I left the old homestead, drove west, past Aunt Helena's farm now also converted to beef production, past the now abandoned one room schoolhouse where Miss Boudegard taught me my ABC's. Soon I reached the upper edge of the Flat and saw that the Old Norwegian Lutheran church appeared vacant with broken windows and the front door missing and the cemetery untended and over grown with weeds. This saddened me because many of my ancestors lay buried there and I wondered if there were any new graves and if anybody ever rang the mournful old bell in the steeple.

Feeling somewhat depressed, I cut across the prairie to the river road and headed back toward Arendal. Soon I found myself in front of what used to be Uncle Ole's farm.

Again I didn't know why, something just drove me to do it. Maybe I wanted to see the well that had ruled my life for so long, or maybe I wanted to visit the cave that had hidden its mysteries. Or maybe it was just curiosity. But whatever the reason, I felt I had to visit the scene of so many of my childhood problems.

I stopped but did not get out of the car. Looking around, I saw where the old house had stood and marveled that the fireplace and chimney still stood, intact after all these years of neglect and exposure to the elements.

Heart pounding, I looked at the hill where the shooter had stood that fateful day, but could see nothing. What became of the old garage where the family furniture had been stored before the fire that caused Poppa and Sheriff Bjornburg such angst? What became of the peach orchard that played such a vital roll that fateful year?

I looked toward where the water well had been and couldn't believe my eyes. Was that the little oak tree Poppa had planted in the well in 1937 in memory of his brother? Just look at it now, fifty feet tall with a trunk that must measure ten inches in diameter. I remember the weekly trips to water the little tree that dry first summer.

As I stood admiring the tree, memories of Cousin Esther overwhelmed me and, though I knew I shouldn't, I decided to go to the Arendal Cemetery and find her grave, the grave I had never visited since she died. It was just too painful.

Feeling as if unseen hands were driving the car, I returned to Arendal, turned right onto the highway and in a few minutes I was at the cemetery. Again turning right, I found myself on the gravel road that wound between the graves and continued until I reached the area where many of my departed relatives, including my parents, rested in Peace.

I stopped the car, got out and looked around. A few clouds and a cool breeze drifted in from the west. The only sound came from a cicada in a nearby cedar tree and an occasional car on the highway. I stood facing the breeze, attempting to sort out my emotions. Should I pack my thoughts and leave? Would I regret yielding to sudden emotion? Unable to decide, I carefully picked my way between the graves until I stood before headstones I recognized: Uncle Ole and Aunt Telinda, Uncle Andrew and Aunt Olivia, Uncle Albert and Aunt Helena, Uncle Helmer and Aunt Caroline, Aunt Thelma and Cousin Gertrude and several others I didn't remember.

In a moment I recognized the family plot with its two graves. I looked at the tiny headstone that read, Baby Alicia, then brushed the dust from the large headstone and read: Gunder Svendahl 1881-1942 and Anna Johansson

Svendahl 1884-1962. Although the day was cool, perspiration soaked my shirt and dripped from my brow.

Like someone in a trance I looked for and found Cousin Esther's grave. Tears filled my eyes as I gently brushed the dust from the marble lamb on the headstone, ran my hands over the inscriptions on its surface, then sank to my knees and allowed my hot tears to fall on the dry soil of her grave, tears I should have shed many years ago but couldn't because of my anger, anger at life in general and anger at God in particular. For perhaps the hundredth time I shouted WHY? And for the hundredth time I received no answer.

After maybe thirty minutes I left the cemetery and didn't stop until I reached the safety of my modest condominium in Dallas. That night, my eyes never closed as I sank in my recliner and began to review the events of that dreadful time in my life. After maybe an hour, I went to bed but when I closed my eyes, I could see her shining face, her friendly smile, her golden hair and her sky blue eyes that sparkled when she listened and teased when she talked. I thought I felt the touch of her soft hand on mine and remembered our first hesitant kiss when we were eleven and our urgent desire when they were eighteen. And when I thought I heard her whisper, "I love you, Jacob," I knew I was in serious trouble. My throat closed, my chest hurt, my heart began to pound and I realized I was again sliding down the slippery slope toward another nervous breakdown. It had been a big mistake to attend the reunion and a bigger mistake to visit her grave. I should have known how painful it would be.

As the hours passed, the black cloud around me grew deeper and more oppressive and I knew I had to do something before the self-destructive thoughts gained control of my mind as they had before. But what could I possibly do?

"Jacob, review your childhood," the psychiatrist advised in 1956 during my recovery from a suicidal attempt. "In my opinion, that's where your problems began."

What a bunch of crap I thought at the time. Now I wasn't so sure. And what better way to review my youth than writing about it. After all, that's my specialty. I got out of bed, went to my desk, booted my new laptop computer, opened my word processor and, to save my sanity, and perhaps my life, I began to write.

Chapter Two
, Threshing time

June 14, 1934

To me, there's nothing as exciting as threshing time on a farm with the giant steam tractor huffing and puffing and blowing black smoke out of the smoke stack and hay wagons scurrying to and from the fields and eating with the workers at the long table made of 2x12's on saw horses under the giant oak tree in the back yard and hiding from my cousins in tunnels dug in the new hay stack and riding on the hay wagons pestering the drivers with stupid questions as they call them. We had anxiously waited for this day and now it's here. And, oh yes, I forgot. Momma says, before you talk with strangers, you should introduce yourself, so here goes.

My name is Jacob Svendahl but most people call me Jake except Momma and Poppa who call me Jacob and Brother Ben who calls me 'Knucklehead' or 'Twerp' or 'Idiot' which ever pops into his feeble brain first. I'm nine and a half years old and my sisters and especially my brother frequently remind me that I'm the baby of the family and am spoiled rotten, but of course I'm not.

I live on a farm with my parents, five miles west of Arendal in central Texas. I have three sisters, Alicia who died as an infant, Selma who is in her second year of nursing school and Sybil who is a freshman in high school and bosses me around all the time. Then there's Benjamin, my totally obnoxious brother who is a senior in high school and must have been adopted or maybe dropped on his head as an infant but Momma said he wasn't.

Our five hundred acre farm isn't the best farm in the area. The best ones are down by the river, but ours is one of the biggest. Two hundred acres are in cultivation where Poppa grows cotton, corn, oats and wheat, barley and sometimes maize; the rest is pastureland where we keep the sheep. Beyond the pasture are the mountains where the rattlesnakes live.

We pray before and after every meal and say our prayers every night and twice a week we study the Bible before we go to bed. We never miss Sunday school or Sunday church services or Wednesday Evening Prayer Services and every time the doors of the Arendal Norwegian Lutheran Church open you will find me in the family pew between my parents.

We have five Jersey cows that we milk twice a day and about fifty calves obtained from other farmers or at auction. We use some of the milk to make slop for the pigs and some is saved for the family, but most is used to feed baby calves.

Farmers in the area know Poppa has a soft heart for baby calves and if one of their cows has twins and the mother rejects one, or if a young cow rejects her first born, which they often do, we get a call unless they plan to feed it themselves. Poppa calls our farm 'the calf orphanage' and we usually have ten or fifteen on the bottle at all times. Fortunately we only have to feed them with a bottle for two or three weeks, then they can get by on their own. There are always a few who would like to stay on the bottle forever and they can get downright ornery when we try to wean them, so we keep them separate.

Poppa says our soil isn't very good, not as good as that in the Arendal Valley but it's good enough to support beef production, but to succeed it is essential that the weather be favorable and the grain be harvested at the proper time. This year Poppa planted over one hundred acres in wheat and oats that now lays cut and shocked, waiting for the thresher.

We haven't had any rain since March and I know Poppa is worried about the crops. "But it's much worse in the Panhandle," he said. "They haven't had any rain since last summer and the wind is blowing the soil away."

Ever since school let out for the summer we've been preparing for this day. Two weeks ago we harvested the wheat and oats. Poppa drove the nearly new Farmall H tractor and I rode the old McCormick binder adjusting the sickle height, watching for snakes and rabbits and making sure that we didn't run out of binder twine. Poppa paid Uncle Ole and Aunt Telinda a dollar a day each plus the noon meal to follow the binder and shock the grain and Momma looked after Cousin Angel while they work.

Before he bought the tractor, Poppa did all the fieldwork using the ten horses and four mules but the tractor was so much better. It cost four hundred dollars and Poppa said it was the best investment he had ever made. All you had to do was keep the tank filled with kerosene and check the oil frequently and it would run all day and you didn't have to let it rest every hour and you didn't have to feed it oats and hay. After we got the Farmall, he sold the mules and all but four of the horses; two to pull the wagon and the one row cultivator and two for rounding up the cows and sometimes riding to school if the bus broke down.

Poppa and Uncle Ole are brothers but they are so much alike, they could have been twins. Poppa is a year older and Uncle Ole wears a bushy coffee stained mustache so people can tell them apart. They are both about five feet nine and weigh about one sixty-five and can work from day light till dark without breaking a sweat. I felt they could outwork anybody in Arendal County except maybe Aunt Telinda and Cousin Gertrude.

Uncle Ole had his own farm but sold it to Poppa in '17 to keep the bank from foreclosing on the loan. With the money, he purchased a narrow strip of land along the river and the adjacent mountain. There he planted his orchard filled with peach, plum, and fig trees but he mostly makes a living helping other farmers including Poppa.

Momma and Aunt Telinda, Uncle Ole's wife, are as different as day and night. Momma is short and fat and outweighs Poppa by twenty or thirty pounds and at fifty her hair is almost white, because of me my brother claims. And her upper plate always falls down when she yawns.

Aunt Telinda is tiny, maybe only five feet in her Sunday shoes if you included the coil of black hair on the top of her head and I don't think she ever saw a hundred pounds except when she was expecting Baby Angel. But she could put in a full days work in the field, go home, feed her husband and child, put out a wash, scrub the floor and be back in the field by sun-up the next morning.

I had trouble sleeping last night because Fritz barked constantly until midnight and the clock in the downstairs hall seemed to tick louder than usual. I guess the dog knew something special was about to happen or maybe a possum was in the henhouse.

About midnight Cousin Esther, who was spending the night so she could help with the morning chores, climbed in the bed with me and we both finally fell asleep. Momma had put her in Brother Ben's bed because he was with the threshing crew and planned to sleep in the hay wagon.

Some time during the night I woke up thinking I heard Poppa in the kitchen but it was Momma going to the bathroom. Finally, at four, I heard him making coffee so I woke Cousin Esther; we put on our overalls and joined him. I wasn't too fond of coffee but it seemed the right thing to do so early in the day.

Together we helped Poppa milk the cows, slop the pigs, let out the sheep, feed the horses, put mash in the hen house hoppers, gather the eggs and as the sun peeked over the hills, we watched the hay wagons with the loading crew turn in our gate and head for the fields. In about thirty minutes, the first wagon returned, fully loaded and stood by the gate to the upper pasture where the threshing would take place. The driver had already climbed down and stood beside the horses drinking coffee from a tin cup and smoking a pipe filled with tobacco from a red Prince Albert can.

Just as we were sitting down to eat breakfast, Sister Sybil dashed into the kitchen screaming, "They're coming, they're coming, the thresher's coming!"

"Can we leave now?" I blurted out.

"Not until we eat breakfast," Poppa growled.

"But I'm not hungry," I replied.

Ignored my response, he said Grace, then Momma put the food on the table.

After devouring, a big bowl of Oatmeal, three sausages and three biscuits and a full glass of milk, I asked, "Can we leave now?"

"Not until everybody finishes and Poppa thanks the Lord for the meal," Momma replied as she blew on her saucer full of hot coffee then slurped it noisily.

Normally no one left the table during meals until all plates were empty. But today was threshing day and I hoped Poppa would make an exception but he didn't.

After everybody finished eating and Poppa said the blessing, we ran to the gate and when we got there, Cousin Esther pointing down the road and screamed, "There they are!" Sure enough we could see the smoke billowing from the giant steam tractor and hear it slowly creep toward our farm. "I can feel the ground shaking!" she said.

"So can I," Sister Sybil said.

"So can I," I added. In my mind I could see the giant wheels digging into the gravel, tearing up the road with it's sharp cleats. And I knew in a few days the county road grader would come and smooth out the ruts.

It wasn't long until we recognized Uncle Andrew's huge frame at the controls of the steam tractor. He's Momma's brother and probably outweighs her by a hundred pounds. Cousin Matthew, Uncle Andrew's oldest son, also considerably overweight, followed driving their Model T truck and nine year old Cousin Joseph, Uncle Andrew's youngest son and my second best friend appeared to be feeding logs into the firebox. He also looked like his father, sorta big and fat.

After a few minutes we could plainly see the threshing machine with the large J. I. CASE sign on its side and the straw pipe curled over its back. "Don't you think it looks like a giant cat getting ready to pounce?" Cousin Esther asked.

"Sure does, a great big cat with his tail curled over his back," I answered and she was right. Momma always said Cousin Esther had a vivid imagination.

The noise of the steam tractor grew louder and louder and by the time it got to our gate, it was almost deafening. Steam bellowed from the whistle when Uncle Andrew announced his arrival and the cows ran to the other end of the pasture and the chickens dashed for the hen house.

We ran along beside it as the machine slowly advanced past the barn, black smoke billowing from the smoke stack. When they arrived at the upper pasture, Poppa pointed to a spot close to the watermelon patch and shouted, "Put her right here!"

"Okay!" Uncle Andrew yelled back as he pulled the thresher into position, unhooked it, then turned the tractor around so they faced each other.

"Don't they look like two wild animals about to fight?" Cousin Esther suggested.

"Sure do," I answered. "One belching fire and brimstone, the other waiting for the charge." We watched as Cousin Matthew slipped the long leather belt onto the power drive of the steam tractor, twisted the belt a half turn, and then slipped the other end of the loop onto the thresher drive wheel. Then Uncle Andrew slowly backed the tractor to tighten the belt.

"Why did you twist the belt?" I asked Cousin Matthew.

"So idiots like you would ask stupid questions," he answered. "Now get out of my way, I'm busy." He raised his hand as if to strike and we backed away.

"Well, phooey on you!" Cousin Esther yelled as we ran to where Poppa was hooking a sack to the grain chute. Apparently he heard the exchange and said, "If you don't twist the belt the thresher will run backwards." Why are older boys always so obnoxious, I wondered?

This was the first time we actually helped with the threshing; me sewing the grain sacks shut and pulling them out of the way, Cousin Esther bringing empty sacks from the barn and threading the crooked sewing needles I used to close the sacks, and Cousin Joseph, red faced and perspiring profusely, hauling wood for the firebox and carrying water for the boiler. And by dinnertime we were really hungry.

I knew Momma, Sister Sybil, Aunt Telinda, Aunt Helena, and Cousin Gertrude had been working all morning preparing the noon meal for the twenty workers. I also knew Momma had been boiling potatoes since daybreak, the potatoes we had peeled last night. When they were done she would mash them and serve them in large bowls with a big dab of butter in the middle and steam rising from of the top.

I also knew Momma had caught two-dozen fryers yesterday afternoon, took them to the block by the woodpile and chopped off their heads with a hatchet. She cleaned and gutted them last night, then separated the pieces and put them in the old icebox on the porch with a fifty-pound block of ice the iceman delivered yesterday. Today, I knew she would roll them in flour, fry the pieces until they were crisp golden brown, then serve them on huge tin platters.

There would be pitchers of rich brown gravy to pour over the potatoes along with beans and carrots fresh out of the garden and biscuits hot out of the oven. Big pitchers of iced tea sat at each end of the table and homemade ice cream would finish the meal. About thirty minutes before dinner I asked Poppa, "Can me and my cousins eat at the table under the tree with the rest of the workers?"

"Depends on how many places there are at the table," In my mind I counted heads and places and had a sinking feeling. "I don't think we're gonna be allowed sit at the main table," I said to Cousin Esther.

"Aw pshaw!" she answered. When I told Cousin Joseph, his comment was, "Well, tarnation!"

Dinnertime finally arrived and, as I suspected, we didn't get to sit at the long table. It was full so we sat on the porch and held the plates in our laps. Before the meal the workers chatted noisily about this and that until Uncle Andrew boomed, "Quiet!" then said Grace.

I was amazed at how much food Uncle Andrew could pile on his plate and he had seconds of everything. No wonder he's so fat. I also noticed that Cousin Mathew and Cousin Joseph loaded their plates and ate every bit plus two bowls of ice cream each. Everybody seemed to have hearty appetites including Cousin Esther and me although she didn't eat as much as I did and definitely not as much as Cousin Joseph. Threshing will do that to you.

After the meal the men sat around in the shade for about thirty minutes smoking their pipes and telling stories from their past. Some fell asleep; others pulled out Bull Durham tobacco pouches and skillfully rolled and lit cigarettes. A few had ready rolls, usually Lucky Strikes or Camels, but most of the workers felt they were much too expensive and didn't taste as good as those made by hand.

I was in the kitchen after the meal when I heard Poppa crank the phone and say, "Hello Central, connect me with Ole Svendahl's house." In a few moments he hung up and said to Momma, "No answer." That's when I realized I hadn't seen him at dinner and realized Aunt Telinda wasn't in the kitchen.

When I asked Poppa where they were, he said, "I don't know. He is suppose to be on the field crew and Aunt Telinda is suppose to be helping in the kitchen."

"Whose keeping Baby Angel?" I wanted to know.

"I guess she's with her parents."

I could tell both Poppa and Momma were a little worried about their absence because they always helped with threshing. "Gunder, where do you thing they've gone?" I heard Momma asked.

"I haven't the faintest idea."

"I just hope he hasn't gone off on another one of his drunken binges,"

It kinda surprised me that they weren't working because Momma had told me how badly they needed the money. I knew Uncle Andrew paid Uncle Ole a dollar a day to work on the loading crew and I think Poppa paid Aunt Telinda a dollar a day for helping in the kitchen.

I found out later that when Uncle Ole didn't show up, Uncle Andrew sent Cousin Matthew to the Hobo Jungle and he brought back a man who claimed he had worked on a loading crew before. I saw him at the noon meal and wondered how in the world such a skinny man could put in a full day in this heat, but apparently he could.

I know Uncle Andrew paid Hobos fifty cents a day at the end of each day because they often did not return the next day. Besides Poppa said they usually needed the money that day to buy food for their families.

Fifty cents didn't seem like much to me but when I asked Momma, she answered, "Jacob, fifty cents will buy you a quart of milk, a dozen eggs, a pound of hamburger meat, and a small sack of flour with a few cents left over. That's enough to feed a family of four for several days." And I knew second Cousin Gilbert Nordahl kept his family grocery store open until ten to accommodate these late shoppers.

"The Hobos never complain about the wages," Poppa told me. "They're happy to get work, any kind of work because paying jobs are scarce and most of the families at the camp have children to feed."

"Why aren't there any jobs? I asked Poppa.

"It's because of the crooks in Washington who don't know what the heck they're doing. I just wish President Roosevelt would hurry and get it straightened out."

The afternoon went about like the morning except the belt broke and one of the crew whose job was to cut the binder twine on the shocks before they were fed into the thresher, cut his hand with his pocketknife. Uncle Andrew poured kerosene on the cut and bound it up with a clean rag and sent him back to his job. It took him about thirty minutes to patch the belt, then the threshing continued until sundown with no further trouble. The wagon crews unhooked the horses, fed them oats out of a bucket then hobbled them in the pasture so they could graze. With these chores completed, they went to the horse trough to clean up.

After a supper of fried pork chop and more potatoes, the men sat around smoking and telling stories. But before the stories started, Momma took us side and said, "Esther, your mother and I have decided it's time for the two of you to stop sleeping together."

"Why?" I asked. I guess she knew Cousin Esther had disobeyed her instructions and had slept with me last night.

"Because Cousin Esther's coming of age."

I didn't know what she meant and I didn't want to expose my ignorance by asking Momma. So I asked Cousin Esther and she said, "I don't know for sure but I think it has something to do with making babies."

"We can't make babies, we're too young," I answered.

"I know," she replied. "Besides I don't even know how."

"Neither do I," I answered which wasn't exactly true.

Actually I knew all about making babies. I had watched the bulls visit the cows and the boars visit the sows and the rams visit the ewes and the studs visit the mares and I knew how they made babies. I also knew that after a certain period of time, babies would come.

I also had a pretty good idea how people made babies. At that time in my life, all the bedrooms were filled, so I slept in my crib in Momma and Poppa's room until I was three. One night shortly after my third birthday I woke up to the sounds of Momma and Poppa playing some kind of game. The bed was bouncing, the springs were squeaking and both Poppa and Momma were making funny noises. Finally the noise stopped and Momma got up and went to the bathroom and I went back to sleep. The next morning I asked Momma what game they were playing and she said, "Eat your breakfast Jacob!" I asked my brother and he said they were trying to make another boy so they could send me to the orphan's home. When I told Momma what he had said and she whipped us both and so did Poppa. That night they moved my crib upstairs to the landing and I never slept in their room again.

Shortly after we were four Cousin Esther and I realized our bodies were different. This happened while we were standing on the porch, drying off after our weekly Sunday morning bath. Although she no longer lived with us, she usually spent the weekends and we took our baths together in a large washtub on the back porch before going to Sunday school.

We ran to the kitchen and I asked, "Momma, what happened to Cousin Esther's peter?" I had learned the word from my brother.

"She doesn't have one," Momma replied.

"Why?'

"Because she's a girl."

"Why?"

Instead of an answer, Momma said, "Children, put on your clothes then go to the orchard and bring me two substantial switches."

"Why?" we said in unison.

"Because it's a sin to look at each other when you're naked. I think it's about time you quit taking baths together."

We took our whipping and cried because we were expected to cry but it really didn't hurt that much. We both knew if we didn't cry Poppa might take over the punishment. Also I cried because I would miss our weekly baths. And I couldn't understand why it's a sin to look at each other when we're naked but Momma says it is so I guess it is. "Maybe we'll understand when we're five," I said to Cousin Esther.

Later, I asked Sister Sybil about it and she replied, "That's what makes her a girl and you a boy."

"Why?" I had asked.

"You wouldn't understand." And that ended the discussion.

When we were seven, Sister Selma told me about Cousin Esther. "She came into this world three days after you were born. Two days later, a tornado killed her father, Uncle Albert. His wheat crop had been a miserable failure that year, so bad that he plowed it under and decided to seek work in the oilfields of West Texas."

"It happened near Wichita Falls," she continued. "The tornado appeared out of nowhere, destroyed his car and drove a fence post through his chest killing him instantly."

"Aunt Helena, Poppa's sister and Cousin Esther's mother, went a little crazy after Uncle Albert's death," she continued. "She took to the bed for nearly two years only trending to the bare personal necessities so you shared Momma's milk with her and you slept in the same crib for three years."

"During this time Aunt Helena dwindled away to nothing even though

Momma cooked two meals a day that Poppa took to her house. He said she looked like a skeleton and all her hair had fallen out."

"Finally she recovered and, on Cousin Esther's third birthday, she took her home. You cried for days after she left and so did Momma and so did Cousin Esther. In fact Aunt Helena brought her back several times hoping Momma could settle her down."

As we grew up, everyone said Cousin Esther and I were so much alike we could have been twins. Our eyes were the same shade of blue; the color of our hair was identical, almost as white as fresh picked cotton. Our noses were alike, not too big and not too small except mine was a little bit crooked because of a disagreement at school. We were almost the same height and Poppa said our soft suntanned skin felt like the fuzz on a peach.

"After she recovered," Sister Selma continued, "Aunt Helena ran her farm by herself with the help of Malcolm Moore, a single man. Everyone knew Malcolm and also knew he had spent three years in prison for exposing himself to a young girl in another city. But he was very strong and could do anything around a farm and, as far as anyone knew, he had learned his lesson."

Cousin Esther told me Malcolm had proposed marriage to her mother several times but she turned him down. "Several years ago, Malcolm told Poppa he would pick all of our cotton for nothing if he'd let him marry me," Sister Selma said. "Thank goodness, Poppa turned him down and Momma said he was a very lonely man."

One day when we were eight, we saw him walking down the road and Cousin Esther said, "I hate that man and I hate his silly mustache. When I was little, he was forever trying to kiss me on my face and when he did, it felt like I was kissing a Prickley Pear leaf. And one day when I was seven, when my mother wasn't around, he made an indecent proposal to me. When I told my mother, she fired him and took me to the sheriff and filed a complaint."

"What happened then?"

"Nothing. The sheriff said it would be difficult to charge him because no one else heard the proposal."

"A week later she hired him back but fired him again after he finished the fall plowing."

"What's an indecent proposal?" I asked.

"You wouldn't understand." I never brought it up again.

Sister Selma also told me about Cousin Joseph, the third member of our little group. "When y'all were three he also came to live with us. That's when his mother, Aunt Olivia, had a miscarriage and went crazy. She disappeared and they found her a week later walking down the highway near Waco in nothing but her torn stockings and an old ragged straw hat. Her hair was a tangled mess and her body was filthy like maybe she had slept in a ditch or in a hog pen. They said when they found her, she was singing hymns at the top of her lungs in some foreign tongue, definitely not Norwegian."

"Then what happened?"

"Well, Uncle Andrew, whose farm was further down the river road, wanted to divorce her, but Poppa talked him out of it and arranged for her to be admitted to the State Insane Asylum."

"Where is she now?"

"She's still there. They say she never got any better and after one visit, Uncle Andrew never went back. She didn't even recognize him and the doctors said he probably shouldn't visit her again, it would only upset her, so he didn't."

Cousin Joseph lived with us until he was seven, then Uncle Andrew took him home. He too often visited our house and Poppa called us his Three Musketeers. And that was when he began to gain weight.

As darkness fell, the men settled down in the back yard and Poppa hung a kerosene lamp on the lowest branch of the oak tree. The crew lit their pipes and cigarettes and soon the yard grew silent. Uncle Andrew stood in front of the lantern and when he moved, spooky shadows danced around the yard. And when he lowered his voice and began to speak, cold chills ran up and down my spine, and my cousins and me huddled together like lost sheep.

For almost two hours he told scary troll stories. And when he finished, the arguments started. "Them stories ain't true," one worker insisted. "They's just fairy tales made up by grown folks to scare their children."

"They's mostly true," another worker answered. "My Momma told me the same stories when I was a child. She said they were true and my Momma never told a lie in her life, God rest her soul."

A third worker interrupted, "Sounds to me like your mother done told you a bunch of lies."

"I'm telling you she never told a lie so just you shut up!"

As the argument grew louder, I was afraid a fight was about to break out and I got scare. I grabbed Cousin Esther's hand, clasped it in mine and felt a little safer.

"Those stories ain't true," Cousin Joseph whispered. "They just make them up to try and scare kids like us." But he stayed close to us and I think he clasped Cousin Esther's other hand. Finally Uncle Andrew called a halt to the argument, lead them in prayer and everybody went to bed. Since Cousin Esther wasn't going to sleep with me, I asked Brother Ben if I could sleep with him in the wagon. "You ain't gonna sleep with me, lard head," he replied. "You can go sleep with the pigs 'cause you smell like one."

"Well, poop on you, fat gut," I answered and ran to the house before he could hit me. I jumped in the bed, covered up my head but I couldn't go to sleep. Maybe it was because of the troll stores but more than likely it was because Cousin Esther wasn't with me and apparently we would never sleep together again. The troll stories really didn't scare me but I left the light on just in case.

Tossing in my hot bed I heard Poppa drive away in the car and in about thirty minutes I heard him return. Curious as to where he had gone, I sneaked down the stairs, hid in the dining room and listened.

"There wasn't anybody at home," I heard Poppa say. "Their truck isn't there and the house isn't locked."

I heard Momma say, "That worries me."

"It worries me too," Poppa answered. "Well, there's nothing we can do tonight. Let's go to bed." And they did and so did I. I assumed they were talking about Uncle Ole and Aunt Telinda.

The next morning Momma got up at four to start cooking eggs and bacon. At five, Uncle Andrew roused the crew with hot coffee and by seven they had eaten breakfast, hooked up the teams and were on their way to the fields. The second day went smoothly and by sundown they finished. Poppa and Uncle Andrew divided the sacks according to the contract and the loading crew loaded his part into our truck and Poppa's part into our wagon. Tomorrow Poppa would take Uncle Andrew's part to the feed mill, sell it and send him the money.

After they finished separating the sacks I heard Uncle Andrew ask Poppa, "How much do you think I'll get for the wheat?"

"I checked with the feed mill yesterday," Poppa replied. "They're paying eighty-six cents a bushel., Twice what we got last year."

"That'll help except, as well as I can remember, we got twice as many sacks last year as we did this year."

"That's right, because of the drought."

"Yep, the drought done it."

"Where you going next?" I heard Poppa ask.

"I got about two weeks more work here in the Flat, then I'm going to

Hamilton County," he replied. "Probably got about a month's work there, then we're coming home. I ain't going to the Panhandle like I usually do, and I sure as heck ain't going to Oklahoma. The drought there is worse than it is here. The wind is blowing away the topsoil and won't nothing grow. Most of the farmers have sold their cattle and many lost their farms to the banks and the loan companies and moved to California. So I reckon we'll just work the Central Texas area and come home, probably by the middle of July. Give me time to work on my own farm but goodness knows there ain't that much to do. We threshed our wheat and planted the cotton before we started out and it ain't time to hoe. Besides, if we don't get some rain pretty soon, they ain't gonna be nothing to hoe."

Again, the threshing crew ate supper, hobbled their horses, lit their pipes and settled down for the night. I wanted to listen to more stories but I couldn't stay awake. Poppa led me to my bed and Cousin Esther went home with her mother. It had been a full day and I was pooped. And Uncle Ole and Aunt Telinda didn't show up today either. Thank goodness the Hobo came back and brought his wife and four children. She helped in the kitchen and the children played in the yard. I don't think Poppa paid her anything but at least they all got two good meals.

The next morning Aunt Helena and Cousin Esther returned at five to help feed the crew and just as the sun rose full and bright in the east, the wagon crews and the field crew finished breakfast, hooked up the horses and away they went.

When the last wagon departed Uncle Andrew climbed on the steam tractor, adjusted the levers, smoke bellowed from the smoke stack and steam escaped from the whistle as he bid us goodbye. By seven he was gone. Poppa said for us to remember the last two days because it would probably be the last threshing we would ever see. "I plan to buy a combine before next harvest and so have some other farmers in the Flat and I've advised your Uncle to sell his rig."

The more I thought about what Poppa had said the more I wanted to cry. Farming was changing and I wasn't sure I liked it. But mostly I wanted to cry because apparently Cousin Esther and me would never sleep together again.

Chapter Three
A Farm House Fire

Once a month Pastor Pierson conducts Sunday evening services at the old Buffalo Flat church fifteen miles west of Arendal where many of my ancestors are buried. The church doesn't have a congregation or a pastor so these monthly services are about all that happens there except at Christmas and an occasional wedding. There are still many older people in the area, including Momma and Poppa, who speak and understand the language so the sermon is delivered and the songs are sung in Norwegian. Attendance for us is mandatory.

I wasn't that interested in learning to read or write Norwegian but I sorta wanted to learn to speak and understand it because my parents and most of my relatives spoke it and when they did, I felt left out.

As we walked in the back door, the old crank phone on the kitchen wall began to ring, two longs and a short, our number. Receptions being poor, Poppa asked that the message be repeated.

"We gotta go," he announced when he hung up the receiver. "Uncle Ole's house is on fire. That was Selmer Griggs, Uncle Ole's neighbor. He already called the Fire Chief."

"Was your brother there?" Momma asked

"Apparently not. Selmer said he hadn't seen him for several days." I had wondered myself why they weren't at work but I hadn't lost any sleep over it. However I had worried about Cousin Angel and had included her in my prayers every night since they didn't show up for threshing.

So we all piled in the Model A; Momma, Poppa, Sister Sybil, and me and bounced across the prairie toward the river. When we reached the top of the mountain and could see the Arendal Valley below, I heard Poppa exclaim, "Lordy, Anna, looks like a big one!" And he was right. I had never seen such a big fire with flames shooting high in the sky illuminating the thick layer of dark smoke that hovered over the area like a giant umbrella. When we reached Uncle Ole's place, we heard the fire truck coming up the river road and when it turned the last corner, we saw the red light flashing, heard the horn honking and siren screaming. In a minute, it rumbled across the cattle guard and stopped in front to the burning house. Immediately the firemen jumped off, drug the hose to the water well and crammed one end into the water and the fire chief started the pump.

But, as usual in rural farmhouse fires, the fire fighters were much too late. Poppa said it took too long to assemble the fire fighting crew summoned by a blast of the big siren on the roof of the city hall. Then they had to get the engine started, load the crew with their gear and negotiate the rural roads to the fire site. "What more could you expect," Poppa said on several occasions. "They don't get paid. All are volunteers and the fire truck is so old and hard to start, it's small wonder they ever get there." And such was the case tonight.

Before they could drop one end of the hose into the water well, it was too late. They were able to save the garage and the barn by dousing them with water so it wasn't a total loss.

It wasn't long until Aunt Helena and Cousin Esther drove up. Like most people on an eight-person party line, when the phone rings, especially at night, they listen in, it's customary and expected. That's how important news gets passed around. If you didn't want your message to become common knowledge, you had to write a letter or deliver it in person.

"We had already gone to bed," Cousin Esther said as she walked up to our car, climbed in and sat beside me. "That's why it took us so long to get here."

After he got everything working, Orvil Hanson, the Fire Chief and rural mail carrier for the area, came to our car, put one foot on the running board and began.

"Howdy, Gunder. Do you happen to know where your brother is?"

"No, I don't," Poppa answered.

"Well, about a week ago, he left a note in the mail box saying they would be gone for a few days and to hold their mail until they got back. He's gonna be mighty surprised when he sees this mess. Looks like a total loss to me."

"I think you're right, a total loss." Poppa answered. "I'll try to find him tomorrow."

"You do that. It's best he knows about it before he gets home."

Poppa didn't say anything else until Momma asked, "Do you know where they went?"

"I didn't even know they were gone."

"And they didn't call you and let you know where they were going?"

"No they didn't! I already told you that several times," Poppa answered and I thought he sounded a little angry.

"Lordy Mercy," Momma said. "I just hope he hasn't gone away on another one of his drunken binges."

"He wouldn't do anything like that, especially on threshing day."

"Then where is he?" but Poppa didn't answer.

This argument made me kinda nervous so Cousin Esther and me got out of the car and walked around looking at the fire from every angle. We watched the roof collapse sending sparks flying in every direction and helped stomp out the many small grass fires started by the sparks.

We followed the hose as it snaked its way around the barn and plunged into the well. I looked in the well through the hole in the top and couldn't see a thing, not even the water. All I could see was the hose and a rope going down into the well.

Shortly, the fire was out so they pulled the hose out of the well and returned it to its place in the fire truck. Then Mr. Hanson walked back to the well and tried to close the lid but it wouldn't close.

"What's wrong with this dang thing," he grumbled. "Hinges must be rusted, probably been that way for months, maybe years."

Watching the fire had made me kinda thirsty and I thought I needed a drink. A full moon shining in the cloudless sky illuminated the area and I could see the spindle and the rope that plunged into the well. I assumed there would be a bucket on the end of the rope, so I tried to turn the crank but the crank wouldn't turn. "Must be broken," I muttered.

"Let me try," Cousin Esther said. "I'm stronger than you are."

"No you ain't. You're a girl and girls are never as strong as boys."

"Just watch," she said as she tried to turn the crank but it still wouldn't budge.

"See, I told you I'm stronger than you are."

I could tell it made her mad because she hit me on the arm and stuck out her tongue so I stuck out mine and we both began to laugh. That's when the Fire Chief blew the whistle indicating departure and we watched as he tried to start the motor. After a few turns of the crank, the motor sprang to life, backfired twice, then settled into a steady rumble. Another loud blast of the horn indicated immediate departure and the firemen climbed aboard. The engine roared as they lumbered across the cattle guard and in a few moments, they were gone leaving us in total darkness except for the light of the moon. I took Cousin Esther's hand and we walked around the area until Poppa called and we went to the car. Aunt Helena and Cousin Esther left and we watched as Poppa walked around the ruins several more times. Finally he returned to the car and we started home. As we drove across the cattle guard, I thought I saw someone or something in the orchard but there wasn't enough light to tell who or what I had seen but when we got on the road it had disappeared.

I fell in bed and tried to sleep but sleep would not come. I knew Momma and Poppa stayed up for a long time talking. But I couldn't hear the conversation.

The next day Poppa went back to Uncle Ole's house and looked around. I wanted to go with him but he said, "You gotta stay here and clean out the chicken house. It hasn't been cleaned in three weeks."

"How come chickens poop so much?" I asked but got no answer.

I didn't know until a week later that, when Poppa went back to Uncle Ole's house, he found all of their furniture locked in the garage. It was even later before I realized the significance of that finding.

Chapter Four
The Well

It had been three days since the fire and I had sorta forgotten about it. Poppa had barely finished saying the blessing when the argument started. Uncle Ole and Aunt Telinda were still missing and I knew he was worried about them and so was Momma. I also knew he had gone to town several times to talk with Sheriff Bjornburg about their absence.

"I told the sheriff he oughta contact the State Police," Poppa began. "I also told him that if the State Police couldn't find them then he oughta call the Texas Rangers."

"Won't do no good," Momma answered. "He's hid out in some bar somewheres and ain't nobody gonna find him until he wants to get found."

"That ain't true! I think something bad's happened to them."

"You shouldn't worry so much. I'll betcha he'll show up one of these days with some ridiculous story, dragging his wife and child behind him."

"But, Telinda never went with him when he got drunk."

"Maybe she felt she could control him," Momma replied. "Maybe she went along to protect him. You remember last time he got drunk he got in a fight and someone broke his jaw."

"That was *before* Cousin Angel was born."

"Gunder, when are you gonna admit he's a drunkard?"

"He ain't a drunkard. He just occasionally drinks a tiny bit too much."

"Like every weekend."

"No, not every weekend. Maybe three times a year, but not every weekend."

"Gunder, you're a blinkin idiot!" Momma said as she got up from the table and walked into the kitchen.

I had never heard Momma and Poppa argue before, not like this and not in front of us kids and certainly not while we were eating and it scared me real bad. I knew parents sometimes had bad arguments, sometimes so bad that their kids got hurt. One of my classmates got hurt so bad he ended up in the hospital in Waco with a broke skull and his father ended up in prison. But in my wildest dream I could not picture Momma and Poppa in a fight. An argument, yes, but never in a fight. Also, I had never heard them discuss Uncle Ole's drinking problem. In fact, I didn't even know he had a problem.

And I agreed with Poppa, something bad musta happened.

In a few minutes, Momma came to the table and filled their coffee cups, then we all joined hands and Poppa led us in prayer. I was so relieved; I didn't even hear what he said.

After we finished the meal and Poppa said grace, they started arguing again. "Gunder, I don't give a hoot about your brother, I just worry about Baby Angel and so should you."

I thought that would make Poppa mad again, but it didn't. Instead, he said, "I AM worrying about her."

"And you didn't find any bodies in the ashes, is that right?" Momma asked.

"No. I didn't find any bodies in the ashes. I already told you that twice."

"Then he musta took his family and left town. You know when he gets drunk he does crazy things. Besides, Sheriff Bjornburg said his truck is missing so they musta took it and gone somewhere. God only knows where they are by now, might be in California for all we know. "

"I think there's gotta be another explanation. He would never leave town without telling me."

"Gunder, you gotta accept the fact that when he's drunk there's no telling what he'll do."

"We don't know that he was drunk," Poppa answered.

"How do we know he wasn't? Answer me that."

"I just know. He's my brother and I know he wouldn't leave without telling me."

"You can think whatever you want to think. He's a drunkard and you know it. You need to spend less time worrying and more time praying."

"Anna, I *have* been praying, and you should too. In fact, all of you should be praying."

We all nodded our heads and I said, "Poppa, I've been praying every night."

"So have I," Sister Sybil added.

Poppa again asked us to hold hands and he led us in an eloquent prayer asking for God's help in returning our missing relatives. "And please God," he added in closing, " Guard and protect Baby Angel whom we so sorely miss."

After he finished the prayer, the argument started again. "Didn't he leave a note in the mail box? Maybe you oughta go look at it. Might give you a clue."

"Orvil told me the note didn't say anything about where they were going."
"Then we're just stuck," Momma answered. "We'll have to wait until they come home and when they do I'll bet you a hundred dollars he'll start asking for money again." It seemed to me Poppa didn't want to argue any more so he stood quietly, his hands behind his back, looking at the picture on the wall of Jesus Christ, nailed to the cross.

After maybe five minutes, Poppa said to me, "Son, I have to go back to my brother's farm tomorrow and make the appraisal for the insurance company. Do you want to go with me?"

"Sure," I answered. I had finished cleaning the chicken house this afternoon and helped Poppa spread the manure in the garden. I was glad for a day of rest but I knew day after tomorrow I would have to start on the sheep shed and Poppa would resume plowing.

After Amos and Andy, we all went to bed, except Momma and Poppa who stayed in the kitchen and talked. I wanted to listen but I was still too tired from cleaning the chicken house. In my prayers I included Uncle Ole, Aunt Telinda and especially Baby Angel. I also remembered to thank God for a day of rest.

Cleaning manure out of the sheep shed was another of my least favorite chores. Sheep manure hardened over time and we hadn't cleaned it out since last summer. Now it was at least a foot deep and almost as hard as concrete. That meant I would be spending the next week or two swinging a pickaxe and wielding a shovel.

I had gone with Poppa before to investigate other fires so I pretty much knew the routine. As appraiser for Arendal County Mutual Fire Insurance Company I knew he would walk around, look at the damage, take a few pictures with the old Eastman Kodak box camera, and maybe ask a few questions if the occupants were around, then leave. Later he would figure each member's assessment and mail out the bills. In a few weeks, reimbursement would be delivered to the insured.

I didn't understand how it worked except that he had been the appraiser for many years and Momma told me his appraisals were always fair and rarely challenged.

From past experience I knew these appraisals sometimes took a little longer than expected, so I decided to take something with me to pass the time.

It took some hunting, but I finally found Brother Ben's football, the football he had received last Christmas. I sneaked it out of the house and secreted it behind the back seat of the car. There was no reason to ask Poppa and I certainly wasn't going to ask Brother Ben. Besides he was still somewhere on the wagon crew so I couldn't ask him even if I wanted to.

It actually felt cool as we drove along in the black Model A Ford Poppa had purchased two years ago. It had cost him four hundred twenty five dollars and he was very proud of it. He did not allow Brother Ben to drive it because he had given him the old Model T. The idiot had already wrecked it twice, but it still ran, even without a front bumper and right front fender providing you threw enough dirt in the gearbox.

When we got to the farm, Poppa drove across the cattle guard and parked in front of what used to be the house. I watched as he poked around in the burned boards, stirred the ashes in several areas and then walking around the house three times. Then he stood back and studied the entire scene for what seemed like an hour but I knew was maybe only fifteen minutes. Then he went to the garage and opened the lock and I tagged along behind.

"I have to do an inventory," he said. "The day after the fire when I opened the garage, I found it filled with Uncle Ole's furniture."

Poppa seemed upset, but I didn't know why. I didn't think he was upset with me; probably he was upset at Uncle Ole because he went away without telling anyone where he was going. Before he said anything else, he took out a pad and a pencil and began to list all the contents of the garage.

Knowing this would take awhile, it seemed like a good time to play with the football so I sneaked it out of the car, went behind the barn and threw it as high as I could. When it came down, I caught it and ran across the field, zigging and zagging, dodging imaginary tacklers on my way to the goal line with Cousin Esther watching from the sideline screaming and hollering and turning flips. I knew when I crossed the goal line she would be waiting for me and would probably give me a great big hug. Now it was time for the kickoff.

I set the ball in the grass, found a rock to lean it against, then sent it sailing high into the air. I watched as it came down, bounced twice then struck the spindle over the water well.

"Oh, God, is the lid still open?" I wondered and in an instant, I knew. Like a rock, the ball fell through the hole and disappeared into the well along with my heart.

"Oh Jesus, what's Poppa gonna say, and what's Brother Ben gonna say?" I ran to the well and peered into its depths. I could see the bucket suspended about a foot over the water and I thought I could see the football.

"Maybe I can lower the bucket and bring it out," I thought. But when I tried, I found the crank still frozen. "Now what am I gonna do?" I tried to untie the rope from the spindle but couldn't.

Where's Poppa I wondered. Did he see what happened? Should I find him and tell him? Or should I pretend nothing happened and hope Brother Ben wouldn't notice until I could figure out a way to get it back or come up with a plausible excuse?

I sneaked back to the car and saw that Poppa was still listing the contents of the garage. In a little while he came to the car and got out the Kodak and began to take pictures, first of what was left of the house, then of the contents of the garage, then from a distance of the entire area.

Poppa still seemed upset and I wondered if he had he seen me kick the football into the well? But surely if he had, he would have said something by now, not stand there with his hands folded behind his back.

In a few minutes, he again walked around the grounds and closely examined the ruins. I didn't realize until later how upset Poppa was at the situation. It did occur to me that Uncle Ole should have been there but I had other worries.

Sitting in the car, waiting for Poppa, I thought I saw something or someone moving in the peach orchard. I looked around for Poppa and saw him back at the garage locking the door. I looked back at the orchard but whoever or whatever it was had disappeared.

What was that? I said to myself. But, I had other more serious worries like a football in the bottom of a well and what I would tell Poppa and what my brother would do to me when he found out.

Finally we left and Poppa didn't say a word on the way home. My anxieties improved slightly because he made no mention of the football. But we didn't go home; we drove to Arendal and Poppa went to Sheriff Bjornburg's office in the County Courthouse. I waited in the hall for what seemed like an hour wondering if they were discussing my punishment. I could have gone outside and found something to do but decided I should stay close by so I could check the situation. But when Poppa came out, he didn't say a word about the football and we went home.

No one spoke during evening chores. Poppa seemed to have his mind elsewhere and thank goodness Brother Ben was still gone. Even Mama and Poppa didn't speak to each other until we had gone to bed. I could hear them talking in the kitchen, but I couldn't understand what they were saying so I quietly crept down the stairs to the dining room, hid behind the table and listened.

My main concern was about the football. Were they discussing my punishment that I knew would be severe, much more than a switch from the orchard? Probably it would involve the razor strop with my pants down followed by a privilege restriction that would probably prevent me from going to town on Saturday, maybe several Saturdays along with loss of my weekly quarter.

"Were there any bodies in the ashes?" I heard Momma ask.

"No. I told you before there were no bodies in the ashes," Poppa answered.

"Then he must have stored the furniture in the garage, set the house on fire, then took his family and ran away. He'll probably come back later for the furniture."

"No," I heard Poppa answer. "He would never do something like that, not my brother. There has to be another explanation."

"Gunder, you've never accepted the fact that your brother is a drunkard."

"He is NOT a drunkard!" Poppa shot back. "He hasn't been drunk for a year and that was only for a day or two. In fact, he hasn't really been drunk since Baby Angel was born."

"Gunder, he's been drunk half the time, ever since you bought his farm in '17. In fact, that's why he had to sell the farm. He couldn't pay off the mortgage and stay drunk all the time. Don't you remember last year, on the Fourth of July? You had to go bail him out of the Hillsboro jail. Cost you ten dollars that we badly needed for other things. And he never paid you back."

"Well, that doesn't count. He just got lost on his way back from Waco and the Highway Patrol picked him up and called me."

"Yeah, and he had a jug of whiskey in the car. When are you going to wake up and admit he's a drunk."

There was no question about it. They were both angry. The argument made me very nervous so I sneaked back to bed. Soon I heard them go to bed but I still couldn't go to sleep. Also this was my first hint that there was something wrong with the furniture being in the garage. However it really didn't sink in because I had other worries, worries about the football and worries about the punishment when my secret was discovered. Thank goodness my secret was still safe but when Brother Ben gets home my goose'll be cooked unless I could figure out a way to retrieve it.

In my prayers I remembered to thank God for allowing me to escape punishment, for now. I also remembered to pray for Uncle Ole and Aunt Telinda and especially for Baby Angel. It took awhile to go to sleep and tomorrow I knew I had to start in the sheep shed.

Chapter Five
Cousin's Advice

Day before yesterday Poppa and me took a load of hogs to market. He said the sheep manure could wait and he wanted me along to help. If Brother Ben had been home I'm sure Poppa would have asked him, but he wasn't, he was still with the threshing crew.

We put on our best weekday clothes because we were going to Fort Worth, the livestock capital of Texas, maybe of the entire country. I wore my new overalls and a clean work shirt and Poppa wore his new brown cotton work pants and a Sunday shirt without a tie. I wanted to go barefooted but Momma made me wear my nearly new high top sneakers.

We backed the truck up to the loading shoot and loaded up ten pigs, a full load, and secured the end gate. Poppa filled three jugs with water and placed them in the truck, one for us and two for the radiator. When Momma brought our sack lunches, Poppa started the motor and off we went.

We followed the dirt road across the Flat until we got to the mountain, crossed it and picked up the river road near Uncle Ole's burned down house. We followed the river northward and crossed it at Iredell. From there we followed the road northeast and soon crossed the Brazos, We continued until we entered Fort Worth, crossed the Trinity River and found the red brick road that led to the stockyard.

The load was a little heavy and twice the truck heated up and we had to stop, let it cool off and add water to the radiator. Also, we had one flat on the way but fortunately we had a spare bolted to the side of the truck. It took four hours to complete the one hundred mile trip and we made it to the auction barn an hour before it closed and Poppa turned the pigs over to the man from the Shirley Commission Co.

We found a picnic table next to the stockyard and ate our lunches and Poppa paid a nickel for a Dr Pepper that we shared. Two hours later we went to the Commission office and Poppa got a check for $210.60. The salesman said the pigs sold for nine cents a pound on the hoof. When Poppa expressed his disappointment, the salesman said too many farmers had decided to sell. The salesman also said he was lucky to get that much because the price fell two more cents a pound before the market closed for the day and some of the farmers took their pigs back home to wait for a better price.

On the way out of town we stopped at Leonard Brothers Store and Poppa looked at work clothes but didn't buy any. Instead, he bought a nickel's worth of rock candy to take home for the rest of the family and two apples for us to eat on the way. He said he had wanted to go by Montgomery Wards but we didn't have time because he wanted to fix the flat tire. "I don't feel safe starting home with out a spare," he said.

So we stopped at a Sinclair station on the way out of Fort Worth and Poppa fixed the flat, filled the gas tank and added water to the radiator. After he paid for the gas, eleven cents a gallon, we started home.

It was so hot on the way, even with the windows open, I nearly croaked. The truck overheated again and we had to put more water in the radiator. I must have drunk from the jug twenty times and we both wrapped wet handkerchiefs around our necks after wiping the sweat off of our faces. I took off my shirt, dropped the bib on my overalls and bathed my chest and finally we arrived home in time for milking.

"I been worrying about y'all," Momma said when Poppa stopped the truck and turned off the motor. "The thermometer on the back porch showed a hundred five degrees today. I was afraid the truck would blow up and you'd both be killed." She paused, then asked, "How much did you get for the pigs?"

When Poppa showed her the check, she frowned. "Shoulda been more than that!"

"I know, but don't you remember last year? We only got five cents a pound."

The next morning, when I went with Poppa to do the chores, he never mentioned the football and Bother Ben still hadn't come home. Momma said she thought he would be home in a couple of weeks. So my secret was still safe, for now.

Before supper, I heard Poppa tell Momma he was going to town tomorrow and talk some more with Sheriff Bjornburg. When I asked him if I could go along, he said, "No, you gotta start on the sheep shed." So, the next morning, he pulled the John Deere manure spreader to the shed and backed it up to the gate and I grabbed the pickaxe and went to work. I only got one small section removed so I knew at that rate it might take a month unless Poppa got some help.

That night, Poppa and Momma talked way into the night, but I couldn't stay awake. Digging manure was harder than cleaning out the chicken house and after just one day, I was exhausted. I had almost quit worrying about the football and tomorrow would be another hard day in the sheep shed. I went to sleep almost instantly and when Poppa tried to wake me the next morning, I couldn't get up. I was still exhausted.

Finally Saturday arrived and as was our custom we quit work at noon and made preparations to go to town. Apparently Poppa was satisfied with my progress in the sheep shed.

After we ate dinner, Poppa lay down on the floor in the hallway and took a short nap. An electric fan in the doorway cooled the air so I lay down beside him and rested. When he finished his nap, we put on clean clothes, he gave me my weekly quarter and off to town we went. As usual, Sister Sybil went with us.

On the way we picked up Cousin Esther and when we got to town we went to the Corner Drug where we found Cousin Joseph. I was a little surprised he was there. I thought he was still with the threshing crew, but he said his father had taken Poppa's advice and sold his steam tractor and threshing machine to a rancher near Weatherford. "He paid off the wagon crew and the field crew and everybody started home. My brother and me came home with Poppa in the truck and the wagon crews will arrive in a couple of days."

When I heard this I knew somehow I had to find a way to retrieve the football or prepare to take the consequences. Maybe my cousins could come up with an idea.

We pooled our funds that amounted to forty-five cents and bought an extra large Dr Pepper float with two scoops of vanilla ice cream and three spoons and three straws, 25 cents please. We took the float to the last table in the back of the store and each of us started sucking on the straws between dips of the ice cream. A ceiling fan, whirling above us, gave some comfort against the heat. There, in hushed tones, I explained my predicament and asked for advice. After discussion, we decided we should ride our bicycles over to Uncle Ole's farm, take a rope with us and lower one of us into the well and retrieve the ball. We elected Cousin Esther for the trip into the well because Cousin Joseph was too fat and too heavy and I didn't think I could climb up the rope to get out. Besides, she was a tiny bit smaller and when she climbed the rope up into the tree house she looked like a monkey.

"But, when should we do it?" I asked. "Probably not until next Saturday," I answered myself. "Cousin Esther and me can ride our bicycles over to Uncle Ole's and you can come up the river road; it's only about three miles. But where are we gonna get a rope strong enough and long enough to do the job?"

"Why don't we use the rope that's there?" Cousin Joseph suggested.

"I tried but I couldn't get it off the spindle," I answered then added. "Besides, it doesn't look strong enough."

"Why couldn't we bring a bucket and lower it into the well?" Cousin Esther asked. "Jacob, I betcha you got a milk bucket we could use."

"Yeah, we do, but where can we find a rope to tie to the bucket?"

"My dad has one in the back of his truck we can probably use," Cousin Joseph replied.

We argued back and forth until we finished the float. On the way out, we each paid a penny for a piece of bubble, then we walked around the square and stopped in front of the Old WW1 cannon sitting in the Court House lawn. We looked in the barrel and saw a bird nest with three eggs. They apparently belonged to a Mockingbird sitting on a nearby limb yelling at us to go away. When we didn't, she swooped down and pecked Cousin Esther on the top of her head. I thought that was hysterically funny and laughed so hard I fell to the ground. Several old-timers sitting around the square chewing tobacco and spitting on the sidewalk, whistled and clapped they hands.

"It ain't funny!" Cousin Esther snarled and kicked my butt and wouldn't talk to me for nearly thirty minutes.

We walked across the street, Cousin Esther tagging silently behind, so we could look at the movie advertisements. 'Cavalcade' with Will Rogers was showing along with the weekly Tom Mix serial. We wanted to see both but we didn't have enough money for all three of us to go.

We decided to save the money we had left and maybe share a hot dog and a Dr Pepper later. With nothing else to do we sat in the shade on the grass and played mumblety-peg. Soon tiring of the game we walked around the square, past the bank, the insurance agency, the five and dime store, a lawyer's office and the barbershop stopping in front of the Mercantile store so we could look at the new green and yellow John Deere tractor in the window. Then we crossed the street, stopped in front of the Texaco station and found a shady place on the sidewalk where we could play marbles.

Cousin Esther, who still wouldn't talk to us, found a chalky rock and drew a circle about ten feet across. We placed our marbles in the circle, picked out our shooters and began to shoot.

Well, it wasn't long until she had all the marbles. Breaking her silence, Cousin Esther taunted, "You both shoot like a couple of old ladies. I'm gonna tell everybody what bad shooters you are." But after a few minutes, she gave us back our marbles and promised not to tell anyone how bad she had beaten us.

We put our marbles in our pockets and walked along the sidewalk, past the dry goods store, passed Dr. Nygard's office, past another lawyer's office, past the beauty shop and stopped in front of the City Drug and sat on the bench left over from Prohibition days where men sat waiting for the drugstore to open so they could buy whiskey. When we heard the whistle announcing the arrival of the 4:10 Express we dashed to the depot to watch the passengers get on or off, curious as to where they were going or where they had been. But today nobody got on or off so the train didn't stop, it slowed to a crawl and the conductor leaned out and threw the mail satchel on the platform, then grabbed the outgoing mailbag with a long hook. Immediately the whistle sounded, steam escaped from the piston and the train began to increase speed.

We watched it disappeared, then walked along the track to the icehouse to watch the men wrestle three hundred pound blocks of ice out of the boxcar and split the blocks into fifty pound pieces and load them on the delivery truck. The boss man chipped off three small pieces, handed them to us and we departed, sucking and licking and rubbing our foreheads with the ice.

With nothing else to see or do, we walked back to the square, sat in the shade of an old oak tree and reviewed the events of the past week. In a few minutes we ran out of anything to review because nothing much had happened and we fell silent. After a few moments Cousin Esther asked if we had heard from Uncle Ole. This surprised me because I didn't think anybody knew he was missing so I told her he was visiting family in West Texas. She asked the same question about Aunt Telinda and I gave her the same response. When she repeated the same question about Baby Angel, I couldn't answer.

We again fell silent for a few minutes, then she asked, "Do you think Uncle Ole set his house on fire? My Momma thinks he did." That thought had never occurred to me and I had no answer. When Cousin Joseph said his father had reached the same conclusion, tears came to my eyes and they both said they were sorry. We agreed to meet next Saturday at Uncle Ole's and try to retrieve the football. Shortly Poppa came out of the Court House and we went home. On the way he told me he had been talking to the sheriff but didn't tell me what they had talked about.

That night, after we finished supper, we gathered in the parlor and Poppa told us Uncle Ole and Aunt Telinda were missing and had been missing since before the fire and so was their baby, Cousin Angel. "Sheriff Bjornburg told me the State Police are looking for them but so far haven't found them."

"Maybe they went somewhere to visit family and just forgot tell anybody," Sister Sybil said. Momma didn't say a word and that surprised me because she usually had plenty to say about nearly everything.

When Poppa didn't answer, Sister Sybil asked, "Did Uncle Ole burn their house down? Aunt Helena thinks he did." She had apparently heard the same rumor Cousin Esther and Cousin Joseph had heard.

Poppa stood for many minutes, hands clasped behind his back, eyes focused on a picture of Jesus Christ nailed to the cross with the crown of thorns on His head and blood trickling down His face. I knew this was Poppa's favorite picture. I also knew he gained great comfort from that picture and often studied it when faced with a serious problem. I had seen him stand this way before.

Then, in a soft serious voice, he answered, "I don't know, Sybil. I just don't know." I thought I saw a tear in his eye as he said, "Let us join hands and pray."

It was an eloquent prayer especially the part about Cousin Angel. Sometimes I thought Poppa should have been a preacher, his prayers were so good. When he finished, I asked Poppa if we were gonna listen to Amos and Andy and he said we weren't. "We're all going to bed and say our prayers." And we did. But it took a long time to go to sleep; Baby Angel was my favorite cousin.

Chapter Six
A Political Meeting

Brother Ben came home last week and thank goodness, he hasn't missed his football. I didn't get a chance to retrieve it last Saturday because I had to stay home and work in the sheep shed. Poppa wasn't satisfies with my progress, so he and Brother Ben joined me for a day or two but then he had get back to plowing in preparation for fall planting.

At supper last night, Poppa announced, "I want all of you to go with Momma and me to the political meeting tomorrow. It's the fourth of July and one of the main candidates for Governor will be there. You need to hear what he has to say. It's time you learn something about politics."

"I was planning to go on a picnic," Brother Ben objected.

"Well, you can just have your picnic at the political meeting. There'll be plenty of food with speeches and singing and maybe some games."

"If you insist. But I'm not gonna like it."

"Benjamin!" That scared me a little because Poppa rarely raised his voice.

"Okay, okay, I'll go. But do I have to sit with that idiot?" he asked, pointing to me.

"Benjamin!! Watch your tongue!" This time it was Momma who yelled and Benjamin slunk in his chair, pouting, but said nothing.

"Do I have to go?" I asked. "Political meeting aren't any fun."

Momma interrupted, "Yes, Jacob, you have to go, all of you have to go."

"They aren't supposed to be fun, they're educational," Poppa added, "That's how we determine the future of the country." I knew by the tone of his voice further argument wouldn't be permitted so I said nothing else.

The meeting would be at the old campground by the Arendal River. I had no interest in the meeting or in the election but thought it might be a good opportunity for my cousins and me to hunt for arrowheads.

Last year, before a Svendahl family reunion, Poppa told us about the campground. In the remote past several Indian tribes used the ten-acre tree covered piece of land by the river two miles north of Arendal as temporary quarters during their annual hunting trips. The Comanche chased off the original tribes and used it for many years until the Army forced them to move to a Reservation in Oklahoma. There were a few who still came to the area every year begging or stealing. Now it was used as a gathering place for church picnics, family reunions and political meetings.

Shortly after we arrived I found my cousins and we walked around and inspected the area. There was a large platform in the middle of the trees with red white and blue banners that said, 'ELECT WAGGNER' or 'ALLRED IS A CROOK'. Another sign said, 'FDR SUPPORTS WAGGNER.' One banner I didn't understand said, 'HAVE YOU HAD YOUR HOOVER CHICKEN TODAY?'

"Do you know what that means?" I asked.

"Nope," both cousins answered.

We went to the barbecue pit and watched Oral Rasmuson use a paintbrush to smear something on huge slabs of meat cooking over a Mesquite fire. He moved one slab that had finished cooking over to a heavy table and the butcher from his meat market sliced it into small pieces and stacked them on a big platter on the serving table. Several ladies from the church stood behind the table ready to load food on the plates and at the other end of the long table, several young high school girls in cute red white and blue dresses were busy filling glasses with ice tea. The smell of barbecue filled the air reminding us how hungry we were so we got in the serving line.

It wasn't long until we reached the table and collected our barbeque, potato salad, baked beans and iced tea then went to the riverbank to eat because all the benches and chairs were full. Just as we dumped out empty plates into a large washtub filled with soapy water and our glasses and silverware into another, the music started so we elbowed our way through the crowd. There was a cowboy band from Fort Worth standing on the stage strumming their guitars, plucking their banjos and sawing on their fiddles while they sang popular cowboy songs. They kinda reminded me of the Light Crust Doughboys but weren't as good.

Suddenly the music stopped and a big man dressed in a Sunday suit climbed up on the platform and began to talk. In a few minutes he took off his coat and I saw that his shirt was soaked with sweat. Nothing he said made any sense to me. Then I noticed the girls.

There were eight of them, four standing on each side of the band wearing ridiculous red white and blue costumes. They had very short skirts and I could see their red and white bloomers. They wore funny little red, white and blue hats and their chests looked really big and their legs were bare clear up to their butts.

"I wish I had a costume like that," Cousin Esther said.

"You'd look ridiculous," I answered.

"No I wouldn't," she answered and hit me on the shoulder.

After about thirty minutes, the man stopped talking, everybody clapped and the music resumed. Then the girls began to dance around the stage getting closer and closer to the edge. Suddenly, the music stopped and the fiddle player made his fiddle screech like a busted axle and the girls turned their backs to audience and bent over until their hands touched the floor and letters on the back of their bloomers spelled W-A-G-G-O-N-E-R. Everybody, especially the men started whistling and whooping and hollering and stamping their feet.

I thought all of this was really interesting until Momma grabbed my arm and dragged me to the car. "You shouldn't be watching that shameful exhibition of nakedness by a bunch of wanton women. Now get in the car and don't you look at the stage." In a few minutes Poppa and the rest of the family came to the car and we went home.

The first thing Momma did when we got there was to give my brother and me a tablespoonful of caster oil. "This'll cleanse the poison out of your systems," she said. Apparently looking at dancing girls was a sin that required cleansing.

For some reason she didn't give my sister any caster oil although I knew she had watched the performance. And she didn't give Poppa any.

"She's got other ways of punishing Poppa," Brother Ben said. But when I asked him what the punishment was, he said, "You wouldn't understand, so just forget about it." And that ended the discussion.

Caster oil was Momma's standard remedy for all ills including evil thoughts and deeds and I guess looking at dancing girls was considered evil. She used caster oil for other ills like laziness, crankiness, bad grades, and failure to say your prayers. Sometimes if the sins were especially bad like cussing, telling lies or running away from home, after the caster oil, you went to the porch, dropped your pants and waited for Poppa and his razor strop. The strop hurt much worse than Momma's switches and the pain lasted long after the effects of the caster oil had worn off. The only consolation was that you usually deserved it.

After the caster oil, we immediately started the milking and finished before dark. After supper and after many trips to the bathroom, we gathered in the parlor, which was unusual because we only used it at Christmas or if we had company. Poppa read from the Bible about sin and damnation and lust and wantonness, none of which I understood. Then he prayed for forgiveness for all his sins of thought and deed and we joined in prayer. And we didn't listen to Amos and Andy.

Brother Ben told me the next morning that Poppa had really gotten in trouble for whistling at the dancing girls and had assured Momma he would vote for Allred.

"There was a big fight after y'all left," Cousin Esther told me the next Saturday. She and her mother had stayed at the meeting but she didn't know what the fight was about. She guessed it had something to do with politics.

Cousin Joseph, who had also stayed at the meeting, said the fights were between the Democrats and a few Republicans who had sneaked into the meeting or maybe it was between the Lutherans and the Catholics, he wasn't sure.

When I told Momma about it, she said, "It must have been the Catholics. They're always causing trouble."

The next Sunday Pastor Pierson preached a sermon I didn't understand but felt it must concern the things that had happened at the meeting ground. There were to be other political meetings before the Democratic Primary Elections, but Momma said we wouldn't be attending. "We already know who's gonna get our vote so there's no use in going."

Poppa told us there would be an election in November between the Democrats and the Republicans. "But that election didn't matter because who ever the Democrats nominated always won."

If that was the case why did they bother to have the election? It seemed stupid to me. I asked Poppa about it and he said it was the law that elections be held in November. Besides, President Roosevelt wanted the elections so he could throw the rest of the worthless Republicans out of Washington.

"That's really stupid," I said and my cousins agreed. We decided that we would never engage in the silliness of politics. And thank goodness, Brother Ben still hadn't missed his football.

Chapter Seven
Hobo Jungle

We were finishing supper last night when Poppa laid down his fork and said, "Son, I've been asked to say a prayer at the burial of a baby from the Hobo Jungle. The funeral is tomorrow and I want you to go with me and sing. I know the family would appreciate it."

"What should I sing?"

"I think 'Jesus Loves Me' would be appropriate."

"Okay," I replied after looking at Momma to be sure she approved. "Should I wear my Sunday clothes?"

"No. Just wear clean overalls and a shirt. And wear shoes."

"Will it be at church?"

"No, it'll be at the cemetery."

"Will Pastor Pierson be there?"

"No. The family asked for me."

"Will we go to the Hobo Jungle?"

"Probably. Momma baked some cookies for the family and we'll deliver them after the funeral."

The thought of visiting the Hobo Jungle thrilled me. I had never been there because Momma had forbidden it. "There's no telling what kind of diseases you're liable to catch in that filthy place," she said on several occasions when the subject came up. I again looked at Momma to make certain she didn't object.

"Can Cousin Esther go along?"

"No," Momma replied. "Aunt Helena's gonna can peas tomorrow and Cousin Esther and me are gonna help."

"Should I take a bath before we go?"

"Absolutely! You can't go to a funeral smelling like a boar hog."

So this morning, after the morning chores and after a bath, I put on clean B.V.D.'s, a clean shirt and overalls and my Sunday shoes, ate a big breakfast and waited for Poppa to get dressed. The funeral would begin at ten.

On the way to the cemetery we talked about the Hobo Jungles and the people in them. "Hobo Jungles are a national tragedy and nobody seems to know what to do about it," he said. "They're mostly families who've lost their jobs, their money, their income, their homes and are forced to travel around the country in old worn out cars and trucks looking for work, any kind of work, and will stay as long as jobs are available. Men without families usually travel by catching rides on freight trains jumping off when the train slows down for a station. They don't beg, they want work, any kind of work."

He continued, "There usually are a few jobs around during threshing, cotton chopping, and cotton picking time. Occasionally there are odd jobs here and there, cleaning weeds out of the orchard, fixing fences and chopping or splitting firewood. Unfortunately many of the local residents are almost as bad off as the Hobos and couldn't afford to hire anyone even at fifty cents a day."

"Sometimes the town folk criticize me for bringing them food. They claim it encourages them to stay and probably attracted others. But somebody has to help, the government can't or won't. They're good people, down on their luck, drifting from one place to another trying to survive until times improve."

"At first they buried their dead, and there were many, especially children, in graves by the river where the dirt is soft and the cat tails grow. But, for health reasons, the county put a stop to it so now the county buries them in pauper's graves. Sometimes Pastor Pierson officiates at these burials but if he can't, the Assistant Arendal Funeral Director who is also a lay preacher conducts the ceremony. This time the family asked me because they heard I could pray real good and didn't charge anything."

When we arrived at the cemetery we found the gravesite in a far back corner in the rocky soil at the foot of the hill. There were no flowers, no music and no mournful church bells tolling in the distance. The family, the assistant funeral director with a disgusted looks on his face, and Poppa and me were the only people in attendance at that lonely funeral. The baby's father wore clean but ragged overalls and a well-worn shirt and a straw hat that obviously had seen better days. The mother wore a faded dress I'm sure came from the barrel of used clothes behind the church. The only decent thing was a nearly new red and blue hat. The three children, a boy and two girls had been scrubbed until they shone and had on clean but ragged overalls and no shoes.

Everybody, except the funeral director, cried when I sang my song. They also cried during Poppa's elegant prayer. There was a deathly silence when the funeral director lowered the tiny coffin made from an apple crate into the grave then hurriedly departed. Everybody, including Poppa and me, cried as we helped the family fill the grave, the grave they has dug yesterday. After we finished that sad task, the family planted a tiny wooden cross with a name scratched on the cross piece at the head of the grave then invited us to share a meal with them at the camp.

I wasn't sure what I expected as we slowly followed the family back to the camp. Poppa offered them a ride but they declined. When we got there I was surprised at how clean and orderly it appeared and I couldn't understand why people called it a jungle. Poppa said that's what they were called all over the country because most of these camps are hidden in the forests.

There were about ten families in the camp and the grounds had been swept and the trash placed in barrels. The children, and there were many, wore ragged hand me down overalls without shirts. None of the children wore shoes but neither did I in summertime. The women mostly wore dresses made from flour sacks; some dyed various colors and some still had the faded label. I guess the thing that impressed me the most was how skinny they all appeared.

We followed the family to their camp, a Model T truck with a shelter made out of an oilcloth suspended from the side of the truck and tied to nearby trees. There were other families in the camp living in lean-tos made from brush, tents made of cardboard boxes or sheets strung over a rope. I didn't see a bed so I asked one of the girls where they slept.

"Up there," she replied pointing to the truck bed. "Poppa sleeps in the truck and Momma sleeps with us."

"Let's eat," the mother said motioning to a table made of an old door suspended across two apple crates. The children and me sat on a rickety wooden bench and Poppa and the man sat on well-worn cracker barrels at each end of the table. Poppa said Grace then the woman picked up a syrup bucket and left saying, "We're gonna have Mulligan stew."

I immediately remembered the story out of a magazine our teacher had read to us last year. At the time I couldn't believe the story but I guess I was about to find out. The story told how to make Mulligan Stew.

First you fill a large cast iron pot with water, place the pot over an open fire, bring the water to a boil, then throw in whatever you can catch like rats, lizards, grub worms, crickets or anything else that's alive. Then you're supposed to throw in cattails from the riverbank and grass from the nearest field and several ears of corn if they're available. When cooked it's called Mulligan stew.

When she returned with the food she looked at me and said, "Son, I saw that look on your face. Don't worry. It's only got vegetables and a pound of hamburger meat. Add some salt and pepper and I think you'll like it." And I did and asked for more.

After we finished eating, Poppa said Grace then presented the cookies to the family. In ten minutes they were gone. The children left to play, then Poppa and me settled down to hear the man's story.

He, at first, seemed reluctant but we both knew he was anxious to talk so we sat quietly and waited. The mother went to the river to wash the dishes and finally he began.

They were John and Mary Archer, a family of sharecroppers from Louisiana with four, now three, children. They scratched out a meager living on a fifty-acre cotton farm until the AAA forced them to plow under half their crop. They expected to get some of the money but they didn't. The owner of the land got all the money and they got nothing. When they harvested the rest of the crop, they only got eight cents a pound or forty dollars a bale for the cotton, which they split with the landowner. That didn't leave enough money to pay off the annual loan for the seed and food for a year. He gave the landlord all the money he had but the man had him evicted and they left the county one step ahead of the sheriff who had a warrant for the man's arrest as a debtor and thief. They didn't follow him because the county jail was already filled with other sharecroppers behind on their debts.

He said they found a little work along the way, a day here, a half-day there but when they reached Arendal, they ran out of gas about a mile away from town and didn't have enough money to buy any more. A man from the Hobo Jungle happened to walk by and helped him push the truck to where it now stood. He said he had been unable to find any work so far and they were down to their last penny and he didn't know what they were gonna do. "Might have to put the kids in an orphanage," he mumbled.

I didn't quite understand the story but I could tell it made Poppa mad. It seemed obvious he was a broken man after the death of the baby and Poppa loaned him ten dollars.

On the way home we talked some more about the Hobos and their problems. "The County Commissioners arranged for outhouses so they wouldn't have to use slit trenches as toilets," he said. "Sometimes ladies from the various church societies distribute food and basic supplies like soap, sugar, salt and pepper. But mostly they are ignored."

When we got home we sat in the car and Poppa continued to talk. It seemed to me that he, for some reason, really wanted to get it off his chest. I just know I felt closer to him than I had ever felt.

"Son," Poppa continued, "Sheriff Bjornburg says crime is not a problem in these camps. The occupants have an honor code and rules of conduct and specific punishment for the transgressors, usually expulsion from the camp."

"Now, south of town there's another camp I want you to avoid. That's where the criminals; mostly thieves, pickpockets, yeggs and muggers gather hoping to hide from the law. They don't seek work; in fact they consider work sinful. They survive by begging what they can beg and stealing the rest. Hobos have no use for them and if one wanders into a Hobo Jungle they are usually beaten and expelled."

We sat quietly for a few moments, then he continued. "There's another camp five miles south of town where murderers and rapists hide. Don't ever go near that place, you might get killed. The Waco police or the county sheriff go there every week and arrest the whole bunch. But within a week another batch shows up."

Poppa stopped talking for a few moments and my thoughts strayed to the children. I remembered what our Sunday school teacher said. "These children are starving for food and they're also starving for some stability in their lives. None of them go to school and the only education they get comes from their parents."

I know Poppa had invited several of the families to church and had suggested the children should come to Sunday school. But they rarely came. Momma said their clothing is not appropriate to wear in church so they stay at home.

Two weeks ago Pastor Pierson brought a boy of about my age from the Hobo Jungle to our Sunday school class. "This is Daniel," Pastor Pierson said to our group. "He wants to visit your class and join in the activities. Please make him feel at home."

The first thing I noticed was his shoes. I think they were sneakers but they were so worn I couldn't tell for sure and rubber bands made from inner tubes held the soles in place. His overalls were clean but worn and were way too big for his frail body and a rusty nail secured one of the shoulder straps to the bib.

"Your name is Daniel?" I asked.

"Yes."

"Does that come from the Bible?"

"I don't know" he replied.

"You know, the story about Daniel in the lion's den?"

"I don't know that story."

After a few minutes, I offered him my Bible opened it to the story about Daniel.

He looked at a few pages, then, with tears in his eyes, he handed it backed. "I can't read," he said and ran out of the building crying.

I wept that might as I said my prayers asking God to help the poor unfortunate child, the young boy whose name is Daniel.

Finally Poppa stopped talking because Momma came to the car to see what was keeping us and to tell us dinner was ready. When he told her he was going to take some milk to the Archer family whenever he could, she asked, "How are they going to pay you?"

"With their gratitude," Poppa answered.

And when he told Momma he loaned the man ten dollars she threw a fit. "Don't you know better than to loan money to them bums? You know you'll never see it again. You need to stop giving it away and think of your own family!" She didn't speak to him the rest of the day.

Two days after the funeral, when Poppa went to deliver a syrup bucket full of milk to the Archer family, they were gone. Someone in a nearby tent said they had pulled up stakes the night of the funeral and headed west. When he came home and told Momma, her response was, "Serves you right!" which made Poppa furious.

Chapter Eight
The Orchard

It had been a tough two weeks digging manure out of the sheep shed. Even with Poppa's help I wasn't making very much progress. Brother Ben was still plowing so Poppa hired two men from the Hobo Jungle and with the extra help we finished yesterday. So today I hoped we would go to town.

Thank goodness, Brother Ben still hadn't missed his football but when school starts in six weeks I was sure he would. I think he was too busy plowing to miss it and too tired to look. But we didn't go to town. Poppa wanted to work on the truck.

I rode my bicycle to Cousin Esther's and together we rode the three miles over to Uncle Ole's. I was surprised when Cousin Esther met me at their gate wearing a flowered green dress. She usually wore bib overalls without a shirt just like Cousin Joseph and me. And sometimes in the summer, just like us boys, she would cool off by dropping the bib so she could bathe her chest. When I asked her why she was wearing a dress, she answered, "My Momma made me wear it. She said I either had to wear a shirt under my overalls or wear a dress."

"Why?" I asked.

"Because she said I'm coming of age."

There's that 'coming of age' business again. I wish someone would explain it to me. Maybe I'll ask Sister Selma the next time she comes home. She knows everything.

"You want to ride to town?" I asked.

"I thought we were going to Uncle Ole's farm and try to get the football."

"You're all dressed up like you were going to town so I thought that's where you wanted to go."

"No, I want to get the football. Come on, let's get going. Is Cousin Joseph coming?"

"Yeah. I called him earlier and he said he'd meet us there, but he said he might be a little late. Some problem at home."

When we got to Uncle Ole's place Cousin Joseph was already waiting. "Poppa took the truck to Fort Worth for repairs and he hasn't got back yet," he said. "He left before I could get the rope, so we ain't got one."

"Well, what should we do?" Cousin Esther asked.

"I don't know," was my response.

"Maybe we could get the rope off the spindle and try to catch the football in the bucket," Cousin Joseph suggested. "It's worth a try."

"Maybe there's a ladder going down into the well," Cousin Esther suggested. "Grandma Svendahl's well has a ladder, I've seen it. I could climb down the ladder and grab the football and put it in the bucket. Then we could haul it up by hand."

"I didn't see a ladder when I looked down in the well," I answered.

"Maybe it was too dark to see a ladder," Cousin Joseph said. "I think we oughta go look." After further discussion, we agreed.

We left our bicycles by the road, walked across the cattle guard, briefly examined the remains of the house and then started toward the well. When we rounded the edge of the barn, I thought I saw someone or something come out of the orchard and dash across the road. I couldn't be sure, might have been a deer and in a moment it disappeared. "Did you see that?" I asked

"What?" both cousins ask.

"Something ran across the road and disappeared up into the mountain."

"I didn't see anything," Cousin Joseph replied.

"Neither did I." Cousin Esther added. "What was it?"

"Looked like a person but it might have been a deer."

We watched for a few moments, saw nothing so we walked on to the well. It seemed unchanged from the day of the football tragedy. The lid was still open and the crank was still frozen. We leaned over and looked into the well. There was no ladder but we could see the football floating in the water and the rope going down to the bucket.

"One of us oughta climb down the rope and put the ball in the bucket," Cousin Esther said.

"I ain't going down no rope!" Cousin Joseph said. "I'd never be able to climb out."

"I don't think I could either," I said.

"Don't ask me to go down into no well," Cousin Esther protested. "It might break and I'd drown."

After lengthy discussion, we finally decided to wait until we could get a better rope so we went to the orchard to maybe get some peaches to eat on the way back.

Uncle Ole had a pretty good size orchard down by the river with about forty or fifty peach, plum and pear trees. In early summer he usually gathered them and sold them at a stand in front of the courthouse. But this year he was gone so no one had gathered the peaches and now they had mostly rotted and fallen to the ground and the ones still on the trees were half eaten by birds or squirrels.

When we reached the center of the orchard, we found a large pile of peach limbs someone had cut off and stacked in a large pile. "Looks like somebody's been pruning out the dead limbs," Cousin Joseph commented.

"But who?" I asked. "Uncle Ole's been gone all summer and these look fresh cut."

We walked around the pile and kicked at the limbs trying to decide the meaning of our find. Unable to solve the puzzle, Cousin Joseph said, "Come on, let's go. We gotta get back before dark." Before either of us could answer, we heard what sounded like a gunshot coming from the hill across the road. When we looked in that direction, we saw a man standing in a little clearing on top of the hill holding a gun. Before we could do anything, he fired another shot that tore up the dirt about twenty yards away. Terrified, we dashed to our bicycles and raced down the river road until we reached Cousin Joseph's house.

Hot, sweaty and exhausted, we dunked our heads in the water trough, shook ourselves dry and then sat on his back porch and discussed the problem.

"Why was that man shooting at us," I asked. "We weren't doing nothing wrong."

"I don't know," Cousin Joseph replied. "Maybe he thought we were stealing peaches. Could you see who it was?"

"He was too far away and I was too scared to look."

"Me too," Cousin Joseph said.

Neither of us said anything for several minutes, then Cousin Esther said, "Something about that man looked familiar."

"So, who do you think it was?

"I don't know. I just know he looked familiar."

"I think we oughta go back out there next Saturday," I suggested. "Maybe we can figure out what's going on."

"I don't know about that!" Cousin Joseph answered, shaking his head. "I'm not so sure we should. We're liable to get shot. Whoever it was seemed mighty serious."

"Maybe whoever did the shooting was just trying to scare us, "Cousin Esther suggested. "But why?"

"I bet he thought we were stealing his peaches," I answered. "But they ain't his, they belong to Uncle Ole."

"Well, I don't know about the peaches. I just don't think we oughta go back unless one of our parents goes along."

"Then I'll just go by myself," I replied. "If I told my parents were we were today, they would throw a fit and I'll get grounded, especially if I told them about the gun."

"If you decide to go, I better go with you," Cousin Esther answered. "I don't think it would be a good idea to go alone."

I thought about that for a moment, than said, "Yeah, you're probably right. I just wish I knew who shot at us," and that ended the discussion. We got a drink of water out of the horse trough hydrant, then Cousin Esther and me headed home.

In spit of the failure, I wasn't ready to tell my brother about his football. And I wasn't about to tell Poppa where we went. And I sure wasn't gonna tell him what happened while we were there. If I did, he'd order me to stay away and I'd never have a chance to recover the football. When we got home, it was almost dark and he asked me where we'd been so I told him a lie. I felt bad about it but I didn't think I had a choice. "We went to town and had a Dr Pepper float."

Pastor Pierson had recently discussed lying in Sunday school. "Tell a small lie and soon you'll have to tell a bigger one to cover it up. Tell a bigger one and pretty soon your whole life will be a lie." This made sense and I believed him. So, I would just keep it to myself for now and address it in my prayers. I hoped my cousins would do the same.

Chapter Nine
Chopping Cotton

The next Monday after our trip to Uncle Ole's, Poppa announced, "We gotta start chopping cotton today. The weeds are about to crowd out the cotton plants."

"Aw Poppa, "I whined, "cain't we wait a day or two? I'm still pooped from cleaning out the sheep shed."

"Son, you weren't too pooped to ride to town on your bicycle last Saturday," Poppa said.

I could tell by the tone of his voice that he didn't believe my lies and further argument might bring punishment so I dropped the subject and prepared to spend the day in the hot boiling sun.

"Who's gonna be chopping?" I asked

"Cousin Gertrude and two men from the Hobo Jungle and of course, you."

"Aren't you gonna be chopping?"

"No son. I have to help Benjamin pull the rest of the corn so he can run the stalk cutter and start the deep plowing. I had planned on you being the boss while I'm helping him. When we finish, I'll help with the chopping. Until then, you're the boss."

"What about Uncle Ole and Aunt Telinda? Will they be chopping?"

"No, Son, they aren't back from their trip."

"And you want me to be the boss?"

"That's right. I want you to be the boss. I know you can do it."

Poppa knew I wanted to help him pull the corn because it was much easier than chopping cotton. Did he really expect me to be the boss of the chopping crew? Cousin Gertrude would never let me be her boss. The Hobos might, but Cousin Gertrude? No! Never! Not in a million years would she take orders from some silly nine-year-old brat like me.

As was our custom, before going to the field, we listened to the weather report. "104 degrees" the man on WBAP predicted.

"Jacob," Momma said, "you gotta wear something on your head or the sun'll bake your brain."

"Don't worry Momma," Brother Ben piped up. "He ain't got a brain in his head so the sun cain't do no harm."

"Yes I do have a brain."

"No you don't. Nobody as stupid as you could have a brain."

"Mine's better than yours, fat gut!"

"Boys! Boys! Stop that infernal bickering and Jacob, I want you to wear my bonnet, the pink one."

I knew that wouldn't work. Not the pink one with the blue flowers. How could I possibly be the boss in a pink bonnet? The other workers would laugh at me and Brother Ben would call me a sissy. "Why can't I wear one of Poppa's old hats?"

"Because they're too big," Momma replied. But in the end we found one that sorta fit after I wrapped a bandanna around my head.

On the way to the field, hoe on my shoulder, I contemplated my new position. I could hear it now. Cousin Gertrude would say, "Don't you go giving me no orders you little twerp" and if she said anything else I might start crying.

But, much to my surprise, she didn't object. I think Poppa probably talked to her and she agreed to accept my suggestions but I didn't have to give her any because she had much more experience in chopping cotton than I did and the Hobos didn't seem to resent my showing them what to do so things went well that first day.

Momma said Poppa was gonna pay Cousin Gertrude a dollar a day like always but he could only pay the Hobo fifty cents a day and the noon meal unless they were really good. She said it was up to me to decide how good they were and if they were really good Poppa might pay them seventy-five cents a day. I asked Momma if Poppa was gonna pay me for chopping and she said, "Probably not." Well, that's okay as long as I get my twenty-five cents every Saturday to spend as I please. And I decided then that the Hobos would have to be really bad before I would tell Poppa they were only worth fifty cents.

I hated chopping cotton almost as bad as cleaning out the sheep shed. It was dull and boring and, even with the hat, the blistering sun and the scorching heat made serious thinking impossible so I spent my time reviewed past concerns; like why did someone take a shot at us at Uncle Ole's farm and why did the government kill all our baby pigs and half the sows last year? And why did they make Poppa plow up half of last year's oats, wheat and cotton and corn. I know they paid Poppa two dollars each for the pigs and seven dollars for the sows. I also know he got paid for plowing up the crops but he wouldn't tell me how much. The whole thing didn't make any sense to me.

When I asked Poppa about it, he said, "To boost prices. I just hope the

JACOB'S CLOAK

heck they know what their doing."

Chopping along, removing the weeds and trying to decide how many cotton plants to leave in each hill, I thought about the next Saturday. Since we probably weren't going back to Uncle Ole's farm, maybe we could we go down to the swimming hole and jump into the cool still waters behind the Arendal dam. Would we finally have enough nerve to swing on the rope and dive into the water? Probably not. Cousin Joseph would and I might but not Cousin Esther.

I learned to swim when Brother Ben took me to the river and threw me in shouting, "Sink or swim, you little twerp!" and I did and so did my cousins except he didn't throw Cousin Esther in like he did us. He carried her into the water and supported her as she screamed and hollered and sometimes cried. But we all learned.

The main problem with the swimming hole was the cottonmouth water moccasins that called it their home. You had to be careful when you dashed along the trail to the river and you had to be careful you didn't land on one when you jumped in. Fortunately they were just as afraid of us as we were of them and Brother Ben told us they can't bite under water but I didn't believe him so I always looked before I jumped.

Continuing to chop, my mind wandered to the task of filling the silo with ensilage made from sugar cane stalks. We did this the week before the fourth of July and it was similar to threshing grain and only took two days. Work all day then sit around in the evening and listen to stories from the past when men were men and Comanche roamed the area.

That's when Poppa told us the story about his sister, Aunt Thelma, who the Comanche kidnapped when she was fourteen, held for four years and then traded her back to her parents for a sack of corn and the colorful wool blanket hanging on the clothesline with the comment that she couldn't be tamed. Some time later Cousin Gertrude was born and she didn't look like a Norwegian but the family accepted her without question because she was an exceptionally good child and grew up to be such a good worker.

After Aunt Thelma's twenty-first birthday, she took her child and visited the Comanche Reservation in Oklahoma but came back in a week very depressed and, according to Sister Sybil, cut her wrists with a butcher knife.

When Cousin Gertrude turned eighteen, Aunt Thelma came down with consumption and spent the rest of her life at a sanitarium in East Texas and finally died when I was three. Cousin Gertrude took over their farm but leased it out to a neighbor and spent her time working for other farmers. Momma

59

said she seemed quite contented. I just knew she wasn't like my sisters and certainly not like Momma. I thought she was a little too bossy, but then, what did I know about women.

One time I worked up enough courage to ask Cousin Gertrude if her father was an Indian. She said it wasn't any of my business. I got the same answer from Momma, but Sister Selma told me, "Her father is a famous Comanche Chief."

The day after we finished filling the silo, Poppa went to Aunt Helena's house to help make molasses using sugar cane but I didn't go along. I had to stay home and clean the chicken house again, a job we usually did every other week. And after he came home, we had to prepare the tractor for heavy plowing by grinding the sleeves and the valves and changing the piston rings.

It took two weeks to chop the cotton and on the night we finished I heard Momma and Poppa talking in the kitchen. I was so tired I went straight to bed. But before I went to sleep, I heard Cousin Angel's name mentioned. I really miss her.

Chapter Ten
Cousin Angel

Beautiful Miss Boudegard, who taught all the classes in Buffalo Flat elementary school and also my first love, nurtured me through letters and numbers when I was six. When I was seven, Sonja Henie replaced Miss Boudegard after I watched her glide effortlessly across the ice at the local movie theatre. Poppa said he thought she might be a distant relative but I think that made Momma mad so I never brought it up but kept her in my dreams.

Later Shirley Temple replaced Sonja Henie and was the last of what Momma called my puppy loves. Cousin Esther came later but she was a cousin so I didn't think about her day and night until we were much older.

Sometimes I sat with Cousin Esther during church services but usually I sat between Momma and Poppa. Once a month the women of the church would spread a picnic either in the basement of the church, or, if it wasn't too cold or hot or if it wasn't raining, they would spread it in the yard beside the parsonage. Every family was expected to bring a dish, some good, some bad, but there was always plenty to eat.

These were the days I really enjoyed. My two cousins and I would go up into the mountain behind the church and have our own picnic with whatever we could steal from the table. We would be ten in December and were beginning to take notice of the opposite sex, not that anything came of it. To me, Cousin Esther was more like a sister than a friend. We just knew changes were occurring in our relationships.

One day, when Momma saw Cousin Esther and me holding hands, she mentioned that cousins shouldn't get married,. "It's okay to be friends," she said. "But that's as far as it should go. Just remember that."

I asked Cousin Esther what she thought about my mother's advice and she said mothers are like that and if the time ever came when we wanted to get married we would just do it. I asked Cousin Joseph what he thought about cousins getting married and he said they shouldn't. "Don't you remember Cousin Sylvia? She married her cousin and when she had a baby it was a monkey."

"Aw, that's not true," Cousin Esther replied. "It wasn't a monkey, it just didn't have a head. Besides she married her half brother, not her cousin."

I thought about asking Sister Sybil but felt she would just laugh at me. And

I certainly wouldn't ask Brother Ben. He would grab me around the neck, rub my scalp with his knuckles and call me a pervert, whatever that meant.

I just knew when Cousin Esther and I were together, I felt good and I think she felt the same way. Cousin Joseph didn't seem to mind that Cousin Esther and I were growing closer. In fact, he seemed to have eyes for another girl, Suzie Swisher whose father was head cashier at the bank making forty-five dollars a month, but he was too shy to approach her. Cousin Esther offered to help but he declined. "I don't think she likes fat boys," he said. I think he just didn't want to risk being rejected. So, Cousin Esther and I usually led the way in our adventures and Cousin Joseph tagged along behind.

Last weekend, at Sunday evening church services, Pastor Pierson offered a prayer for Uncle Ole and Aunt Telinda and a special prayer for Baby Angel asking God to guide and protect them wherever they may be. I noticed Poppa and Momma were both crying. I had never seen Poppa cry before so I cried too. And on the way home I could think of nothing but Baby Angel.

She came to Uncle Ole and Aunt Telinda three years ago and everybody said it was a miracle because Aunt Telinda was forty years old at the time and maybe too small to bear a child. We visited her several times during the pregnancy and Momma kept saying how blessed she was. Poppa kept congratulating Uncle Ole and everybody seemed so happy. When I asked Momma why Aunt Telinda never had any children, she answered, "It was God's wish. Now God wants her to have a child before she gets any older."

I didn't really understand any of this, but Cousin Esther said they couldn't have any children because Uncle Ole was a drunkard. I didn't understand that either but I was glad everybody was so happy.

When the baby arrived after what Momma called a long and painful delivery at home, it was obvious they had been blessed. At her Baptism six weeks later Pastor Pierson said she had been sent from heaven and they should call he 'Angel' and they did. Poppa said he had never seen such a beautiful baby and Momma agreed.

Uncle Ole couldn't stop showing her off by taking her to town on the flimsiest excuse. Poppa said he even quit drinking except maybe a nip or two at Christmas and the Fourth of July.

That night I said a special prayer asking God to protect and defender her and bring her back safe and sound. If He did, I promised God I would dedicate my life to her protection. Then I went to sleep and dreamed some really frightening dreams. After maybe an hour I woke up and heard Momma and Poppa arguing in the kitchen. Both sounded kinda mad so I sneaked downstairs and listened.

"Your brother is a drunk!" I heard Momma say. "When are you going to accept that and quit worrying so much about it."

I didn't hear his response but I heard what Momma said next. "I want you to spend some time with Pastor Pierson. Maybe he can beat some sense into your thick skull." I heard a door slam so I slipped back to my room and tried to go back to sleep.

Chapter Eleven
Radio

We started the afternoon milking early today because Poppa wanted to listen to a 'Fireside Chat' by President Roosevelt. "We got serious problems in the country and I hope he has some new ideas about how to fix it," Poppa said. So I didn't get to listen to 'Jack Armstrong, the All American Boy' that came on at five. The only reason I listened to the President was because Poppa insisted. However, I understood little of what he said and I could tell Poppa was disappointed. After the speech we did get to listen to Allen's Alley with George Burns and Gracie Allen followed by Amos and Andy.

Momma threw a fit last year when Poppa went to Montgomery Ward's in Fort Worth and paid twenty dollars for an Atwater-Kent radio. "That thing is an instrument of the Devil and I oughta make him take it back!" Momma barked when he hauled in the house. "Every one of our children need new shoes and winter coats, now they won't get them because you squandered all of our money."

Poppa and Brother Ben strung an antenna made of copper wire across the roof and brought one end into the house and hooked it to a screw on the back of the radio. Then he plugged an extension cord into the three way light socket on the ceiling, and plugged the other end into the radio. Holding our breath, we watched Poppa turn it on and clapped when we heard the music. Momma began to cry and we knew that within an hour, she'd be in the bed with a wet rag over her eyes and Sister Sybil standing by her side holding the vomit bucket and fanning her with a Ladies Home Journal.

Later, after the vomiting started, Brother Ben said to me, "She's that way because you're a spoiled brat who came too late in Momma's life and wasn't wanted in the first place. I think they oughta put you in an orphanage."

The next day, when I told Poppa what Brother Ben had said, he took him to the back porch and whipped his butt even though he outweighed Poppa by thirty pounds. Brother Ben didn't speak to me for weeks.

Momma took the problem to Pastor Pierson who assured her God didn't object to radios unless it interfered with prayers or Bible studies. And by the end of the first month she began to brag to friends and relatives about the wonderful programs we could hear.

We were seven, Cousin Esther, Cousin Joseph and me, when they brought electric lines to our farm. We ran down the road and watched the men dig holes and sink tall poles in each hole. Then they strung wire from pole to pole and when they got to our house, they hooked the wires to something they called a transformer. We followed as they marched across the Flat, hooking one house after another to the line until they stopped for the day. We raced back to the house in time to see Poppa and the man from the electric company string lines from the transformer to the house, the milk barn, the sheep shed and the chicken house, hooking each line to a fuse box. Then they strung wires from the fuse box on the back porch to the kitchen, the dining room, the parlor and their bedroom. We watched as Poppa screwed the fuses into the box and waited anxiously as he pulled the cord that hung down from the ceiling light. Then, like magic, the room was flooded with the brightest light I had ever seen. Momma, of course, immediately came down with a sick headache and Sister Sybil dashed for the vomit bucket. "That light is gonna cause us all to go blind," she sobbed. But in a week she acted like she couldn't get along without it.

After Poppa bought the radio our nightly routine rarely changed. Finish the chores, eat supper, clean the dishes then gather in the dining room. Poppa would sit in his easy chair by the window and read his Bible or the Progressive Farmer magazine and Momma would lie down on the divan and look at 'Woman's Home Companion' and we children would sit around the table and start our homework. If we didn't have any, we would pretend that we did.

Soon Poppa would doze off and his Bible or magazine would fall to his lap and sometimes to the floor and Momma would begin to snore and her upper plate would fall down. Then the argument would start. "It's my turn to choose tonight and I want to listen to the Jack Benny show," I whispered. I knew if I didn't express my choice first I'd never get to listen to anything I liked.

"That doesn't come on until tomorrow night, stupid." Brother Ben said. "It's my turn and I say we're gonna listen to the baseball game!"

"You're both wrong," Sister Sybil interrupted. "It's my turn and I say we're gonna listen to the Texaco Hour."

If we got a little too loud Momma would wake up and say, "Children, if you don't stop that infernal arguing I'm gonna have your father take that thing to the wood pile and smash it to bits. He shoulda never bought in the first place. All it's ever done is cause trouble in the family." I knew this wasn't true; she enjoyed it just as much as we did.

If our arguing woke Poppa he would say, "You're wasting your breath quarrelling about it. We're gonna spend the rest of the evening studying Revelations."

One night I made the mistake of saying "Poppa, we've already studied Revelations twice this week" which earned me a trip to the back porch with my pants down and a week's loss of selection privileges.

There was one program we never argued about. It was the nightly 'Amos and Andy' show. It came on six nights a week and we never missed it. We would anxiously watch the clock and when the time came, we would turn to the right station, turn up the volume and wake them up.

The program featured the characters Amos & Andy, two black men who drove a window-less taxicab for the 'Fresh Air Taxi Company'. Other characters on the program were Kingfish who was a member of the 'Mystical Knights of the Sea' and Stonewall, a scheming crooked lawyer. Momma and a girl friend named Sophia also participated on the program. The program was so popular that, on Saturday night when it came on, they stopped the movies in the theatre so people could listen. When the program was over they would restart the movie.

I couldn't believe it when Poppa told me that 'Amos and Andy' were two white men pretending to be black. "I saw their pictures in the Star Telegram and they're as white as you or me."

Electricity changed our lives in so many ways. It changed how Momma cooked our meals and the electric lights eliminated the smoky coal oil lamps and made reading and studying much easier. In the winter we still heated the house with the Franklin wood-burning stove but in the coldest weather, she warmed our beds with bricks heated in the electric oven.

The electric refrigerator, a Kelvinator with the funny round thing on the top, kept the milk from turning blinky and kept our food from spoiling and eliminated the need for a fifty-pound block of ice delivered every other day. And the electric stove prevented the kitchen from being so hot in the summer.

The daily routine rarely changed. Get up at five, eat a slice of bread with butter, milk the cows, fix bottles for the orphaned calves and take enough to the house for family needs. What was left, Poppa would mix with ground wheat and oats, add the table scraps, and feed it to the pigs.

At six o'clock, we would always stop work and go to the house and eat breakfast while Poppa listened to the stock market and the weather report. After breakfast we would finish the chores and Momma would listen to The Early Bird program with Jimmy Jeffries. We had to finish all these chores by seven thirty so we could catch the school bus during the school year or start with fieldwork during the summer. At dinnertime Poppa again listened to the noon news and the weather and stock market report.

The evening routine usually started about five. Saddle up the horse and round up the cows and the sheep, milk the cows, take the milk to the house, fill the bottles for the calves, feed the horses, slop the pigs, pen the sheep and fill their water trough, haul mash to the chicken house and fill the hoppers, throw down ensilage for the cows, feed the baby calves, help Momma run the milk through the separator, then eat supper hoping we could finish in time to catch the eight o'clock radio programs.

I guess living on a farm had its advantages. We never went hungry like a lot of people, especially the people in the Hobo Jungle and I almost always got my twenty-five cents every Saturday. But I was beginning to think I didn't want to be a farmer when I grew up.

Chapter Twelve
Wages of Sin

Sometimes there are moments on a farm when the chores are caught up and there's time to relax. Yesterday Brother Ben finished the first plowing and the second plowing with the double disk harrow and the toothed harrow in tandem could wait a day or two with plenty of time left for planting.

It rained a little bit last Thursday but Poppa said it was still too dry and if we didn't get some more rain pretty soon, the cotton might not mature. The tank in the upper pasture went dry last week and now we have to carry water to the sheep pen every day.

"Son, it ain't as dry as it was in '17 when it didn't rain a drop for six months," Poppa said when I complained about carrying the water. "That year most of the farmers, including us, lost their crops and had to borrow money from the bank. Many farmers sold their livestock and some lost their farms."

Last week we sprayed the cotton for boll weevils and, because of the drought, Poppa said there weren't enough weeds to justify hoeing the cotton again. Hurrah for the drought, I thought, but I didn't say it out loud. Day before yesterday, we dug up all the potatoes and now we have twenty sacks stored in the smokehouse.

About a month ago, when they were ripe, Momma and Sister Sybil picked all the Mustang grapes from the vines covering the oak trees around the tank in the upper pasture, They brought three large tubs full to the house and used them to made grape jelly, jam and grape juice for us and gave some of the juice to Pastor Pierson who would use it to make Communion wine.

Week before last, Momma and Sister Sybil picked all the peas, the beans, the sweet corn and the okra. They shelled the peas, snapped the beans, boiled the okra and shaved the corn from the cob then sealed each item in cans and cooked them in the pressure cooker.

Last week Momma and Aunt Helena and Sister Sybil gathered the peaches, pears, apricots and figs, cooked them and stored them in one quart Mason jars. Now we have forty-eight jars of four kinds of preserves. They also gathered the plums and made plum jelly and jam and poured them in one-pint Mason jars and sealed each jar with hot paraffin. They used what was left of the tomatoes to made ketchup and now the vines were ready to be pulled. Cousin Esther and I helped by hauling the jars and cans to the pantry and now it is full and the garden is ready to be plowed but that would only take a day.

With these tasks complete, both Momma and Poppa felt we had sufficient food to last until next summer. So Poppa decided this would be a good day to go to Waco.

"I'm having trouble reading the paper so I want to go to Woolworth's and get a new pair of glasses."

"I want to look at a new school dress for Sybil and new Sunday shoes for Jacob," Momma said, "and I want to get pencils and writing pads for school."

From the last cold spell in spring until the first cold spell in the fall we went barefooted except on Sunday. That's when we wore dress shoes. And in the winter we wore high top sneakers to school and at home.

Momma bought the sneakers from Mr. Wolinski, owner of the Dry Goods Store in Arendal, for a dollar ninety-nine. Once a year, usually in June when everybody started going barefoot, Mr. Wolinski would have a sale and you could get them for a dollar forty-nine. That's when we usually got new ones. Momma always bought my shoes one size too big so I wouldn't outgrow them before I wore them out except they fell off when I ran and everybody laughed at me.

I didn't think I needed new Sunday shoes this year because my old ones still fit although the sole on one shoe had come loose and flapped when I walked and the heels are kinda worn down. "Poppa can take my shoes to the cobbler and have them fixed," I told Momma. "That won't cost near as much as new ones."

We had definite positions in the car for the trip. Brother Ben sat by the window behind Poppa and Sister Sybil sat by the other window behind Momma and I sat in the middle.

"Sit over there and don't you dare come any closer," Brother Ben snarled, pointing to the space beside Sister Sybil.

"Why don't you stand on the running board? Then I won't be so close?" I replied. "Children, stop arguing!" Momma yelled.

Cousin Esther sorta had a standing invitation to go with us when we went to Waco and such was the case today. She always sat in the front seat between Momma and Poppa. I thought that's where I oughta sit but Poppa said, "I can't shift gears if you sit there because of your long legs and bony knees" which wasn't true. We were still about the same size and my knees weren't bony. I think he just wanted her by his side.

I noticed Cousin Esther was wearing the dress she wore when we rode our bicycles to Uncle Ole's farm, but today she had a red belt around her middle.

I thought she looked kinda cute. I told her so and she blushed.

Both Momma and Poppa always got their glasses by going to the counter at the Woolworth's store filled with all shapes and strengths and sizes. An eye chart on the back of the counter provided a way to test your vision and sometimes it took half a day before a satisfactory pair could be found. A sign tacked to the table stated, "If you can't find a fit on this table, Dr. Arald, Certified Optometrist, whose office is in the back of the store, would be happy to assist."

The road to Waco was narrow and rough and I got a little carsick. On one particularly bad stretch near China Springs we had to stop so I could puke which everyone except Momma thought was hysterically funny. But, by the time we got to Waco and parked behind the Monnig's store, I had recovered.

We all went to the shoe store and I was thankful Momma didn't try to fit me with new shoes. We did look at them but Momma said, "We can't afford those. Four ninety-eight for a pair of shoes! Preposterous! We'll just send yours to the cobbler" like it was her idea in the first place.

Then we went our separate ways, Poppa and Brother Ben headed toward Montgomery Wards to get a new fan belt for the tractor, Momma and Sister Sybil went to Monnig's to look at the ridiculous clothes as Momma called them, and Cousin Esther and me went to Kress's and paid twenty five cents for a double banana split and a nickel for a sack of horehound candy. Nobody wanted us tagging along so Cousin Esther and me pretty much went our own way with certain restrictions. "You can go into any store, admire but not touch any of the merchandise and you're not to leave Austin Avenue," Momma said. "Meet us in front of Kress's at three for the trip home. And behave yourselves."

"Okay," we both replied.

Momma said we would probably stop at Hillcrest Hospital on the way home to see Sister Selma. She was in her second year of nursing training and Momma thought she might be a little homesick.

I knew Momma had prepared lunch so I felt sure we would eat on the way home, maybe in Cameron Park by the Brazos River where the CCC boys were working. At least I hoped that's where we would eat.

Poppa had told me that the CCC employed boys age twenty to twenty five to work all over the country on forestry projects, flood control and beautification of roads and parks. They built fire brakes and lookout towers in the National Forests and bridges, campgrounds, trails and museums in the National Parks. They were paid thirty dollars a month and were required to send twenty-five dollars out of each pay check home to their families. It seemed to be a very popular program and, according to Poppa, they had already hired over a million boys. "It also helped support a million destitute families." Poppa added.

He also said the twenty-five dollars they sent home was all the money some families had to live on. Poppa said he was strongly in favor of the project and that it was one of the few things the government got right.

After the banana split and after we selected the candy, we moseyed along looking at the store windows, admiring the many shinny black cars parked along the street and looked in the barbershop and the beauty shop next door. We studied the movie marquee and the advertisements for coming attractions and decided what we wanted to see if we ever got the chance. Sometimes we held hands, most of the time we didn't.

We went to the Amicable Building and rode the elevator to the top. The elevator lady, a friendly little woman who kinda reminded me of Aunt Telinda, wouldn't let us out of the elevator unless we had an appointment at one of the offices which we didn't, so we rode back down to the main floor and continued our tour.

Finally, the August sun got the better of us and we returned to Kress's because it was cooler than most of the other stores. We went in and wandered around inspecting the merchandise. Whirling ceiling fans rustled the many dresses hanging on the racks and a large fan over the front door provided some comfort.

We watched the metal cylinders whisk payments on a wire from the sales counters to the second floor offices in the back of the store. Some of the other stores use vacuum tubes, but Kress's still used wires.

We stopped in front of the candy counter and looked at the many delicious goodies and admired the display of Baby Ruths, the candy bar named after the famous baseball player.

"Momma told me they weren't named after the baseball player," Cousin Esther commented. "She said they were named after President Cleveland's baby daughter whose name was Ruth.

"That ain't true. Brother Ben told me they were named after Babe Ruth. He read it in the paper so you're wrong."

"I ain't wrong. Momma told me and she knows everything."

"Well she don't know nothing about baseball and she sure doesn't know about Baby Ruths."

"Yes she does! She knows more than your stupid brother."

Tired of arguing we again looked at the tantalizing red and white wrappers and decided we wanted one but when we counted our money, we only had four pennies and the candy cost a nickel. We looked around, then Cousin Esther whispered, "Let's steal one. There's nobody around."
"I don't know about that. I sure don't want to get caught," I answered.
"We won't get caught. Look, there's nobody in this end of the store. We can grab it and just sorta sneak out."
"You do it," I replied and she did. She just reached over the counter and took the nearest piece, slipped it into her pocket and we hurried toward the front door. But just as we got there a huge man grabbed each of us by the collar and escorted us to the back. Cousin Esther started crying and I sure didn't feel very good.
"Where are your parents?" the huge man rumbled. When we didn't answered, he added, "Guess I'll have to call the police and have you locked up in jail till we can find them." Then we both started crying, me softly, Cousin Esther in near hysterics.
Sobbing, I blurted, "They're coming here to get us at three."
"Well, Sonny, we'll just wait for them. We'll go to the front of the store and wait." And we did, and when Poppa got there and heard the man's story, I knew I was in serious trouble and I imagined Cousin Esther was too.
Nothing was said on the way home. We stopped at the park and ate a tasteless sausage sandwich and didn't visit Sister Selma. Both Brother Ben and Sister Sybil knew we were in trouble and Brother Ben whispered in my ear, "Boy are you gonna catch it when we get home." And he was right.
Poppa didn't wait until after chores which was his usual routine when punishments were in order. As instructed, I went straight to the back porch, dropped my pants and received the worst whipping of my entire life. Between sobs, I could hear Momma in the kitchen wailing, "My baby is gonna end up in prison just like Cousin Thadius." I remembered he had been sent to Huntsville for stealing chickens from a neighbor's farm. I ate standing up for a week and carried a pillow to Sunday school the next weekend and didn't leave the farm by myself until school started. I never knew what Cousin Esther's punishment had been because she wouldn't tell me.
I knew I got what I deserved. Stealing is a mortal sin and I couldn't blame it on Cousin Esther. It was my responsibility to stop her from taking the candy; as a matter of fact, I had suggested it so it was my fault.
I remember Pastor Pierson talking about Adam and Eve and how Eve tempted Adam with an apple and they committed a sin that I didn't

understand. I knew what sin we had committed and I knew it wasn't Cousin Esther's fault. It was mine.

By the next day, I realized I had a new worry; I couldn't go to Uncle Ole's farm and try to retrieve the football. Also, I couldn't try to find out why someone shot at us and when Poppa found out about that, in addition to the whipping I would get, I might not get off the farm for a year. Pastor Pierson was right, a sinful life is a wasted life and I was certainly wasting mine.

Chapter Thirteen
Brother Ben

Finally the hot summer is over and school started today. This was my first day at the Arendal School because my school on the prairie had closed. Poppa said they couldn't keep it open because of the depression. Sister Sybil went with me on the bus and showed me around, but said she couldn't go home with me because she planed to go by the church and do some typing after school and Pastor Pierson told her he would take her home. Brother Ben drove his wreck of a car to school and said I could ride home with him. And he still hadn't missed his football.

Bouncing along in the bus on the way to school, my thoughts turned to Uncle Ole and his family. No one had heard from them and, of course, Cousin Angel was still missing. Pastor Pierson included them in his prayers at Sunday Evening Services last night because they were members of his congregation. I certainly included them as I knelt beside my bed every night praying.

"Now I lay me down to sleep. I pray the lord my soul to keep. If I should die before I wake. I pray the Lord my soul to take. God bless Momma, Poppa, Baby Alicia, Sister Selma, Sister Sybil, Brother Ben, Grama Svendahl, Grama and Grampa Yo, Pastor Pierson and all my relatives and all the angels in Heaven and Hell. And please God, bring Uncle Ole and Aunt Telinda home and please God please protect Cousin Angel" All these names were mandatory in our prayers, Poppa insisted on it.

As the bus began to climb the hill, my thoughts drifted to Poppa. I know he still worried a lot about his brother. Thank goodness I don't think he and Momma argued about it any more, at least not so we could hear. The insurance company paid off the mortgage on the house. Although we never talked about it, I think Poppa now felt something bad had happened to them.

He also said he couldn't move the furniture from Uncle Ole's garage so, last week, he bought a heavier lock and we went to the farm and installed it. He also nailed a two-by-four across the garage door. While he was working, I looked at the mountain but saw nothing. As we were crossing the cattle guard I looked out the window and something caught my eye. I wasn't sure, but it looked like somebody or something crossed the road behind us and headed for the orchard. I punched Poppa and pointed but when he turned around, whatever it was, was gone.

"I thought I saw something," I said.

"I guess you didn't," was his reply, and that ended the conversation. But I knew I had seen something, I just didn't know what. I thought briefly about telling him about the gunshots but decided against it. I was already in enough trouble and I didn't need to add to it.

I wanted to tell Cousin Esther about it yesterday at Sunday school, but she said she wasn't interested. I guess this was further punishment for my sins.

Coming down the hill into Arendal, my thoughts turned to Uncle Ole's farm. But before I could do any serious worrying, we the reached the school yard and Sister Sybil showed me around.

When she took me to my assigned class I immediately sensed trouble. The teacher's name was Birdie Hawk and she looked exactly like a witch with her tiny glasses perched on her hooked nose and long black hair that looked like a horses tail as it cascaded around her shoulders. She was barely four feet tall and couldn't weigh more than eighty pounds. She carried a hickory stick around the classroom using it to get attention and wore a long black dress that swept the floor when she walked.

Looking at the back row, I recognized some of the students and decided I had better sit in the front of the class. I knew they were trouble makers and couldn't pass up the chance to comment on her looks by probably chanting, "Bubble, bubble, double, trouble." And they did, not at first, but toward the end of the first day when she chastised one of the girls for passing a note to one of the boys between subjects. This prompted a visit to Superintendent Roberts's office for a stern lecture and three licks with the school paddle.

Brother Ben told me at lunchtime that he was leaving early because his last class of the day had been cancelled so I couldn't ride with him and in my confusion, I missed the bus and realized I would have to walk home. I was hoping Cousin Esther would walk with me but her mother picked her up and did not offer me a ride. So, I had no choice but to walk the five miles by myself.

Momma had asked Brother Ben to take me by the Wartman's house on the way home from school. She said it was right on the way home and she wanted him to work on the new crop of warts I had grown during the summer. Sister Sybil said it was from playing with frogs. Brother Ben said it was from playing with myself whatever that meant. But since Brother Ben went home early I went there by my self.

The Wartman must have had a name but nobody seemed to know what it was so everybody called him the Wartman. He claimed, and many people confirmed, that he could remove warts and he only charged a nickel.

When I arrived at his house, I walked up the steps to the front porch and knocked. In a moment the door opened and I held out my hands and said, "Mr. Wartman, my mother wants you to remove these warts."

Although his appearance was a little frightening with a dingy scraggly beard, ragged pants, faded shirt and a black hat with what looked like a bullet hole in the crown.

"Sonny, you got a nickel?" he asked.

"Yes sir." I reached in my pocket and extracted the nickel Momma had given me and handed it to him. "Here," I said and he took it and put it in his pocket.

"Now, you sit there and wait," he said pointing to the swing. He went in the house and in a few minutes he came back holding a tobacco sack and a small bottle of funny looking bad smelling greenish yellow liquid. He opened the tobacco sack and extracted a bright new penny that he rubbed vigorously on each wart. Then he poured some of the funny looking liquid into a saucer sitting on the porch rail and dropped the penny into the liquid and stirred it with the stem of a wooden match. After about a minute he poured the liquid back in the bottle then put on a pair of work gloves and rubbed the penny on each wart. It kinda stung for a moment and he said, "Now, don't wash your hands for an hour and don't put them near your mouth or eyes." Thank goodness I wasn't going back to school because my hands smelled like rotten egg or maybe like I had caught a polecat.

He put the penny in the sack, removed the gloves, tied the string, then said, "That'll do it." He turned and went in the house and closed the door. I looked at my hands and the warts were still there so I left and continued on my way home.

There was a fairly large bridge over a dry creek bed on the road out of town. I had heard that wild animals sometimes hid in that culvert. So, being in no hurry, I stopped and slid down the embankment to have a look. Instead of an animal, I found Malcolm Moore standing in the shade with a large piece of paper rolled up like a tube.

"Hi, Jake," he said. " I got something I wanta show you."

"What?"

"This," he answered as he unrolled the tube and held it in the light. I think my eyes nearly popped out of my head when I realized it was a picture of a naked lady and they got even bigger when I saw that Malcolm was playing with his peter. I immediately turned and started up the embankment. "Don't tell your parents," he yelled as I reached the top. "They won't believe you and you'll get in trouble and probably get a whippin!" I ran the rest of the way, over the hill, down the other side, across the Flat until I reached home, totally completely exhausted.

Well, gosh, I guess trouble is my middle name because when I got home, Brother Ben had trashed my room looking for his football. Everything I owned, my clothes, my few books, my old toys long stored in a box hidden in the closet lay scattered on the floor and he had even torn up my bed.

Before I could do anything, he stormed into my room yelling, "WHERE IS IT?!"

"Where's what?" I answered. But of course I knew what he meant. He had missed his football.

"You know what I mean, you dumb head!"

"No I don't," I answered and began to cry.

"MY FOOTBALL, STUPID!" he yelled. "NOW WHERE IS IT?"

It scared me that he was so furious and I continued to cry. After a few moments he took off his belt and threatened to whip me and I cried even louder hoping Momma would come and rescue me before he killed me. I tried to leave but he barred the door. He continued to harangue me and I cried even louder until Momma came to see what was wrong.

"This idiot stole my football!"

"No I didn't," I sobbed.

"Yes you did."

"No I didn't,"

"Then where is it?"

"I don't know."

Finally, he calmed down as I continued to insist I didn't know anything about his football and offered to help him hunt for it. Later, after Poppa got home from the field, he asked me about the football and I told him the same lie. I guess three lies won't send you any deeper into hell than one. But, I felt horrible about it and added it to my prayers that night asking God to forgive me of my grievous sins as Pastor Pierson called them. And, I think Brother Ben was ashamed of his outburst and treated me real nice for the rest of the day, even helped me with my chores and helped me straighten up my room. Maybe Poppa had talked to him about his behavior, but whatever the reasons I felt better about my situation.

Because of Brother Ben, I forgot about Malcolm Moore and what I had seen under the bridge. On the way home I decided I should tell Poppa, but when I got home and faced my brother's fury, I forgot. Now it was too late to tell him and I was actually afraid of his reaction. He probably wouldn't believe me and might even extend my punishment for the candy theft. So I never told him but I planned to tell Cousin Esther if we ever speak again. I really miss her company and companionship.

Chapter Fourteen
Doctors and Grand Parents

Sister Selma, who was at Hillcrest Hospital in Waco training to be a nurse, often told us stories about the doctors who had come to Arendal before Dr. Nygard. She was writing a paper about it for school and when she read it to us, I thought the stories were kinda interesting, especially the part about Doctor Bastrop.

Prior to 1925, the only doctor in the area was Doctor Bishop, an elderly, cranky old gentleman in his eighties whose office was in his home and made house calls in his horse and buggy pulled by Dobbin, an ancient gray mule who was said to be older than the doctor. He looked like the man on the label of the Smith's Brother's Cough Medicine bottle and carried a six-shooter in his doctor bag and treated all illnesses with laudanum and mustard plasters. He received his degree in 1880 after a year of training under a New Orleans surgeon. Few of the area's residents used him preferring the medicines available from the Watkins man who came once a month in his covered wagon. The farmers eagerly looked forward to his visits because his wagon contained needed items like Sloan's Liniment for sore muscles and Udder Balm for chapped teats and materials for making clothes and condiments for the kitchen and grease for squeaky axles and Paregoric for the squirts.

In 1925 Dr. Bastrop came to Arendal and opened an office in the back of the City Drug. It was said that an irate family in Quanah, upset over a botched delivery, ran him out of town at gunpoint and actually fired a shot or two at him.

He was short and fat and sported a goatee and always wore a dirty black suit and smoked awful smelling cigars. It was common knowledge that he was an alcoholic and stayed drunk most of the time except on weekends when he would sober up enough to go to his 'office' and take care of his 'patients'. His only function at the drug store and in the community was to write prescriptions for medicinal whiskey because of something called Prohibition. This kept him busy on weekends when men came from all over the area including Waco and Hillsboro seeking his services because that was the only place in Central Texas where you could legally buy whiskey.

I still remember the line of men on Saturday afternoon shuffling along, smoking their pipes and spitting on the sidewalk as they snaking their way to the drugstore. When they arrived at the front door they entered and wound their way between the soda fountain and the tables to the center isle that led to the doctor's 'office' where Dr. Bastrop sat at a desk writing prescriptions for 'Medicinal Whiskey' for treatment of the croup, "fifty cents please." Occasionally he would feel of a 'patient's' pulse and maybe listen to his chest but usually the line was too long for such niceties. The 'patient' then went to the liquor counter in the front part of the drugstore and got the 'prescription' filled, one dollar a pint.

When Doctor Bishop died in 1929, Dr. Nygard, having just graduated from University of Texas Medical School, arrived to take over his practice. He wasn't very busy at first mostly because people felt he was too young to know what he was doing and his prices were too high. Few of the residents of the area could afford to pay fifty cents for an office visit and seventy-five cents for a house call and he charged ten dollars to delivering a baby. So most people continued to treat themselves using Patent Medicines from the drug store or something obtained from the Watkins Man.

In those days, most people really didn't trust doctors and they only called one when they needed a Death Certificate so the deceased could be buried or when there was a complication with a delivery. Normally, relatives or midwives delivered the babies and frequently no one filled out a Birth Certificate, but they always listed the birth in the family Bible. Poppa said any court in the land would recognize that as a legal record.

In 1933, when Prohibition ended, Dr. Bastrop closed his 'office' and disappeared leaving Dr. Nygard as the only physician in the county. "He told me his birth name was Leonardo Romano," Poppa said. "He claims his maternal grandmother was a Norwegian and Nygard was her family name. He liked it so much he legally changed his name before he came here. He thought people might accept him better with a Norwegian name. I told him it wouldn't make no never mind if his name was Romano but he said he felt better when people referred to him as Dr. Nygard."

"Well," Momma said when the subject came up. "he don't look like a Norwegian to me with all that black hair, them black eyes and olive skin. Looks more like an Italian to me."

"He is an Italian, mostly," Poppa said. "He doesn't deny that but wants to be called Dr. Nygard.

"I hear he sometimes gets drunk," Momma said.

"Heck, like most Italians, he loves wine and sometimes he maybe drinks a little bit too much," Poppa replied. "When he makes a house call at night, he uses Sen-Sen to sweeten his breath. If he drinks a bit too much and if his medical services are needed, his wife will tell the patient 'He isn't well today' and they would understand. If the medical problem is urgent, she would suggest they go to Hillsboro or Waco."

But, by the time he had been in Arendal for a year, people began to trust him and utilize his service even with his 'problem'. And when I caught pneumonia in 1930, Momma called on him and he probably saved my life; at least Sister Selma says he did.

It was the first week in January when we had a three-foot snow that almost covered the fence around the house. When Poppa waked me and I saw the snow, I ran outside and, of course, had a snowball fight with my brother then helped him build a snowman. When I returned to the house complaining of my frozen hands and feet, Poppa took me to the back porch and whipped my butt. Two days later, when my temperature hit 104, Momma called Dr. Nygard who came immediately in his Model T Ford and diagnosed pneumonia. Sister Selma told me later that I was one of his first really sick patients.

About all I remembered for two weeks was Dr. Nygard coming to the house every day to take my temperature and listen to my chest. Then he would empty a packet of bitter white powder into a glass of hot water, add a drop of something from a brown bottle and made me drank it. In about an hour the coughing would stop, I would get sleepy, and begin to sweat and my fever would go down. After each visit Momma gave him and a quarter and a dozen eggs or a quart of milk. Two weeks later, after what Dr. Nygard said was the 'crisis', I finally began to improve and he only came twice a week.

I was in the first grade at Buffalo Flat at the time and missed six weeks of school. On my first day back, I came down with red measles and missed two more weeks. One of my classmates died while I was out of school, probably from pneumonia, so I guess I was lucky. I think I actually flunked first grade but Poppa talked miss Boudegard into promoting me. Also, I think my survival maybe helped Dr. Nygard's reputation, at least Sister Selma said it did because the student that died was not seen by a doctor.

Last month Grandma Johansson (we called her Grandma Yo) fell and injured her hip. After five days in the bed without any improvement, Uncle Andrew called Dr. Nygard who came to the house, diagnosed a broken hip and prescribed laudanum for the pain. He suggested they take her to Waco for an x-ray but Grampa Johansson (we called him Grampa Yo) refused. "They ain't nothin they can do," he said and Sister Selma agreed.

"Grampa, just keep her as comfortable as you can, and try to get her to eat," she advised.

However this presented a problem because both Momma and Uncle Andrew felt Grampa Yo couldn't look after her and there wasn't anybody who could stay with her day and night. Momma said she could do it if they would come live with us and Grampa Yo agreed.

I knew this would require some shifting of sleeping arrangements and I suspected Grampa and Grandma Yo would sleep downstairs in Momma and Poppa's room and they would move upstairs to Brother Ben's room.

I had slept on a cot on the landing until Sister Selma left for nursing stool, then Sister Sybil moved into her room and I got hers. Now it looked like I'll have to share mine with Brother Ben.

I asked Momma why Brother Ben couldn't sleep with Sister Sybil, she said it wouldn't be proper but she wouldn't tell me what was improper about it. I asked Poppa if I could sleep in the barn with the cats. I told him I could never sleep in the room with Brother Ben because he snored all the time, which wasn't true and Poppa knew it, so he also turned me down.

Mostly I didn't want to sleep with Brother Ben because several times in my life I had talked in my sleep. Both Brother Ben and Sister Sybil had teased me about it and said they were going to find out about all my secrets. At the time I had no secrets so it didn't worry me but now it was different. I had secrets I wanted no one to know and if I talked in my sleep they would be revealed and I would probably be kicked out of the family and sent to the Orphan's Home in Waco or maybe to the one in Dallas where a distant cousin had been sent.

Actually, it sorta worked out okay. My bed wouldn't hold me and blubber-gut so we moved Brother Ben's bed in with mine. Although the room was crowded we had enough space to walk between the beds and room enough to say our nightly prayers. And as far as I know, I never talked in my sleep.

Before they moved in, Momma told us they both came from Norway and Grandma Yo had never learned to read or speak English, Grampa Yo took care of everything, Besides it was customary for Norwegian wives to remain illiterate.

Chapter Fifteen
A Sad Day

Grandma Yo died on the first day of October, of pneumonia Dr. Nygard said. We could never make her comfortable and she just seemed to fade away. Also she had a foul odor about her that Dr. Nygard said was from something he called a bed sore. Momma blamed herself for Grandma Yo's death, but Pastor Pierson said it was her time and that the Lord needed her in Heaven and for us not to grieve. "She's happy now and free of pain," which seemed to make Momma feel better.

We buried her in the cemetery behind the church on The Flat where most of the old settlers and many of my ancestors rested in peace. Pastor Pierson conducted the services in Norwegian and a quartet of Norwegian men sung two songs in the native tongue.

While the service was going on, it began to rain. After the services, we got soaked before we could get to the tent over the grave and I caught a bad cold that lasted a month. After a brief ceremony, they lowered the casket and we all went home. Relatives would fill the hole and cover the casket after the rain stopped. The bell in the old church tower tolled it's mournful sound every thirty seconds for an hour before and after the services.

Momma may have been devastated but I didn't think Poppa was too upset. I've seen him more upset over losing a calf or a sheep and much more upset over the death of a cow. I asked Sister Sybil about it after the funeral and she said it was Poppa's way of dealing with grief. I didn't understand but assumed she was right.

School would be out in a week or two so students could pick cotton. Poppa planned to hire a family or two from the Hobo Jungle if Uncle Ole and Aunt Telinda didn't return and I still missed Cousin Angel.

Most people felt Uncle Ole had taken his family and skipped the country because of financial problems like most people in the area, but Poppa knew better. He continued to write letters to relatives in various parts of the country. He even wrote to distant relatives in Norway assisted by Pastor Pierson who was fluent in the native language. All inquiries proved fruitless.

There was another problem with their disappearance. His truck was gone. It wasn't that much of a truck, a Model T Ford cotton truck probably at least twenty years old. Most people felt he had used that vehicle to leave the country, maybe to California. Also most people felt he would return by winter and every thing would be cleared up. Maybe he put the furniture in the garage and somebody; maybe one of the transients drifting around the area, started the fire trying to keep warm. After all, the house was unlocked. "But why hasn't he written to someone explaining his absence?" Poppa asked. "It just doesn't make any sense."

Cousin Esther was still grounded but she would talk to me during recess and sometimes we ate lunch together. One day last week, we purposely missed the bus so we could walk home together. I think she did it without her mother's permission because the next day, her mother picked her up after school and didn't offer me a ride.

On the way, we talked of many things but I didn't bring up the football and we didn't talk about Waco. I did mention I had seen Malcolm Moore standing under the bridge but I didn't mention the picture or what he was doing. She remained silent so I didn't pursue it.

Grampa Yo sold their farm and finished moving his things to our house a few days ago and seemed to be settling in nicely. Poppa said he knew all about trolls and I should spend time with him listening to his stories. He would be lonely with Grandma gone. So I did. And it opened a new chapter in my life.

The first night he talked about life in Norway and about rolls. "They is many kinds of trolls," he said, "Veta, Nesse and especially the Haugfolk." I had heard these terms before when there was some calamity or natural disaster like a tornado, hailstorm or when grasshoppers destroyed the crops. In the past, I rarely paid much attention to these discussions because I didn't understand what they were talking about. But now, right here in our house was an authority that could teach me about trolls that suddenly seemed important considering the mess I was making out of my life.

Before we could get very far, Grampa Yo went to sleep in his chair and began to snore. I called Poppa who helped him into bed and covered him with a light blanket. Then Poppa patted me on the back and led me to my bed and kissed me on the forehead. He had never done that before and it made me feel good. Maybe my troubles weren't so bad after all, but only if I didn't talk in my sleep.

Chapter Sixteen
Chopping Cotton

The last day of October school let out for three weeks so the students could pick cotton. This was also on my list of least favorite chores and by the time we finished, I had lost most of the skin on my fingers and could hardly tie my shoe laces or use a pencil at school. Some of the pickers wore cotton gloves but I didn't have any.

Uncle Ole and Aunt Telinda still hadn't returned from their trip so Poppa hired a Hobo family of seven, two adults and five children, who claimed they had picked cotton before. He agreed to pay them forty cents a hundred pounds and two meals a day and most days the five of them earned at least five dollars.

Two of the children were too young to pick but the rest were actually pretty good. We returned to school after three weeks but the Hobo family stayed for the second picking. When they finished, Poppa paid them over a hundred fifty dollars. The next morning, they packed their truck and headed west.

I was glad when we finished but a little sad to see them go. They had a daughter about my age who could pick cotton better than me. She had hair the color of a fresh scraped carrot and freckles on her face and arms to match and her eyes were bluer than Cousin Esther's. I saw her frequently at the weighing scale but when I tried to talk to her, she always blushed and ran away. When I told Cousin Esther about her, she threw a fit and wouldn't talk to me for a week. I'll never understand girls.

Cousin Gertrude was the best cotton picker around and Poppa paid her fifty cents for every hundred pounds she picked because she was careful and never picked the hulls. He didn't pay me by the pound; he paid me twenty-five cents a day and by the time we finished I had five dollars hidden under my mattress.

The fifty acres of cotton yielded thirty bales and Poppa sold it to the gin for twelve cents a pound or about sixty dollars a bale. A week later he received a check for seventeen hundred dollars. That seemed like a fortune to me but he said he barely broke even. "All that work and expense and not a lick of profit," he said to Momma. "I ain't gonna plant cotton next year." To me, that was the best news I had heard in a long time.

Halloween came and went with few surprises. Three seniors got expelled from school for stealing an outhouse from behind a house across the railroad track. The house belonged to a colored man who worked at the feed mill. His wife cleaned houses for white folks and their three children went to the black school on the other side of the river. All were well liked in the community.

They hauled the outhouse in a wagon and dumped it on the sidewalk in front of the school. Sheriff Bjornburg, who had been cruising around looking for trouble, caught them in the act. He made them return it to its rightful place then locked them up in jail for the night. Next morning, they appeared in court and the judge fined them twenty dollars each for vandalism.

Brother Ben was supposed to be in on the prank but, thank goodness, he had enough sense to back out. He said he thought it was a cruel joke to play on the nice family who never caused anybody any trouble.

Election day came and went and James Allred was elected Governor of Texas. Both Momma and Poppa were happy about the results and Momma said she was sure D.E. Waggner was a Republican and maybe even a Catholic. Sheriff Bjornburg and Judge Christenson were also reelected and that also made Poppa happy.

A rattlesnake bit my old dog Fritz, who had helped me learn to walk by allowing me to hang on to his tail. He was also my trusted companion when I was old enough to go 'rabbit hunting' with my homemade bow and arrow. Poppa said he was my guardian.

The fight occurred at the woodpile where snakes liked to hide because of the many rats that called it their home. When I heard the frantic barking I knew he had a problem because he never barked like that unless he had something cornered like a rat or a squirrel or maybe a possum.

When I arrived at the woodpile Fritz had apparently enticed the snake out onto open ground. His knew how to kill rattlesnakes by challenging them to strike and when they did he would dance backwards. Then, before the snake could pull back for another strike, Frank would grab it by the neck and violently shake it until it died. Then he would carry it to the back porch and wait for our praise.

I had seen him do this many times so I had no fear for his safety, but this time was different. I guess maybe age had slowed his reflexes or maybe his eyes had gone bad because on the last strike he didn't dance back quickly enough and the snake sunk his fangs into his nose. He fell backwards, let out a pitiful scream, dislodged the snake with a mighty shake, and then ran to his bed in the barn. Before I could do anything, the snake slithered back into the woodpile and disappeared. I ran to the barn to comfort him but there was nothing I could do. He whined and whimpered the rest of the day and by bedtime his head was swollen twice its normal size. By the next morning his eyes were swollen shut and his tongue looked like a rotten cantaloupe. I asked Poppa if we could take him to the doctor in Waco and he said, "There's nothing he can do." He couldn't eat or drink and that night he died.

Cousin Esther and me held a little funeral for him, and sang 'Jesus loves me.' We wrapped him in a gunnysack and buried him in the flowerbed by the back gate. Then we held hands and I said a prayer and we both cried. I felt really bad about it.

I hadn't been able to listen to any more of Grampa Yo's stories; I was just too tired in the evenings from picking cotton Finally, after we finished, I got a taste of Grampa Yo's magic tales. It was Saturday night and there was no Sunday school tomorrow, some kind of a special meeting at the church.

In his heavy Scandinavian brogue he began with the setting. He said the stories should only be told on long winter nights when the sky was clear and the moon shone as bright as day and a north wind whistled through the cedar. That's when the trolls came out to do their mischief.

His first story was about the Haugfolk, the Underground People who live in castles built under the mounds that one often sees in most fields. The Haugfolk men are handsome and rich and the women are beautiful. It is said that you should never pour water or urinate on a mound for fear that it might contain a castle. If you did you should expect some natural disaster to befall your family like a locust infestation or a hailstorm or a tornado in the summer or an ice storm in the winter. If you plowed up the mound that contained a castle you should expect your house to burn to the ground before the first frost. Custom required you to leave at least one row of corn or wheat unharvested for their satisfaction. That's why you see one or two rows of corn along the fencerows of most farms. Mostly they are peaceful as long as you don't violate their homes.

There is another clan of trolls that are the most feared of all the trolls. They have many names but most people call them the Skogstrollet. When God banished their parents, Adam and Eve, from the Garden of Eden, He sent their children to live in Hell for a thousand years. There they learned the evil ways of the Devil and, at the end of the thousand years, brought that knowledge back to the earth to help the Devil do away with Christianity. They established themselves in the Norwegian fiords and were ugly and mean and turned over the ships so they could eat the crewmen. They spread up into the mountains and tried to demolish the Stave Churches. They hid along the mountain trails and devoured the travelers of all races and creeds but much preferred the flesh of Christians, especially Christian children who ran away from home and ended up in the forest. They especially love Christian blood that they would suck out through the victim's nose. And if they capture a beautiful child, they would often take that child to their castle and turn it into slave. So, if your child is beautiful, never, never allow it to go into the forest alone.

But the Skogstrollet have one weakness. If the first light of morning happened to strike them, they turn to stone so they only do their dastardly deeds at night. And, if you happen to see a large stone in the path, leave it alone for fear it will come alive and eat you.

Then there are the Nisse or Tomte, sometimes called Attic Trolls or Barn Trolls who inhabited every barn and farmhouse. These mischievous little creatures turn over the milk pails, knock over the pots and pans in the kitchen, and let the cows out of the pen during the night. They could keep the bread from rising, cause the milk to sour, pull the cats tail, and cause various other events designed to disrupt the household. They could be appeased by leaving food for them on the kitchen floor or on the porch.

These little guys come at Christmas dressed in red suits and a red tassel hat and leave presents for the children who had been good. If you've been bad, you got nothing.

They expected something in return like rice pudding with a glass of whiskey or rum. If they were pleased with the gift you left for them you could expect the next year to be fruitful, if not, disaster would surly strike.

Grampa Yo sat quietly in his chair for maybe twenty minutes, tapping his cane on the arm of his rocker. Then he continued with stories about the Haugfolk women who were very ugly and had ugly babies. Sometimes they would swap their ugly baby for a pretty one and leave the ugly baby in its place. So, if you had an ugly baby you could say, "The Haugfolk took mine."

"Many of the Haugfolk is fallen angels sent to earth to multiply," Grampa Yo continued. "Most has got tails that they try to hide under their clothes and if they marry a human man the tail vill fall off and you cain't tell them from a human women except they has very bad tempers and always vant their vay about everything. So if your new wife is disagreeable and argues vith you all the time, you could say, "I married a Haugfolk" and everyone vould understand."

Puzzled, I interrupted, "I thought you told us the Haugfolk women were beautiful."

"They is, if they comes from Norway. Them what comes from Sveden is always ugly," he explained.

It was getting late and I was getting sleepy but what he said next kept me awake for hours.

"Vell, Yakob, you know, don't you, the Skogstrollet done got Baby Angel?" Dumbfounded, I didn't have time to ask any questions because he immediately went to bed and in a moment he began to snore.

Chapter Seventeen
Crazy Clem

Shortly after school reopened I developed a big sore on the top of my head about the size of a silver dollar. Dr. Nygard said it was ringworm and gave Momma a small jar of medicine with instructions to apply it twice a day. He said I probably caught it from one of the cats. But after two weeks it was no better so Grampa Yo said he could cure it. "I done cured a many of them ven I vas in Norvay," he explained.

He went to the upper pasture and cut off a prickly pear leaf, brought it home and removed the thorns. Then he sliced it in half and placed the raw surface of the leaf on the sore and wrapped a white rag made from a bed sheet around my head and tied under my chin.

"Yakob, you got to vear this for two veeks and don't you take it off." This presented a problem because after a few days it stunk so bad that no one would sit near me in school. Miss Hawk wanted to have me declared contagious and sent home until I was cured but Mr. Roberts refused saying, "If we sent every body home that had ringworm there wouldn't be anybody left in school." So I sat in the back of the classroom by an open window until the mess was removed. I was very disappointed that the prickly pear didn't cure the sore. Momma finally cured it with a mixture of sulfur and lard that she applied every morning. It also stunk but not as bad as the prickly pear leaf and it did the job and now the sore is gone and a new growth of hair could be seen. But I still had the warts and Grampa Yo said he could cure them with a mixture of horse manure and tobacco juice but I declined. I felt I had stunk up the schoolroom enough for one year.

The Arendal Armadillos played their final football game of 1934 on Thanksgiving afternoon. They lost and Brother Ben broke his ankle. Dr. Nygard set the fracture and applied a cast up to his hip. Poppa said it was a good thing we had almost finished the plowing and planting and all the other chores were pretty much up to date.

There wasn't much a person could do around a farm if you were on crutches but Brother Ben helped where he could and Poppa placed me in charge of milking and feeding the calves. Fortunately we only had a few on the bottle so I used the extra milk to make extra slop for the pigs because they were always hungry.

Uncle Ole and his family were still missing and Grampa Johansson had gone to stay with Uncle Andrew for a few weeks, maybe until Christmas. Momma said they had worked out an arrangement with other members of the family to help in his care. I never got a chance to follow up on his statement about Baby Angel before he left.

Remembering Grampa Yo's stories, I asked Momma about the Haugfolk. "Were the women pretty or were they ugly. Grampa Yo says the ugly ones come from Sweden. Is that right?"

"'Jacob, don't pay too much attention to your grand father. I've listened to his stories all my life and mostly he just makes them up as he goes along and sometimes he gets all mixed up. They're mostly fairy tales with little if any substance." I sorta wanted to ask her about Baby Angel and the Skogstrollet but felt she would just laugh and if she told the family my brother would call me a stupid imbecile.

When I asked Pastor Pierson about trolls, he said it was a sin against God to even listen to such pagan nonsense. But they seemed so real when Grampa Yo told the stories and I wasn't sure I believed everything Pastor Pierson said.

But why would the Skogstrollet want Baby Angel? She was only three and unable to do any housework. She couldn't cook, she couldn't wash dishes, she couldn't milk cows and she was too young to work in the garden, and she still wore diapers, so what possible use could she be to them. I wish there was someone who could explain it to me. Or is it just another fairy tale?

I really wasn't too worried about Uncle Ole and Aunt Telinda, they could look after themselves, but Baby Angel was another matter. And I always shed a few tears when I reached her name at the end of my prayers.

Cousin Esther's mother finally released her from bondage and we again spend time together. Last weekend we hiked up into the mountains behind our house to look at the rattlesnake den. Poppa said we were going to blast it to smithereens soon because two of our calves had died of snakebites. After visiting the snake den we planned to visit Crazy Clem, a disabled war veteran living in seclusion in a tin shack on top of the mountain.

When I told Poppa where we were going he advised caution around the snake den because it was a sunny day and they would probably be out warming themselves on a rock or curled up in a bush. He didn't say much about Crazy Clem except that we should be careful. He didn't say why, just that we should.

We reached the snake den without incident and stood on the edge of the rocky bluff overlooking the area. We could see several snakes coiled up on flat rocks seemingly asleep. There was one particularly large snake close to the slit under the ledge whose head was weaving back and forth and we could see his tongue flicking in our direction. Just looking at him sent shivers up and down my spine.

I truly hated snakes ever since one stuck at me from a hen nest when I was gathering eggs. It was only a grass snake but it scared the life out of me and I have hated snakes ever since. I ran screaming to the house and Poppa came and shot it with a shotgun. The blast killed the snake, blew up the nest and left a hole in the henhouse wall the size of a football. I wish I had the shotgun now. Instead, we picked up a few rocks and chucked them at the large snake. He shook his rattle and struck at each rock then slowly slithered into the hole. This aroused the other snakes and they also disappeared.

Tiring of that sport we headed toward Crazy Clem's house if you could call it a house. We had both been there before so we knew the way and what the shack looked like but we had never been inside. We followed the trail across the mountain, through the wire gate, across the pasture being careful not to disturb the goats. When we reached the gate surrounding his yard, several cats dashed for the nearest tree.

The yard contained a wide assortment of broken farm implements and the remains of two cars none of which could possibly be in working order. We saw the donkey he always rode to town standing in a small corral behind the house. The house itself was made of corrugated sheet metal patched together in a haphazard fashion with open areas for a windows and a door. Sunshine filtering through the trees illuminated the packed dirt floor.

We opened the gate and stood inside the yard surveying the many objects. Suddenly, Crazy Clem was behind our backs growling, "What you kids want?"

"N-nothing," I stammered. "Just visiting."

"Then get the hell off my property," he snarled.

I had seen the man before from a distance riding down the road on his donkey but this was the first time I had seen him up close. I don't think I have ever seen anybody so ugly and terrifying. Long black hair framed an angry face covered with a dirty scraggly beard. He had a huge wart on his nose and wore a pair of the dirtiest coveralls that I had ever seen and a dirty shirt with holes in the elbows, neither of which had been washed in weeks, maybe months. He appeared to have lost most of his teeth and the remaining ones looked like rotted tree stumps and he smelled like he hadn't taken a bath in weeks.

I saw all this before I saw the gun in his hand and when I did, we turned and ran out of the yard, across the goat pasture, through the gate, down the hill not stopping until we reached the back porch of our house. When we told Momma what had happened, she thought it was kinda strange. According to her, the man had always seemed friendly. "Besides, it isn't his land," Momma said. "It's part of our farm he rents from Poppa. Maybe Poppa oughta go up there and talk to him." In a moment, she added, "You sure y'all didn't aggravate him in some way to make him mad? Did you maybe chase the goats or throw rocks at the donkey?"

"No ma'am," Cousin Esther replied. "We was just standing there and he started yelling at us."

"Well I expect you better stay away from him until Poppa has a talk with him."

With that out of the way, we each ate a peanut butter and jelly sandwich, drank a glass of milk and then went to the barn. We climbed up to our favorite place, the hayloft, and sat with our feet swinging over the edge.

"I wonder what's wrong with that old fool?" Cousin Esther began.

"I don't know. I just know I was plenty scared when I saw that gun."

"Me too," she said, then added. "You know what? I think he's hiding something in his house."

We both considered it for a few minutes, then Cousin Esther whispered, "I bet you he's got Baby Angel. I bet he has her locked up in his house so he can violate her. What do you think?"

"Violate her?"

"Yeah, violate her. I bet that's what he was doing when we arrived."

"What does violate mean?"

"If you don't know, I'm not gonna explain. Ask your brother."

I sat for many moments thinking about what she had said. Finally I asked, "What should we do?"

"I guess we oughta go up there some day when he's gone and look around. What do you think?"

We talked long and hard about how and when we should do it but couldn't come up with a suitable plan. Neither of us knew his schedule of comings and goings nor did we know anything about the inside of his house. We knew the house wasn't locked because it didn't have a door."

"Probably there's a room of some kind or maybe he has a cage where he locks the poor baby. He probably keeps her doped up all the time so she won't cry."

Although I didn't understand the term 'violate' I figured it had something to do with making babies. But Baby Angel was so young she couldn't possibly have a baby. Maybe I should ask Poppa or Pastor Pierson but I'm not gonna ask Brother Ben. He'd call me a pervert and try to give me another knuckle haircut.

We finally decided we should think about it and maybe try to find out when Crazy Clem goes to town. Poppa probably would know but how could I ask him without making him suspicious. I took the problem with me to bed as I prayed extra hard for God to protect the poor child and to guard her from being violated, whatever that meant.

On the weekend before Thanksgiving I went with Poppa to help him fix the gate at Uncle Ole's farm. Orvil Hanson had called and said someone had cut the wires. He also said, last week, he seen a Model T truck parked next to the barn and he assumed Uncle Ole had returned. He left a note in their mailbox saying he would bring their mail the next day.

"I honked my horn," he said, "but no one responded. The next day, when I returned with the mail, the truck was gone and I haven't seen it since. I left the mail but it remained in the box for several days so I brought it back to the post office."

I knew Poppa had locked the gate with a chain and I saw that the lock and chain were still in place. Someone had apparently cut the wires to gain entrance, but why? There was nothing of value except the furniture in the garage and it was still locked.

As we finisher repairing the gate, I looked up at the mountain and there he stood, partially hidden in the scrub cedar. I wasn't sure because of the distance but to me he looked like the man we had seen before, the one who took a shot at us in the orchard.

"Poppa," I whispered, "there's somebody up on the mountain watching us." But before he could look, the man disappeared.

"Who did it look like?"

"I don't know."

"Probably it was a hunter."

"But it ain't hunting season."

"Don't you know there are people in the area that don't pay any attention to the hunting laws."

Should I tell Poppa the man shot at us before? Probably not, I'm in enough trouble already. So I didn't and we went home and I again addressed the problem in my prayers.

Chapter Eighteen
Christmas in Arendal

It was two weeks before I had enough courage to ask Poppa about Crazy Clem. We had just finished the evening milking when I popped the question. "Poppa, when does Crazy Clem go to town?"

"On the first of every month. That's when he gets his government check."

"Is that when he buys his food?"

"Yeah. He cashes his check, buys his groceries and carries it home in a gummy sack. Why do you want to know?"

"Just wondering," I answered. I couldn't come up with a reason without telling a lie and I figured I had done enough lying for one year so I dropped the subject. Also my warts still hadn't gone away, in fact I had more now than before but I wasn't ready for the horse manure and tobacco juice.

I don't think Poppa ever talked to Crazy Clem. If he did, I knew nothing about it. I wanted to ask Momma but kinda felt, in view of my delicate position I should leave well enough alone. I just hoped he wasn't doing anything bad to Cousin Angel.

We blasted the snake den the first Saturday in December. Poppa loaded six sticks of dynamite and an extra long fuse in the wagon along with a long cane pole and two large washtubs. We drove up to the top of the mountain and tied the horses to a tree about a hundred yards away then crept to the cliff and looked over the edge.

The day was fairly cool and clouds filled the sky so the snakes would probably not be out. However the big snake we had seen before was again laying on his rock and Poppa shot him with the shotgun. Then he climbed down the cliff, stood at the bottom and slid the dynamite attached to the long cane pole as far into the den as it would go. He lit the fuse, climbed back to the top of the cliff and we hurriedly left the area. In a few moments the ground shook, the horses tried to run away and the mountain erupted in a cloud of dust, rocks and rattlesnake parts and the whole front of the cliff disappeared.

We waited for a while, then Poppa and Brother Ben slowly crept to the edge of the cliff and examined the blast site. Seeing nothing moving they cautiously climbed down and picked up two washtubs full of snake parts and twenty-three rattlers. Each would bring a twenty-five cent bounty from the County Agriculture Agent. The rest of the parts we ground up and fed to the pigs. When I told Cousin Esther about it she got mad and wouldn't speak to me for a week because I hadn't invited her.

One day last week Sheriff Bjornburg came to the house and told Poppa that some kids from Somerville County had discovered a Model T truck submerged in the Paluxy River near Glen Rose. The river was down and they were looking for dinosaur tracks when they saw the upper edge of the sideboards. It was too cold to swim, so they rode their bicycles to Glen Rose and reported it to the sheriff. When they hauled it out they found it to be a Model T cotton truck with no license plates.

"We're checking with Austin to see if they can identify the owner. It might have belonged to your brother."

I had my tenth birthday last week and so did Cousin Esther. Her mother baked a cake and Momma made ice cream and they sang 'Happy Birthday.' There were no gifts but I knew my Christmas present would read "Happy Birthday and Merry Christmas" and that was okay with me. It had always been that way, I didn't expect more.

Grampa Yo was scheduled to return the day after Christmas so we would return to the crowded sleeping arrangements. I looked forward to asking him more about trolls and Baby Angel. Uncle Ole and his family were still missing and I continued to include them in my nightly prayers.

The Christmas routine had never varied since as far back as I could remember. The day before Christmas Eve, Poppa would hitch the horses to the wagon and we children would go with him up into the mountains to find a suitable cedar tree. After considerable argument one would be selected, Poppa would saw it off even with the ground and we would help carry it to the wagon.

When we got home Poppa would nail the wooden foot piece to the tree stump and stand it in the parlor and Momma would cover the foot piece with a white sheet. Then she would drag out the box of decorations we used every year and we would wrap the silver and gold ropes around the tree then carefully hang the many colored glass balls on the limbs. Finally we would hang the tinsel we saved from year to year and place the Silver Angel on the top branch. After we went to bed Poppa would place our gifts around the tree and the next morning we each would examine the boxes and secretly guess what they might contain.

I didn't know what I was getting. I knew there was one package under the tree with my name on it. I had shaken it and turned it this way and that suspecting it might be a new coat.

I knew Brother Ben was getting a new football; Momma had told me that and Sister Sybil was getting a new pair of dress shoes to wear to church and to the Luther League Christmas party. I knew she had a crush on Alton Anderson, a member of her high school class who would also be at the Christmas party and I teased her about it.

Up until two years ago we had candles on the tree until a neighbor's house burned down when their tree caught on fire. "Some of the families in town have electric lights on their Christmas tree," Poppa said. "Maybe that's what we'll do next year."

For our Christmas Eve supper, we always had a huge steaming bowl of rice mush with a spoonful of butter in the center and a generous sprinkling of cinnamon and sugar on the top. We finished the meal with Kringle or Spritz. Sometimes Momma would bake a Julekake if she didn't have a headache.

Poppa always bought a crate of fruit, usually grapefruit or oranges that we shared after the meal. He had read somewhere that citrus fruits would protect a person from colds and pneumonia so we would probably be eating them all winter.

After Momma and Sister Sybil cleared the table and washed the dishes, we gathered in the parlor. Sister Sybil played the upright piano and we sang Christmas songs taken from the Lutheran Hymnal. After several songs, Poppa would read the Christmas Story from the Second Chapter of the Gospel of St. Luke that began, *"And it came to pass in those days, that there went out a decree from Caesar Agustus, that all the world should be taxed."*

After the reading, we sang another song or two and if Poppa was pleased, we opened the gifts. If he wasn't pleased with our singing or felt our attention had wavered during the reading of the Christmas story, he would read it again and we would sing more songs.

Since I was the youngest I passed out the presents so I didn't get to open mine until last. Brother Ben got his football and Sister Sybil received her new shoes and one Nancy Drew book. When I opened my present I found a new black Sunday suit with long pants, the first long pants of my life. I inherited the one I had been wearing from Brother Ben. The coat was so worn and the pants were so short, I was ashamed to wear them and every body teased me. Now maybe I'd get some respect. Also the package contained a red wind up car.

Thanks were exchanged and Sister Sybil went to her room to read and I went to the back porch, turned on the light and played with my car.

Momma and Poppa received no gifts because they said they didn't want any, besides, none of us had any money to buy them a gift. Momma said our good health and presence was all they needed. She always said Christmas was strictly for children.

I asked Momma if she was going to leave some rice mush for the Tomte. She laughed and said, "You've been listening to Grampa Johansson again, haven't you?"

Last week, the subject of Santa Claus came up at school. When I asked Momma about it, she sent me to the orchard for a switch. "That's nothing but pagan nonsense and it's a sin to even listen to it."

On Christmas Day, we went to church and participated in the traditional rituals that I felt were way too long, especially the sermon. We had stayed up late the night before and I actually fell asleep during the sermon and almost fell out of the pew. When Poppa popped my butt, I woke me up.

After the services we went to Grandma Svendahl's house for a traditional Norwegian Christmas Dinner. Before the meal Pastor Pierson gave the traditional Norwegian blessing used by most Norwegians before meals that went:

J Jesu Navn gar vi til bords
Spise og drikke pa ditt org
Deg Gud til aere, oss til gavn,
Sa far vi mat I Jesu navn

I could recite this blessing in Norwegian by the time I was four. And by the time I was five I knew that it meant:

In Jesus name we take our place
To eat and drink upon Thy grace
To Thy honor and our gain
We take our food in Jesus' name

Grandma Svendahl is nearly eighty years old but you would never know it by looking. Her hair is still dark, not gray like most old people and she moves around like a teen-ager. Clear of mind she still manages her affairs and is said to be one of the area's best horse traders.

She sorta resembles Poppa and Uncle Ole, thin and strong, without an ounce of fat and she often laughs and jokes with her grandchildren but we know to behave in her presence or there would be trouble. She firmly believed in 'spare the rod and spoil the child'.

Aunt Caroline and Uncle Helmer live with Grandma Svendahl or maybe she lives with them, I was never sure. Together they prepared the meal with a little help from Aunt Helena and Cousin Gertrude. They serve all of the food in huge platters that are passed around the table to the right starting with Grandma Svendahl. She always takes careful notice than everyone receives a generous portion of each dish and everybody understands that all plates must be empty at the end of the meal. If not, you could expect a tongue lashing before you left the table and might be demoted to the third serving next Christmas. She always remembered your transgressions.

I knew when we came in the front door that we were having lutefisk, the smell was unmistakable. Brother Ben told me lutefisk was a Norwegian favorite made from dried Cod soaked in lye for three days, soaked in water for three more days, then hung in a tree for three days to cure. Next it should be boiled in salt water, baked until soft, and served hot. It smelled so bad I could hardly stand the stuff even swimming in melted butter but I ate it anyway. I had great respect for Grandma Svendahl's tongue.

The main course was usually a huge platter of Kjottboiler, a Swedish meatball, accompanied by a heaping platter of Lefse. Next came potatoes, gravy and green peas along with a platter of Hvetebrod. A pound of butter sat at each end of the table.

Desert varied from year to year but always started with a slice of Julekake and my favorite, Sotsuppe, a delicious mixture of fruit and pearl tapioca. Last year I made myself sick because I ate so much of this delicious dessert. Sandbakkels, Rosettes, and Fattigmannbakkels were placed on a table in the hall as snacks during the afternoon if there was any room left in your stomach.

Adults sat at the big table in the dining room and children our age ate at the second serving. When her grand children reached twelve, she would put them on the list for the first serving but somebody had to die or leave the family before you could claim a chair.

After the meal, the older boys shot off fireworks and us younger boys pestered the girls by pelting them with water filled balloons. The men gathered in the upstairs parlor, smoked their pipes, exchanged gossip, and played card games. I think there must have been fifty people there for the meal because Grandma Svendahl had a very large family.

Before anybody left, Grandma Svendahl always gathered the Grand Children in the parlor and told us about our ancestors. Great Grandfather Isaak Svendahl, born in 1822 in the small Norwegian village of Arendal, immigrated to America in 1846 and settled in what was to become Texas. After he grew up, Axel, his eldest son, known to us as Grampa Svendahl made a fortune selling land out on the Flat he purchased for a dollar an acre. Unfortunately, he lost most of his fortune in a failed oil venture. He died three years before I was born so I never knew him.

I had heard the story several times so I wasn't really interested. I wanted to watch the card games being played in the upstairs parlor. But when I tried to sneak up the stairs, Grandma Svendahl saw that I was missing and sent word for me to return immediately, and I did. After she finished the story she gave each of the grand children and great grand children shiny new silver dollars and a hug and a kiss on the cheek.

There was a large picture of Grandma and Grampa Svendahl hanging on the parlor wall over the fireplace. He sported a huge mustache stained by coffee or tobacco juice but Poppa said he never chewed or smoked.

When I looked at the picture it actually frightened me, he looked so stern and forbidding and Grandma Svendahl looked so unhappy. But it seemed to me all old people looked that way in pictures. Maybe it was the hard life they had endured, at least that's what Poppa said.

I loved Grandma Svendahl's two-story house. You could see it for miles with its gleaming white exterior and the split shingle roof. It had a well in the kitchen and a huge dining room and many rooms upstairs and a big porch across the front. It sat on the edge of the Flat and was the first house on the other side of the mountain from Arendal.

The dining room easily seated twenty-five people and she welcomed company at any time and insisted on feeding them without prior notice. If visiting preachers came to town they usually stayed at her house.

Aunt Caroline and Uncle Helmer lived downstairs in the back part of the house. Upstairs there were several bedrooms reserved for overnight guests and an indoor bathroom with a commode, a tub and hot or cold running water. Grandma Svendahl lived downstairs in a bedroom next to the parlor. She had her own personal bathroom across the hall from her bedroom that she shared only with Aunt Caroline and Uncle Helmer.

That night we went back to the church for the Christmas Pageant put on by the various Sunday school classes. Each grade sang separately, then all grades sang one song together. Miss Boudegard played the pipe organ while I sang my solo, 'Away In A Manger'. Momma always said I had the sweetest voice this side of heaven.

After the singing, we put on a Christmas Pageant about the birth of Jesus.

I played the part of Joseph and Cousin Esther played the part of Mary. Last year cousin Angel was baby Jesus but this year we used a doll. It didn't seem right but there were no other children of that age in the congregation. Momma said it was because of the depression; nobody had any money. I didn't understand why the lack of money would cause no children to be born but I didn't dispute her.

Finally, at bedtime, exhausted but happy I went to my room and prepared for bed. It would be my last night alone for some time so I prayed out loud. When I finished my prayers I began to think about Cousin Angel. And, for the first time in my life, I experienced a twinge of doubt about God.

I truly believed in *God the Father Almighty, Maker of heaven and earth.* I also believed in *Jesus Christ, His only Son, our Lord, conceived by the Holy Ghost, born of the Virgin Mary, suffered under Pontius Pilot, was crucified, dead and buried. He descended into Hell.* I also believed that *on the third day he arose from the dead and ascended into heaven and sitteth on the right hand of God The Father Almighty; from thence He shall come to judge the quick and the dead.*

And, though I didn't understand it, I believed in *the Holy Ghost, the Holy Christian Church, the Communion of Saints, the forgiveness of sins, the resurrection of the body and the life everlasting.*

I believed that God ruled heaven and earth and all the stars in the firmament and all the Angels in heaven and hell and all the ships at sea. I believed that He knew our every thought and deed and that we were beholden to Him in our daily lives. I had been taught this at home, in school, in Sunday school, in Parochial School, and in church and I had no reason to doubt it.

But why would God allow a sweet young child like Baby Angel to be subjected to unspeakable danger and unknown perils and possibly death? She could not have sinned in her young life so why was she being punished. Or was she being punished for the sins of her father as it says in Exodus; Chapter 20, verse 5, *"I, the Lord thy God am a jealous God, visiting the iniquity of the fathers upon the children unto the third and fourth generation of them that hate me."* That just didn't seem fair to me. Why punish her? She had no control over her father even if, as Momma said, he was a drunkard and a debaucher, whatever that meant. I know the Bible says we are born in sin but does a baby have to suffer for that?

Surely she isn't being punished for my sins, which were many, especially this year. My grief over her absence was my punishment, not hers. I pondered these thoughts during my prayers and when I finished I asked God to forgive me for my doubts and all my sins and to spare Baby Angel from punishment for my sins and the sins of her father. Then I promised God I would commit my life to finding her and restoring her to her family and her friends. Feeling at peace for the first time in weeks, I went to sleep with a new resolve that would perhaps assuage my guilt. And when I got up the next morning I noticed that my warts were gone.

Chapter Eighteen
Crazy Clem Again

January 1, 1935

It turned very cold yesterday and Momma felt a headache coming on so we didn't go to church. Instead I rode my bicycle to Cousin Esther's house so I could show her my wartless hands. We played with the new board game she had received for Christmas, but it wasn't much fun so we quit.

"Come on, let's go outside," Cousin Esther suggested.

"We better put on our coats. I don't want to catch pneumonia again,"

We went to the back porch, sat in the swing and talked about the many things that had transpired since we last spent any time together. I showed her my wartless hands then we began to talk about our plans for the New Year and I told her about my pledge to find Baby Angel. After a few moments she said, "Why don't we go up on the mountain and spy on Crazy Clem?" She paused then added "Why don't we do it today?"

"Okay, but it'll be cold up there. We better get gloves and something to cover our ears."

We rode our bicycles to our house then headed for the mountain. It's a good thing we did because by the time we got to the top of the hill, it began to drizzle and the cold north wind picked up strength. I wanted to turn back but Cousin Esther called me a sissy, so we plodded on.

At the gate to the goat pasture we stopped and looked around. We didn't see any goats and the donkey wasn't in the corral. The door and the window were covered with heavy cardboard so we couldn't see if there were any lights in the house.

We slipped around the pasture into the cedar that ran behind the house and slowly crept closer. The wind whistling through the trees sucked a thin wisp of smoke out of the chimney.

When we got within twenty feet of the house we stopped and listened for any activity. Suddenly we heard what sounded like a baby crying and then it stopped only to be repeated. I grabbed Cousin Esther's hand that was as cold as mine and whispered, "We better go."

"No, we gotta go in that house and see what's crying. It might be Cousin Angel."

"Maybe it's a baby goat," I suggested. Then we heard it again, seemingly

103

much closer and from a different direction and we both said in unison, "That ain't no goat!"

I let go of her hand and put my arm around her shoulder and felt her shivering. She leaned closer and whispered, "I think it's Cousin Angel. Let's go in and maybe we can save her."

Silently we crept closer toward the house. When we were about ten feet from the door, I stopped and whispered, "Before we go in let's throw a rock on the roof and see what happens." And when we did, all hell broke loose. The cardboard flew out of the door and the donkey followed by about a dozen goats came charging out into the yard and ran into a large water barrel knocking it over, spilling water everywhere. Several chickens also dashed out the door followed by a mother cat and three half grown kittens. Crazy Clem followed, gun in his hand and when he saw us he pointed it at my chest and snarled, "I thought I told you kids to stay away!" Then we heard it again, something crying and definitely coming from the house. "W-what was that?" I asked.

"None of your damn business!" he yelled and discharged the shotgun into the air. The screaming became much louder, the donkey let out a whoop that sounded like a train whistle, the goats broke down the fence and ran away and the chickens took flight into the cedar. Then the crying stopped.

Crazy Clem again aimed the gun at my chest and rumbled, "If y'all ain't off this property in one minute they'll be picking bird shot out of your belly for a year. Now, GET!!" and we did. We ran as fast as our legs would carry us all the way back to our house and I noticed she had no trouble keeping up with me. In fact, she beat me there.

Later, after we rested and after we ate a piece of Julekake and drank a glass of milk, we talked. "What do you think was crying?" Cousin Esther asked.

"I don't know. It sounded like a little baby. But it might have been Cousin Angel, " I answered.

"It sounded more like a baby than Cousin Angel, but what ever it was, I bet he was violating it."

After a pause, she continued, "I bet he was violating it when we got here. I bet it's Cousin Angel and he has her locked up in a cage," Cousin Esther said with a quiver in her voice. "What are we gonna do now, tell our parents?

"Probably," I answered. This question had been running through my mind all the way home and at the moment I couldn't decide what we should do. Poppa would be mighty displeased because he had told me to stay away from the man and I had disobeyed. He probably wouldn't believe we heard a baby crying, that seemed too preposterous. But we did, I just know we heard a baby or somebody crying and I knew we couldn't ignore it. "Now that I think about it," I said, "it sounded just like Cousin Angel right after she was born."

"But where would Crazy Clem get a baby?" Cousin Esther asked. "He ain't even married."

"I don't know. Maybe he stole it."

We puzzled about this for several moments, then I looked out the window and saw it had began to snow, not a lot but I was sure it more would follow. "You better get on home while you can," I said, helping her with her coat.

Watching her ride away into the swirling snow I pondered the problem. I gotta tell somebody, I thought. I had asked her to call when she got home to let me know she was safe, and when she did, I told her my decision.

Chapter Nineteen
Grampa Yo Explains

Later That Day

After chores and after supper I went to Grampa Yo's room to ask his advice. I explained the problem as carefully as I could, trying to remember every detail. I tried to imitate the crying sound we had heard but I just couldn't duplicate it to my satisfaction.

Poppa came to the door when he heard my efforts and I explained that I had heard something in the upper pasture that I didn't recognize. He asked me to repeat the sound and when I did, he shook his head and said, "You mustsa heard a hoot owl."

After Poppa left, Grampa said, "Vell, son, vot you heared vere a baby Haugfolk, one of them underground peoples. They come out ven bad veather is acomin to varn the farmers to cover their crops and to bring I der animals."

"But why did it sound like a baby?" I asked fascinated.

"It vere a baby, the Haugfolk has babies just like ve does." He paused for a moment, and then continued. "That happened today?"

"Yeah, we nearly froze before we got home."

"Did you see any animals in da house?"

"Yeah, his donkey, all of his goats, some cats and bunch of chickens ran out of the house when we threw a rock on the roof."

"Vel then, you definitely heard the Haugfolk. They come out to varn the man about the bad weather." Grampa scratched his head a moment then continued, "Vell I never seen one in Norvay but my brother did and he never told a lie." He paused, tapped his cane on the arm of his rocking chair, then continued, "A man over in the Hamilton county has one that lives in his vater vell. Comes out before every norther. He sometimes brings a baby with him to sound the alarm. That man is a preacher so I knowed the story ver true." Grampa Yo stopped, lit his pipe with a kitchen match and began to puff. The smoke was so thick I nearly choked so I left.

Grampa Yo didn't smoke regular pipe tobacco. He ordered cigars from a company in Minnesota that advertised in the Decorah Posten. The cigars came by mail in a square tin can. When he opened the can he would take one out, cut it in half and stick one of the halves in his pipe and light it. Each half would last for days and you could smell it all over the house.

I wasn't sure what to make of the story but tended not to believe it. But what had we really heard? Maybe I better ask Poppa.

It took me several days to work up the courage and when I did, he laughed so hard he almost fell off of his milk stool. After he stopped laughing he asked, "I thought I told you to stay away from Crazy Clem. Did you forget?"

"Yes sir." I lied and I think he knew it but he didn't threaten to get out the razor strop and he didn't threaten to ground me. Maybe it had something to do with the Christmas spirit Pastor Pierson talked about in his last sermon. Whatever the reason, I was greatly relieved but I was disappointed that he had no answer and apparently didn't believe me. Maybe if Cousin Esther and I talked to him together, he would listen. And when I told him what Grampa had said he laughed even harder.

Chapter Twenty
Butchering Time

By the next morning there was an inch of snow on the ground and the temperature hovered around freezing so Poppa decided it would be a good day to butcher a hog. Our meat supply was running a little low because it could only be done in cold weather and this was the first cold spell of the winter. If the cold weather holds I'm sure we'll butcher a calf in the next few days.

It took until noon to get everything ready: fill the scalding barrel with water and bring it to a boil, scrub the pot Momma used to boil our clothes so she could make lard, sharpen the butchering tools, select the pig to be butchered, call the relatives and by noon there were ten or twelve men standing around the fire, drinking coffee and smoking their pipes, helping where they could for a share of the meat.

The process took all afternoon and by sundown we were through. The body had been quartered, the fat removed and the quarters salted and hung in the smokehouse to cure. The slabs of bacon with the skin in place had been salted and hung beside the quarters. Poppa stripped the fat away from all the pieces except the bacon and set it aside. Some of the helpers wanted to split the pig's head and remove the brains but Poppa didn't approve. "That ain't no way to treat a pig," he said.

Every step of the way, Grampa Yo muttered, "That ain't the vay ve done it in Norvay." After the fourth such remark Poppa mocked, "Vell, ve ain't in Norvay, ve's in America and this is the vay ve's gonna do it!" I think it made Grampa Yo mad because he went to his room and didn't come out the rest of the day. The next morning we stoked the fire under the black pot and when the water began to boil, Momma used the lard from yesterday and ashes from the stove to make lye soap.

The next day the weather was still below freezing so we butchered a calf. The process was about the same as the pig except Poppa skinned the hide, scraped the fat away. Later he would use it to make harness leather. Later in the day, tiring of the butchering process, I went to the back porch and sat with Grampa Yo. I knew he was still a little peeved at Poppa and I thought maybe I could cheer him up. He pouted for a few minutes, then began to tell me more troll stories, some I believed, most I didn't, like the story about the old man who got lost in the woods and the Skogstrollet stole his head and replaced it with a horse's head but his body remained the same. There was no way I could believe that story but he swore on Grandma Yo's grave that it was true.

"It's not possible to take a man's head off and replace it with a horses head," I protested.

"Son, the Skogstrollet can do anything they vants to do," he answered. I knew arguing would do no good so I remained quiet. Maybe Momma's right. They're nothing but fairy tales.

He went on with more stories, all as unbelievable as the first story but I listened politely until he finished. He said nothing for a few minutes, rocking back and forth, tapping his cane to the rhythm of the chair. Then he stopped, turned to me and asked, "Yakob, you know that garage out at your Uncle Ole's farm?"

"Yeah, I do." How could I forget?

"Vell," he continued, "the Skogstrollet done broke in and stold all the furniture and has took it to der castle."

"How do you know?" I asked.

"It ver revealed to me in a dream." When I didn't respond, he continued, "Your Uncle Ole and Aunt Telinda is dead and buried somewheres and they ain't never gonna get found." He stood up, adjusted his pants and headed toward the bathroom and I went to the barn to start my chores.

There was no way I could believe the things he had said either about the Skogstrollet or about the garage or Uncle Ole and Aunt Telinda. He was just making all this up about having a dream. Nobody believed in dreams. Poppa said so and so did Pastor Pierson.

After dark and after the evening meal I again went to Grampa Yo's room and sat beside him. Neither of us said a word for many minutes, until I asked him if he was sure about Uncle Ole and Aunt Telinda. He again said he had seen it in a dream. He said he knew the Skogstrollet had put the dream in his head so folk's vould qvit looking. Then he said something that shocked me even further.

"The Haugfolk has got has got Baby Angel."

"But you told me before that the Skogstrollet had her."

"Vell they did but the Haugfolk done bought her from the Skogstrollet before she got kilt. They is holding her in one of their castles and someday they's gonna ask for ransom. If the family won't pay no ransom, they'll turn her into a slave."

"How do you know?" I asked.

"I seen that in the same dream. I seen a man come and give the Skogstrollet money and took the child to a castle up in the mountain and he ver a changeling."

"What's a changeling?" I asked even though I thought I knew the answer.

"Vell, a changeling is a Haugfolk who can change hisself into a human. He is immune to the effects of sunlight."

"Where is Baby Angel now?" I asked hoping to hear something encouraging.

"Like I said, they has got her in their castle high up on top of the tallest mountain."

"You told me the Haugfolk live in caves under the ground."

"If they is a Changeling, they can live in the mountains." I listened quietly but began to suspect he was making it up as he went along. But what if he wasn't? So I asked, "Can we get her back?"

"The Haugfolk vill let us know in good time vot the ransom vill be. She von't be harmed because it vould bring them bad luck."

"How did they get her to their cave and where is it?"

"They took her up into the mountain where they is a hidden entrance that no body but Changelings can see."

"How do you know she's safe?"

"I know Haugfolk and I know they vouldn't harm a young child because she is free of sin. Your Uncle Ole committed the unforgivable sin and had to die. And your Aunt Telinda tolerated this sin and made no effort to seek his redemption so she also had to die." He paused for a moment, then said, "May God rest their souls and grant them eternal peace. Amen."

"Amen," I answered.

We both fell silent. And when he lit his pipe, I left and went to bed not knowing what and how much to believe and wondering what Uncle Ole's sin may have been.

Chapter Twenty-One
An Empty Garage

It took me two days to work up enough courage to tell Poppa about Grampa Yo's dream. I expected him to laugh and ridicule me for even listening to the ridiculous story. But much to my surprise, he seemed interested, "I reckon we better go out there and have a look," he said. "I ain't been there since Christmas and I really should look the place over." So, on Saturday, Cousin Esther and me went with Poppa to Uncle Ole's farm.

When we got there everything seemed the same except the gate. The wires had again been cut and when we reached the garage, we immediately saw that the two-by-four had been pried off and the lock had been broken and lay on the ground and when he opened the doors, he found the garage empty except for a broken chair and several empty kerosene cans. Everything else, the beds, the table, the chairs, the stove, the icebox, the dresser and all the pictures were gone. Even the clothing that had been packed in boxes was gone.

Poppa examined the lock and could see it had been opened probably with a hacksaw. There were tracks on the ground where the furniture had been dragged and many footprints in the soft dirt. There were tire tracks in the soft dirt leading away from the garage but they disappeared once the vehicle reached the gravel drive way.

"Looks like somebody's stole the furniture," Poppa said and I could tell he was upset.

"What are we gonna do?" I asked

"Guess we better go to town and find the sheriff " But before we left, Poppa took out the camera he usually carried in the car and took several pictures of the empty garage, the marks on the road and a picture of the lock. Then he picked up the broken lock and put it in the car.

Instinctively, I looked at the mountain and there he was, the mountain man, and he definitely had a gun. I grabbed Cousin Esther's hand and pointed.

"Who's that," she whispered.

"It's the man that shot at us."

"Could you tell who it is?"

"No, he's too far away."

Before I could tell Poppa, the man disappeared but I told him anyway and he answered, "Probably that hunter again." That ended the discussion and we went home.

When we got there Poppa said he was going to town and report the missing furniture. "I reckon me and the sheriff will go back to the farm and check it out."

"Can we go along?" I asked.

"No. You need to stay here and help Brother Ben with the milking. We might be late getting back." I didn't answer; I had other things on my mind.

When we arrived home, Poppa let us out and went to Arendal. Cousin Esther and I went to the house, drank a glass of milk then sat on the front porch and sulked.

"Why don't we follow them on our bicycles and watch what happens?" Cousin Esther suggested.

"But Poppa told me to stay here and we're liable to get caught."

"We won't get caught. We can stop at the top of the hill and watch. Won't anybody see us."

"Well, okay. But if I don't get back in time for milking, I'll be in big trouble."

"Don't worry so much Jacob, You sound like my mother; worry, worry, worry, all the time worrying." So we sat and watched the road.

It wasn't long until we saw Poppa drive up and park in the back yard. In a few minute, the sheriff arrived and Poppa got in with him and they drove toward Uncle Ole's farm. I knew we should have told Momma where we were going but I was afraid she would tell Poppa when he got home and I would be in trouble again. Besides, she would probably forbid it and if we went anyway I would be in double trouble and so would Cousin Esther. But I didn't want to miss the excitement. And with a little luck, no one would know we were gone.

As planned, we stopped at the top of the hill overlooking Uncle Ole's farm.

We saw Poppa and the sheriff standing in front of the garage apparently talking. I looked at the well and saw that the lid was still open and saw that the rope still plunged through the hole.

Suddenly a gruff voice close by growled, "You kids better get the hell out of here before you get hurt!"

At first we didn't see him, then we did, partially hidden by the cedar about fifty or sixty yards away. It was the mountain man and he had a gun that looked like a 30-30 Winchester. I had seen one like it in a hunting magazine and felt it was the prettiest gun I had ever seen. I tore out the picture and kept it hidden in my closet.

"I SAID GET!!" the man yelled and we did, on our bicycles, peddling as fast as we could until we got to home.

We drank a glass of milk then sat on the back porch until we saw them drive into the yard. Poppa got out and the sheriff headed for town.

"Who do you think it was?" Cousin Esther asked.

"I don't know. I never saw him before."

"Didn't his face look kinda funny?"

"Yeah, I guess so. I was too scared to look closely."

"Are we gonna tell your father?"

"I don't know, maybe we better not. If we do, he'll throw a fit because he told us to stay at home."

Sneaking away without asking permission was kinda like running away from home and I knew that called for a trip to the back porch with your pants down. It didn't matter that we had returned before we were caught, we had gone without permission.

I didn't fear the strop that much. Sure it hurt and you were sore for a week but the consolation was that you usually deserved it. I guess the thing I hated the most was the thought of not seeing Cousin Esther for weeks or even months. And if her mother found out what we did, and I knew she would, Cousin Ester would also be in big trouble. Her mother had her own means of punishment that I considered worse than a whipping.

So, in the end, I told no one, not even Grampa Yo but I carried the burden in my heart and thanked God for delivering my cousin and me from harm and asked His forgiveness for my sins. But, somehow, I knew we had to discover the mountain man's identity and figure out why he's so interested in Uncle Ole's farm.

I did consult Grampa Yo about one thing. That night I asked him, " Do trolls carry guns?"

"No, but changelings does. They is just like peoples. They can carry a gun but they don't never use them except if they is in mortal danger. They is afraid of guns."

The next day, which was Sunday, Cousin Esther and I again went with Poppa to Uncle Ole's farm. Poppa said he wanted to put a new lock on the garage even though it was empty He also said he wanted to put some penetrating oil on the hinges of the well lid so it would close, then put a lock on the well lid and repair the gate.

After church we went to the farm and Poppa put the new lock in place and again tried to close the well lid. It still wouldn't close so he squirted on a generous amount of oil and tried again but it still wouldn't close. I kinda wanted to look in the well but I was afraid Poppa would start asking questions that I couldn't answer without lying and I felt I had lied enough for this month.

Waiting for him to finish, I glanced at the hill and there he was, the mountain man. "Look! That's him," I whispered to Cousin Esther pointing toward the mountain. But before she could look, he was gone and I still didn't recognize him.

"Who," she whispered back.

"The mountain man but he's already gone."

In a few moments, Poppa gave up on the well lid and we went home. For some reason we didn't tell him about the man and when we got home, Poppa went to town and Cousin Esther went home.

We had just finished milking when Poppa came back accompanied by Sheriff Bjornburg. He asked me to sit on a milking stool and he pulled up a feed bucket and sat beside me.

"I understand you've seen a man up in the mountain at your Uncle Ole's farm. You know his furniture is missing and we're trying to find out what happened to it."

"Yes sir, I know" I replied.

"When did you last see him?" he continued.

"Today."

"Where was he?"

"Standing at the top of the hill."

"What did he look like?

"I couldn't tell, he was too far away."

"Could you tell what kind of clothes he had on?"

"Overalls and a brown shirt, I think."

"Was he wearing a hat?"

"Yes sir, I think so."

"Did you see a car or a horse near by?"

"No sir."

"Have you ever seen this man in town?"

"No sir."

"Have you seen him on the hill at any other time?"

I knew this question was coming but I didn't know what to say. We had disobeyed Poppa's direct orders and sneaked out here yesterday. Should I try to lie my way out of it? Would he talk to Cousin Esther? Would her answers jibe with mine especially if I lied? If I told the truth what would be my punishment?

Poppa knew I was struggling with an answer and I think he knew there was a lie somewhere in my story. After maybe a minute, Poppa said, "Tell the truth son. Just think about Cousin Angel. Your answers may help save her."

And that did it. No more lies. I told the truth about the football in the well and the day when the mountain man fired a gun at us. I told him about yesterday when the man chased us away. The story poured out like water out of a rain barrel and when I finished I felt as if a great weight had been lifted from my shoulders.

Poppa didn't seem too angry, at least not at that moment. But I wasn't sure what would happen after the sheriff left.

"Would you recognize the man if you saw him again?" the sheriff asked.

"I think so."

"And you're sure you've never seen him anywhere else?"

"Yes sir, I'm sure. I've never seen him anywhere else."

"Were you close enough to be sure you didn't know him?"

"Yes sir."

"How close were you?"

I hesitated then replied, "Maybe fifty yards yesterday, maybe two hundred yards the other times."

"And he was fifty yards away when you saw him yesterday?"

"Maybe sixty, I'm not sure, I was so scared."

"Could it have been your Uncle Ole?"

Too stunned to answer immediately, the sheriff asked again, "Could the man you saw on the mountain have been your Uncle Ole."

"No!" I could tell the sheriff didn't believe me so I repeated, "I know it wasn't Uncle Ole. I know that for sure. He didn't look at all like Uncle Ole."

"You're sure about that?"

"Yes sir, I'm sure."

The sheriff thought for a few moments then said, "Okay son. That's all for now. I'll probably talk to you again in a few days. Until then, I want you to think real hard and see if you can remember anything else."

"It wasn't Uncle Ole," I repeated as tears began to stream down my cheeks.

"Okay son," he said as he patted me on the back. In a moment he was gone.

"Poppa, it wasn't Uncle Ole. I know it wasn't. I could see him real good and it wasn't Uncle Ole."

"That's okay," Poppa answered. "I know it couldn't have been your Uncle Ole. He has no reason to be up on the hill and he would never shoot a gun at you. I think it must have been a hunter who mistook you for a deer. After supper we'll talk some more." And we did. We sat on the back porch and talked.

We had never talked like this before and it felt good. He again assured me it wasn't Uncle Ole I had seen and I agreed. Then we talked about the football.

"Son, I'm not gonna tell your brother, it would only create needless problems. I know you didn't do it on purpose but I wish you had come to me when it happened. Maybe we could have retrieved the ball then."

He paused, then continued, "It's probably ruined by now and he already has a replacement so why don't we just call it our little secret." I cried until he patted me on the back, then put his arm around my shoulder.

Then he said he was going back to the farm tomorrow and look around. "Funny things seem to be happening out there and I'd like to find out if I can who that man is that you and Cousin Esther saw on top of the mountain. Maybe he can tell us who stole the furniture. Maybe he can tell us who started the house fire and maybe he can tell us about Uncle Ole and he might even know about Baby Angel."

We sat for many minutes, and then Poppa continued, "The whole thing doesn't make any sense. The only thing that makes a lick of sense is if maybe my brother removed the furniture from the house, stored it in the garage and started the fire. But I just can't in my wildest dreams believe he would do something that stupid. I know he's done some foolish things in his life, but I just don't think he would burn down his own house. What would that benefit him? As for the insurance money, it would only pay off the mortgage with nothing left for him." He repeated, "It just doesn't make sense."

He was silent for a few more minutes then he continued, "No, son. My brother didn't do it! I think there's a good possibility someone killed both Ole and Telinda and buried them somewhere, maybe in the orchard. I think the same person moved the furniture to the garage then set the house on fire. Later he stole the furniture from the garage and probably took it somewhere and sold it. And that person may be the mountain man as you call him."

"What about Baby Angel? Do you think somebody killed her and buried her in the orchard?" I asked with tears in my eyes.

"I just don't know. But we're going to find out." With that, he went in the kitchen to talk with Momma and I went to bed and immediately fell asleep.

Chapter Twenty-Two
More Gun Shots from the Mountain

I guess Poppa and the sheriff must have talked some more about Uncle Ole and maybe about the mountain man. He may have even told the sheriff about Grampa Yo's's dream. I wasn't along so I don't know what they decided but he apparently felt it deserved an investigation.

For the first time that I can remember, we skipped Church and I went with Poppa and the Sheriff to Uncle Ole's farm. Cousin Esther's mother wouldn't let her go even though the Sheriff said she might be of some help. It hurt Brother Ben's feelings because he wasn't invited and he sulked all morning during chores and sorta refused to go to church, but in the end, he went.

Poppa put two shovels and several two-by-fours in the truck. I wasn't sure what he planned to do with the two-by-fours. Maybe he wanted to nail them across the garage door again.

I noticed the Sheriff had his pistol strapped to his belt and a shotgun in his car. I guess he expected trouble and so did I.

When we arrived at the farm, Poppa opened the garage so Sheriff Bjornburg could see it was empty. They looked for the tracks we had seen before but they were gone. Someone had apparently erased them.

"Let's look around a little," the sheriff suggested. "You never know; might find something interesting."

"Okay," Poppa answered.

"I thought I saw someone in the orchard when we were here before," I mentioned. "Maybe we oughta look there."

"Son, that's a good idea. Let's go," the sheriff answered and we followed him across the yard and into the orchard not stopping until we reached the pile of brush in the center. The sheriff pulled a few of the branches away, then fell to his knees and examined the ground. "Gunder, help me get these limbs out of the way. I think we may have found something."

Before either could act, the pile sorta exploded and Poppa fell to the ground. In a second or two, I heard what sounded like a shot coming from the mountain. I looked in that direction and saw a man standing in a little clearing with a gun. Before I could say a word, the pile of brush exploded again and I heard another shot. In an absolute panic I ran as fast as my legs would carry me and when something kicked up a shower of dirt behind me, I ran even faster.

I don't think I had ever run that fast and in less than a minute I was out of the orchard and crouching behind the car. I heard several shots coming from the orchard and several more coming from the hill. It sounded like when Tom Mix fought the bank robbers in the Saturday afternoon serials, only louder and more terrifying.

Through the windshield I could see the hill and there he was, the mountain man, and he was definitely doing the shooting and I guessed the sheriff was shooting back. After a couple more shots, he disappeared. Maybe he ran out of bullets or maybe he got hit, I couldn't tell for sure.

In a few minutes the sheriff, who outweighed Poppa by a hundred pounds, came out of the orchard carrying Poppa in his arms. He placed him in the back seat of his car, then took off his belt and wrapped it around Poppa's thigh just above a big bloody spot that grew larger as he worked. I glanced at the hill to be certain the man was gone, then ran to meet Poppa and the sheriff.

"What happened, Poppa? Are you okay?" I yelled.

"No I ain't okay. The son of a bitch shot me in the leg."

I had never ever heard Poppa utter a cuss word in my life except for a word that sounded like 'dreet' that he used when a cow stepped in the milk bucket, or if a tire on the car or truck blew out. Once I asked Momma what the word meant and she gave me a dose of caster oil and sent me to the orchard for a switch so I knew it must be a cuss word.

"Sonny," the sheriff said, "he's got a hole clean through his leg, just above the knee. We gotta get him to the doctor." He grabbed a stick to tighten the belt, then said, "You know we nearly got killed," then added, "Did you see the shooter?"

"Yes sir, I saw him," I answered. "It was the mountain man."

"The mountain man? Who's that?" the sheriff asked.

"It's the same man I seen before, you know, the man I told you about."

"Did you recognize him?"

"No, but I know it's the same man and I know it wasn't Uncle Ole."

With the tourniquet in place, we left, leaving the garage door open and the gate unlocked. We bounced across the cattle guard, followed the river road, not slowing down until we reached Arendal and found Dr. Nygard in his office busy filling packets with white powder.

The first thing he did was to cut open Poppa's pant leg and examine the injury. I could see dark blood oozing out of wounds, the one on the front of the thigh and the one on the back.

"Gunder, you got a hole clear through your leg and I think it may have broken you femur, you know, the thighbone. Did somebody shoot you?"

"Hell yes somebody shot me! Cain't you tell? Nearly got killed."

"Where did it happen?"

"At Ole Svendahl's place," the sheriff answered. "I got a feeling bad things have happened there so we went to investigate and somebody tried to kill us."

"How about my leg?" Poppa said. "Can you fix it?"

"No, I can't fix it," the doctor replied. "But I am gonna put on a bandage and a better tourniquet. Then I'm gonna give you a shot of morphine and send you to Waco. They can fix it there. Your liable to pass out on the way 'cause you've lost a lot of blood, so I think you better go by ambulance. Sheriff, you call his family and I'll call the funeral home and tell them to hurry up, they got a hot trip to make."

I watched as he applied a new tourniquet, then gently cleaned the wound and packed it with something that smelled like iodine. Watching him work, I got kinda sick at my stomach but I didn't vomit. In a few minutes he applied a large wooden splint up the side of his leg from the ankle to the armpit and secured it in place with heavy tape. Then he gave Poppa a shot in the butt.

I watched, fascinated, as he cleaned up his tools and dropped then in a pan of boiling water sitting on a little electric stove. By the time he finished, the ambulance arrived and they strapped Poppa to a rolling bed, rolled the bed to the ambulance and lifted him in.

"What should I do?" I asked. I kinda thought I should go with Poppa but I wasn't sure.

"You come along with me in the ambulance," Poppa mumbled then seemed to go to sleep. The driver put me in the front seat and the helper sat in the back beside Poppa. The driver revved up the engine, turned on the siren and off to Waco we went. Poppa groaned every time we hit a bump and I got a little sick on the winding road but I didn't vomit. I was too scared. Or maybe I was just too worried about Poppa.

We went really fast over the bumpy road and in what seemed like fifteen minutes we screeched to a halt outside the emergency entrance to Hillcrest Hospital. The driver jumped out and they unloaded Poppa and wheeled the bed inside.

Sister Selma was waiting at the door and went with Poppa to the Emergency Room. Immediately several nurses gathered around and moved Poppa from the ambulance bed to a rolling hospital bed. An older nurse unwrapped the bandage, removed the packing and examined the wound. Then she reapplied the tourniquet and the bandage, went to the phone and made a call. In a few minutes she came back and took Poppa down the hall to another room so they could make an x-ray picture of his leg.

Sister Selma asked me what happened and I told her as best as I could considering my shattered nerves. She said Momma and the rest of the family were on the way and that the Chief Nurse had called Dr. Bassett who would probably take Poppa to surgery tonight. I asked her where I could find a bathroom and she took me down the hall and showed me a door with the picture of a man. Only then did I realize I had wet my pants, probably at Uncle Ole's, but it was already dry and I needed to go again. I almost didn't make it inside but I did and when I finished I went back to the Emergency Room and found Sister Selma. She handed me a candy bar that I devoured, then I asked to see Poppa but she said he was asleep. "Maybe you can see him when the rest of the family gets here."

The surgeons, Dr. Will Bassett and his twin brother Dr. Bill arrived at about the same time as Brother Ben, Momma, Sister Sybil and Grampa Yo. After the doctors examined the wound and looked at the x-rays they came to the waiting room to met the family. Sister Selma introduced everyone, then Dr. Bill began.

"We need to take him to surgery so we can control the bleeding and clean out the wound. Thank goodness, the x-rays are negative, nothing is broken and the pulses in his foot are good so I think the artery is okay. But I suspect the vein is injured judging by the amount and character of bleeding and we might have to tie it off. We'll talk with you again after surgery and give you a more accurate prognosis. Also, he may need a blood transfusion."

"I'll give some!" both Brother Ben and I said at the same time.

"I got more blood than you got so I'm the one should give," Brother Ben said.

"But mine's better than yours," I retorted. I wasn't about to let that tub of lard best me.

"Boys, stop it!" Momma warned. "We'll let the doctors decide."

"We'll talk about that later," one of the doctors said. "Now we need to get him to surgery so we can stop the bleeding and remove the tourniquet. It's already been on longer than it should."

"Doctor, how long will it take," Momma asked.

"Probably about two hours," one replied and they both turned on their heels and walked out.

We followed the rolling bed to the swinging doors that said, "SURGERY NO ADMITTANCE. Poppa was asleep but Momma kissed him on the forehead, then he was gone and we went to the surgery waiting room and waited.

"Who's gonna milk the cows?" I asked.

"I called Uncle Andrew," Brother Ben replied. "He's gonna look after the milking and other chores until we get back. Cousin Joseph is gonna help and probably stay at the house."

We sorta settled in and Cousin Selma found us some coffee then began to tell us about the Basset brothers. They were identical twins who practiced surgery together and were called Hekyll & Jekyll by the staff because they looked like a couple of black crows marching up and down the halls in their black suits, starched white shirts and narrow string ties with their long black hair greased and parted in the middle, but she said they were very good. If any of the staff required surgery they were usually called.

She said they had married identical twin sisters and it was rumored that they sometimes swapped wives. But this had never been proved and did not effect their reputations. So, she assured us that Poppa was in good hands. I noticed Momma was crying, and when Sister Selma finished, Momma sobbed, "How are we gonna pay for all this?"

"Don't worry," Sister Selma said. "I know Poppa's credit at the bank is good."

I noticed that Grampa Yo had fallen asleep so I removed his hat and placed it on the floor beside him. He opened his eyes and mumbled, "It ver a changling vot done it," then promptly want back to sleep.

As promised, after about two hours, the surgeons returned in their bloody operating gowns and bloody gloves and sat down beside Momma, one on each side. From the looks on their faces, I thought they were bringing bad news, like maybe Poppa had died, but they didn't. Sister Selma said later they always wore their bloody gowns when they came out of surgery in an effort to impress the families. She also said if they removed an organ like a uterus or a gall bladder or a big ovarian tumor during the surgery they would sometimes bring the bloody mess to the waiting room and show it to the family. It apparently didn't bother the doctors if one or two members of the family fainted.

"He's okay," Dr. Will said. "We got the bleeding stopped but we had to tie off the femoral vein, the main vein from the leg. That could cause some complications but it was the only way we could handle it. The bullet missed the artery by less than an inch and missed the bone by even less."

"What would happen if the bullet injured the artery?" Brother Ben wanted to know.

The other doctor answered, "He would probably have lost his leg. He's very lucky but he may have some complications from the surgery."

"Praise God," Momma murmured.

"What complications?" Brother Ben asked. I knew he was worrying about when Poppa could resume working.

"He might have some significant swelling of his foot and leg. If he does it should go away in a year or two."

"Does he need a blood transfusion?" Sister Selma asked.

"I don't think he will, but he did lose a lot of blood. We'll just have to watch his blood count."

"When will he be able to work?" Brother Ben asked.

"Son, I can't answer that now. It depends on if there are any complications and how fast he heals. I don't know much about farming so I don't know what would be required to do."

I could tell Brother Ben expected a better answer. A member of his class had dropped out of school half way through his senior year to run their farm after his father's sudden death from a farm accident so I'm sure he was worrying about the same thing.

Momma probably read his mind and said, "Don't worry Benjamin, the Lord will provide. He will never put more on us than we can carry."

The doctors stood up and shook everybody's hand, then left. One of the doctors said we should go home after Poppa returns to his room. We could come back tomorrow.

In about thirty minutes they brought him back to the room reeking of ether and we left, all except Momma who said she wanted to stay with him until he came home. Sister Selma said she would arrange for a bed in the nurses's quarters and she could get her meals in the staff dining room. With that settled, we waked Grampa Yo and went home.

When we got home at midnight a crowd greeted us: Uncle Andrew, Cousin Joseph, Aunt Helena, Cousin Esther, Cousin Gertrude, Sheriff Bjornburg, Pastor Pierson and Johan Olstad, the president of the bank. We stayed up until two telling the story and answering questions.

Finally everybody seemed satisfied and they got ready to leave. That's when Sheriff Bjornburg announced that he was going to call in the Texas Rangers, swear in some deputies and take Uncle Ole's place apart and get to the bottom of this nonsense. Everybody clapped and then they all left except Cousin Joseph who would help with the morning chores. Cousin Esther wanted to stay but her mother wouldn't let her.

We never visited Poppa while he was in the hospital. I wanted to go every day but Momma sent word that we had to stay in school and make sure the chores were done. That really didn't leave any time for driving back and forth to Waco. And the cows still had to be milked and the calves fed twice a day.

On Saturday, a week after the injury Poppa came home by ambulance with a big bandage on his thigh with instructions to use crutches and see Dr. Nygard every other day for a dressing change. To me he looked really sick, pale and gaunt, and I told Momma so.

"Give him a week or two and he'll look as good as new," she said and I believed her. Momma and Poppa moved back downstairs and Grampa Yo slept on a bed we set up in the parlor. On Saturday night, after Poppa rested a while, Sheriff Bjornburg came to the house and talked with Poppa. I hid in the closet outside the bedroom and listened.

"Gunder, I have four deputies and one Texas Ranger lined up for a week from Sunday and we are gonna take Ole Svendahl's place apart. We're gonna scour the hill across the road, dig up the orchard and tear down the barn if we have to. We're gonna solve this mess one way or another. I might even ask Governor Allred to supply a few men from the National Guard. I don't want to get shot at again. I might not be as lucky the second time."

"Well, I wish I could go with you but I'm too weak, but maybe I'll feel better by next week end. If I cain't go, I would appreciate it if you let me know what you find. You do have a search warrant, don't you?"

"Oh yeah. Judge Christenson gave us one allowing us to plow up the entire farm if necessary. He doesn't like for his sheriff to get shot at, and he certainly doesn't like for one of his constituents to get injured by gunfire."

"Well, good luck," Poppa said and the sheriff left. But in a moment he stuck his head in the door and said. "If we find anything important, I'll let you know." Then he left and I sneaked out of the closet.

Five days after Poppa came home the hospital a bill arrived: one hundred and fifty dollars, one hundred for the hospital and fifty for the surgeons. When Momma opened the letter, she began to cry and called Sister Selma who told her she would look into it. In about an hour the hospital cashier called, "You can pay it out over time," the kindly lady said. "Just try to send a little every month."

Chapter Twenty-Three
Dead Calves and Crazy Clem

Toward the end of January Poppa received a letter from the Agriculture Extension Service Agent stating that the government planned to kill half of our calves to help raise the price of beef. He wrote that the government would pay the going market price for the destroyed calves, and like with the pigs, none of the meat could be sold or given away.

When Poppa objected, the Agent said the orders came from the AAA in Washington and that compliance was mandatory, not voluntary. After Poppa's injury, Brother Ben called the County Agent and tried to postpone the event, but the Agent said it couldn't be postponed and they were coming on Thursday and to get things ready as instructed in the letter. When Brother Ben told Poppa, he said, "I just hope the heck they were doing!"

So, on Thursday, Brother Ben and I stayed home from school and waited for the Agent and by nine, they arrived; the agent and three helpers all with 30-30 Winchester rifles. We had separated the calves into two pens, one for those to be killed and the other for those to be saved including the ones raised on a bottle because they were our pets. The County Agent counted all the calves, found twenty one in each pen, Then Brother Ben had to swear that we hadn't hidden a few calves elsewhere. The agent went to his truck and wrote out a check for two hundred and ten dollars and gave it to Brother Ben who took it to the house and gave it to Poppa.

After the first shot, I covered my ears and tears came to my eyes as the slaughter progressed. The calves raced around the pen, dropping like stones as the bullets hit their mark. It took about an hour because of the dust and by then, the ground was covered with blood and dead calves and horse flies filled air. High in the cloudless sky, a circling buzzard showed interest and soon ten or fifteen more joined in and the circle grew lower and tighter.

Soon a bulldozer arrived and dug a gigantic hole in the upper pasture that looked big enough to bury an elephant or a hippopotamus. They used log chains and the bulldozer to drag the bodies to the grave, then covered them with the dirt they had dug out. When the hole was full, they drove the bulldozer back and forth and you couldn't even tell it was a grave. Then they left, the bulldozer, the County Agent and the deputies.

When we went back to the house Momma and Poppa were both crying and

I didn't feel so good. I felt a personal loss because I had watched these calves grow and they were kinda like part of the family.

On Saturday after the killing of the calves, Cousin Esther and I, upon Poppa's suggestion, went to see Crazy Clem again. Brother Ben went with us, as a chaperone I guess, but he waited for us at what was left of the snake den. He said he wanted to see if any snakes were still alive.

Poppa said he had talked to Crazy Clem before his injury and the man indicated he would welcome a visit from us and was sorry about our previous trouble. "He told me he didn't know who you were; he thought you were some of the kids that had been pestering his donkey."

When we arrived at his pasture, we saw him waiting outside the shack. "Y'all come on in," he yelled. "Don't pay no attention to them goats. They's harmless."

The goats stopped grazing and watched us with suspicion as we walked across the pasture. And when we stopped at the gate around the yard, he called, "Come on in and set a spell." Then we heard it, the sound of a baby crying.

"W-What was that?" we both said

"That? Oh, that's Popsicle. She's a parrot thinks she's a baby. Actually I got him from my sister who had a new baby and Popsicle made so much racket imitating the baby they couldn't sleep so they gave her to me. She still thinks she a baby, yells like that all the time. I oughta cook her and eat her but she does keep me company."

With that, he invited us into his house, a one-room shack about twenty by twenty with one glassless opening for a window and a second opening that apparently served as a door. The first thing I noticed was the earthy smell; a mixture of animal dung, unwashed bodies, and maybe spoiled food. When Popsicle let out a loud screech we both jumped about a foot and backed out the door. Crazy Clem draped a dirty towel over the cage and the crying stopped.

"Come on in, she ain't gonna make no more racket." Cousin Esther and I exchanged glances and I knew she wanted to leave. Not wanting to offend the man, we stayed.

Crazy Clem had to stoop to keep from hitting his head on the doorsill. A potbelly stove stood in one corner beside a wood box. I assumed he used that to cook his food because I didn't see another stove in the room. A small table that had once been blue stood against the other wall. Several shelves filled with canned goods hung over the table and a shotgun hung on nails over the door. Two pickle barrels sat under the table and a small icebox, barely large enough to hold a twenty-five pound block, sat in the corner. A baby goat lay sleeping on a filthy overstuffed chair by the window opening.

His bed appeared to be a straw filled mattress spread on three 2x6's suspended on two ancient sawhorses and covered by a threadbare patchwork quilt. The only clothing I saw was a pair of overalls hanging on a nail, filthier than the ones he was wearing and a ragged blue shirt that had also seen better days. I didn't see a closet or a trunk so I assumed he had no other clothing. In a moment he pulled out the pickle barrels and told us to sit and we did.

"Come on Elmo," he said as he picked up the baby goat and carried it to the pasture. "You need to go see your mother." When the baby began to cry, the mother came running and the baby immediately began to nurse.

With that done, he settled in the chair and began to tell us what he had done in the war and what the war and the government had done to him.

"They tried to lock me up in some insane asylum, said I was crazy. But I ran away and came to Arendal and rented this little piece of land from your Pa. Built a house on the land and been livin here ever since, raising goats and collecting my government pension. My donkey, who's got better sense than them idiots in Washington, is my best friend."

While we were sitting around listening to him talk, several chickens and three cats came into the house, examined us, and then ambled away. The mother goat jumped the fence and came to the door; the baby stood outside the fence crying.

"Get out of here, Precious!" the man shouted and the goat walked out, jumped the fence and the baby again began to nurse. "I call her Precious but she ain't. She's meaner than a snake and gets mad if I call her anything else."

There were no further interruptions and after several hours of listening, I looked out the window and saw that the sun was about to set so we left.

Crazy Clem followed us to the gate and as we walked away, he yelled, "Y'all come back sometime soon. If you let me know ahead of time, I'll bake you a batch of cookies." That ended our immediate concerns about Cousin Angel and, from the looks and smell of his house; I didn't think either of us wanted any of his cookies.

When we got back to the snake den no snakes were evident and Brother Ben was gone. So we walked home comparing our impressions of Crazy Clem's house.

Chapter Twenty-Four
Another Trip to the Orchard

The Next Day

When I got home after the visit, I went to Poppa's room. Since the visit was his suggestion, I felt I should tell him how it went. I told Poppa about Crazy Clem's house, his furniture and the parrot. I told him about the goats and our desire never to return. Poppa listened patiently but I realized he had something else on his mind.

When I finished my report, he said, "Son, the sheriff came by this afternoon and told me he was gonna take some men tomorrow and search my brother's farm. Somebody seems hell bent on keeping us from moving the brush pile and there's a good possibility your aunt and uncle are buried there, that is if they're dead. I cain't think of any other reason why someone would try to kill us."

I immediately called Cousin Esther who asked, "Are we going?"

"I don't know if Poppa will let us."

"Well, if he won't, we can ride our bicycles and watch from the hill like we did before."

"What about your mother? Will she let you go?"

"She's going to a quilting party at Grandma Svendahl's house. I just won't tell her."

"Should we ask Cousin Joseph if he wants to go with us?" I asked.

"He's going with his father to Waco tomorrow," Cousin Esther answered. "Besides if we called him on the phone, someone would listen in and tell our parents. Then we would be in trouble."

"Yeah, I guess you're right."

However, the next day, things didn't go as planned. Poppa decided he wanted to go to church. It proved difficult because he couldn't walk so Brother Ben picked him up and carried him to the car and off we went. When we stopped in front of the church, people began to clap and Uncle Andrew lifted him out of the car and carried him to our customary pew.

Pastor Pierson led a long and very emotional prayer and preached a sermon filled with messages about bravery, thanking God for sparing Poppa's life and asked God to insure his swift recovery. Everyone wanted to talk to him after church and it was over an hour before we got home. When

Brother Ben carried him into the house he sorta passed out and ended up in bed with a cold rag on his forehead and Sister Sybil fanning him with a Progressive Farmer magazine. Momma wanted to call the doctor, but, in a few minutes, he perked up and seemed okay.

We were late eating dinner and before we finished, Grandma Svendahl arrived driving her shiny black Model T. She said she had postponed the quilting party until next Sunday because she had to see her son. I just hoped this wouldn't upset our plan.

I knew I shouldn't have done it, but after Grandma Svendahl got in the house and sat down by Poppa's bed, I sneaked out the back door, jumped on my bicycle and rode across the Flat to where we had planned to meet. I was already an hour late and I wasn't sure she had waited.

As I cleared the front gate and turned up the road I heard Brother Ben yell from the back porch, "Where do you think you're going?" I pretended not to hear him and I knew I was in trouble, big trouble. But I also knew Poppa couldn't whip me, at least not now, maybe later when his leg healed.

When I got to the rendezvous site, Cousin Esther was waiting and I could tell she was mad.

"Where have you been?" she snarled. "I've been waiting for an hour! I was about to decide you had chickened out."

"I'm sorry. I had problems getting away." And when I added, "That's sure a pretty dress you have on, you look real cute," she blushed and began to calm down. I had learned about flattery, but when I explained what happened when I left the house, she suggested, "Maybe you oughta go home before you get in trouble."

"No, " I replied. "I'll just take my chances. I don't want to miss the excitement. I want to see what they find. But maybe you should. Grandma Svendahl said she called off the quilting party and if your mother comes home and finds you gone, we'll both be in trouble."

"I'm not going home, I'm going with you," she replied. "If we get caught, I'll tell her some lie that will cover both of us." So we went on across the prairie until we reached the top of the hill overlooking Uncle Ole's farm and found an area were we could watch.

We saw two men in the center of orchard apparently digging a hole and next to where they were digging we could see another hole. The limbs from the brush pile were stacked neatly in the next row.

"That looks like a grave," Cousin Esther said and she was right, it looked like an open grave.

In a few minutes the men began to fill both holes and when they finished they replaced the brush pile and walked to where the sheriff was standing. Together they walked to the well and talked to a man in a uniform. "He looks like a Texas Ranger," I whispered to Cousin Esther and she agreed.

In a minute I saw several men come down out of the mountain threading their way through the scrub cedar. They crossed the road and went to talk to the sheriff. In a few minutes, the Texas Ranger got in his car and left.

Cousin Esther said it was kinda like a Tom Mix serial with a barn in the middle and river in the background and people scurrying here and there. I agreed but I was not interested in the picture, I was too busy looking for the mountain man. But, he was nowhere to be seen.

"I want to get closer," I said to Cousin Esther. "Something seems different and I don't know what it is. You want to come along?"

"No. You go on, I'll stay here and guard the bicycles."

"Okay." I left and crept through the cedar toward the road in front of Uncle Ole's farm and soon I reached the fence across the road from the farm. Feeling I couldn't get any further, I hid behind some bushes, squatted down and watched. The sheriff was still standing by the well talking to the other men. I could catch a few words, especially the words of one of the men that had been digging in the orchard. "They looked like graves but they was empty," I heard him say.

The sheriff said something, then the digger answered, "Yeah, we filled them back in and put the brush back where we found it." More words I couldn't hear, then someone said, "I wish I could get a drink of water out of that well but it looks like somebody nailed it shut."

I immediately looked at the well and saw that the lid no longer stood open. The rope and the bucket had been removed and lay on the ground beside the well. Should I run to the sheriff and tell him that the lid was open and the hinges were frozen two weeks ago. Someone must have closed it and nailed it shut. Then I heard the sheriff say, "Yep, somebody nailed it shut and that's a good idea. It'll keep some dumb kid from falling in. If you gotta have a drink, get it from my jug."

After a few minutes, they all got their cars and left. As soon as they were gone I dashed across the road and examined the well. He was right. Someone had closed the lid, placed two-by-fours across the lid and nailed them in place with large nails and what looked like heavy screws.

"Why? Why would someone shut the well so securely," I puzzled. Trying to decide what to do, I looked at the mountain and there he was, the mountain man, and it looked like he was laughing at me. But in a moment he disappeared.

I dashed up the hill to where Cousin Esther was waiting, but she was gone. Frantic, I began to scream her name while walking along the crest of the hill. In a few minutes I thought I heard someone close by calling my name. I hurried in the direction of the voice and soon found a deep ravine and saw Cousin Esther lying at the bottom. I slid down the slope on my butt and there she was, sitting on a log, sobbing softly and holding her ankle.

"Esther! What happened? Did you fall?"

"THE BASTARD TRIED TO RAPE ME AND I THINK I BROKE MY ANKLE!"

"WHAT?"

"I said the bastard tried to rape me. He sneaked up behind me and grabbed my braid and threw me to the ground. He flipped me over on my back but when he tried to pull down my bloomers, I kicked him in the crotch so hard he fell backward and I run away. That's when I slipped and fell into this hole."

"Who did it," I asked

"I DON'T KNOW!" She screamed. "After I fell, he came to the edge, looked at me and started to climb down grinning from ear to ear. I was sure he was gonna try to rape me and I began to cry. But in a minute, he climbed out of the ravine and disappeared. I think something spooked him."

"Was it the mountain man? I saw him on the hill awhile ago and he seemed to be laughing at me."

"It wasn't the mountain man. I know that for sure. But I don't know who it was."

Through the fog of my anger and confusion I heard a car horn honking near by and a voice yelling "JACOB. ARE YOU THERE?" It was Brother Ben.

"I'M HERE!" I yelled. "COME AND HELP ME! COUSIN ESTHER'S BROKE HER LEG."

In a few moments, he found us and I told him what had happened. "Somebody tried to rape you?" my brother asked.

"He tried but I got away. That's when I fell and broke my leg."

"Who was it?"

"I don't know. I never saw him before."

"Well, let's get you to the car and take you to the doctor."

He lifted her gently, climbed out of the ravine and carried her to the car. She continued to cry as he gently placed her on the back seat and I climbed in beside her. Her foot looked kinda crooked and she had a bruise on her cheek and a skinned elbow." What about our bicycles?" I said to my brother.

"I'll come back and get them later. Besides, you ain't gonna need yours. You're in such deep trouble I doubt you'll be allowed off the farm by yourself until you are twenty-one. Poppa and Momma are mighty furious, and so is Grandma Svendahl."

I didn't say anything until we got home and Brother Ben went in the house and told Momma what had happened. Sister Sybil grabbed some ice and a towel and ran to the car. She applied the ice pack then asked, "Did he penetrate you? You know what that means, don't you?"

"Yeah, I know what that means. No, he didn't penetrate me but he was getting ready to try when I kicked him. I think I hurt him pretty good because he yelled and grabbed his crotch."

I went in the house and in a moment they left. I heard Momma talking to Dr. Nygard and when she finished talking, she called Aunt Helena, told her what had happened. "Get to Dr. Nygard's office as fast as you can," Momma said. Then she turned to me and I could tell by the look on her face that I was in deep, deep trouble.

"Poppa is waiting to talk to you now," she said. "He's in the bedroom."

I was glad he couldn't whip me because he mighta killed me, he was so mad. Never, never have I received such a tongue-lashing, a whipping might have been better. And I could hear Momma in the kitchen crying and begging God to cleanse me of the Evil that had taken possession of my soul.

When it was over, I was grounded for a year except for school and church affairs. I was not to see or talk to Cousin Esther and I was instructed to confess my sins to Pastor Pierson, probably in front of the entire congregation. That depended somewhat on the outcome of Cousin Esther's injuries. Then I was sent to my room and told to fall on my knees and earnestly pray for God's forgiveness.

I knew what I had done was a grievous sin and I knew my sin had caused great harm to Cousin Esther. I was sure she would hate me and I might never see her again. That seemed an extremely severe punishment but I realized I deserved it. I couldn't blame her. It was all my fault.

After about an hour on my knees I ran out of anything to pray about so I began to review the events of the day. Who coulda done it? What gave him the right to try to mess with Cousin Esther? She's only ten and according to Momma hasn't come of age whatever that means. Could it have been the mountain man? I know she said it wasn't but maybe she was mistaken.

Unable to answer my own questions, my thoughts changed to the events that transpired at Uncle Ole's farm. Who had closed the well lid and nailed it shut? What about the empty graves in the orchard? At least they looked like graves. And who is the mountain man and why is he so interested in Uncle Ole's farm?" I could think of no answers to any of these questions so I gave up and went to other problems.

The door opened and Momma came in with a dose of caster oil I swallowed without vomiting. Then I said, "Momma, I need to talk with Poppa and tell him about something I saw at Uncle Ole's farm. I think he would want to hear it, maybe tonight."

"It's too late, he's already asleep. Your foolishness has made him sick and I doubt he will talk with you for several days."

"But, Momma, I think it's real important."

"You should have thought of that before you took your cousin and ran away today."

"But, Momma, I didn't know about it until we got to the farm."

"Jacob, you father is asleep. Now just forget about it." I knew she was still angry and further argument would be useless and might even increase my punishment. But there was one question I wanted to ask and I did. "Is Cousin Esther gonna have a baby?"

"You should have worried about that before you took her up into the mountain and left her by herself."

"I know and I'm sorry."

"Well, you should be and you can apologize to Aunt Helena after church next Sunday. You will also apologize to Cousin Esther if she's there."

"Yes Momma and would you tell Poppa something, maybe tonight?"

"I will, but not tonight and maybe not tomorrow. I don't want to upset him any more than he's already upset."

"Would you tell Poppa someone nailed the well lid shut at Uncle Ole's farm? He'll understand."

"Okay, I will, but not tonight. He's already asleep."

"Thank you Momma," I said, then added, "I love you." She left but in about thirty minutes she returned with a platter of fried chicken and a glass of milk. I didn't realize how hungry I was as I attacked the chicken and washed it down. And when I finished, I felt better.

Chapter Twenty-Five
The Furniture

It has now been three months since Poppa placed me in solitary confinement. Sure, I went to school every day and to church every time the doors opened. And I continued to help with the chores.

Poppa was still using crutches but seemed to be getting better. And as usual Momma cried every day and worried constantly about who was gonna run the farm and how much all this would cost and how would we ever be able to pay it and her headaches seemed more frequent.

Sheriff Bjornburg and his deputies had scoured the area around Uncle Ole's farm several times but never saw the mountain man or a hunter. "I think they just made it up," I heard him tell Poppa, but I knew we had seen someone. And they never found a rapist.

Several times he went back by himself but never saw anyone on the mountain and after a few trips he quit looking.

Last Saturday Brother Ben took Momma to town so she could talk with Mr. Olstad. "Don't worry," he told her. "Gunder's credit is good." He could just as well have given that advice to a fence post for all the good it did.

Poppa still couldn't do anything so Brother Ben and me and sometimes Uncle Andrew did all the work. It wasn't time to plant corn and Poppa said he hadn't planned to plant any cotton. The grain fields were up and the cows and calves were grazing and we only had three on the bottle. So I guess this was the best time of the year for Poppa to be laid up.

I was not allowed to talk to anybody on the phone including Cousin Esther. The night of the assault, Aunt Helena, on Dr. Nygard's recommendation, took her to a hospital in Waco to see a bone doctor about her broken ankle. He took her to surgery and reduced the fracture and applied a cast. While she was in the hospital, a female specialist examined her and confirmed that she had not been raped. They never told me about it but I heard Momma and Poppa discuss it one night when I hid in the closet after they went to bed.

During the first days after the assault, everyone seemed to have a different version about what had happened, especially at school where secrets grow like rabbits and rumors fly like angry bees. Some said she had been thrown off a cliff, some said she had been raped, some said she was critically injured and not expected to live.

Anton Heidl, the classroom bully, suggested that I had raped her, beat her up and threw her off a cliff. He also suggested she was already pregnant and off somewhere getting an abortion. This of course precipitated a fight, first in study hall then on the playground and the two of us ended up in Professor Roberts's office for the required three licks with the school paddle. I was glad Poppa couldn't repeat the punishment when I got home.

Mr. Roberts did not render judgments in these schoolyard fights. In his opinion, if there was a fight, all parties were equally guilty and deserved equal punishment.

Anton and I had fought several times in the past. The last time was when he called Cousin Esther a tomboy. He usually won because he was year older and outweighed me by at least twenty pounds. But I won that fight because I was very angry. He had soiled Cousin Esther's honor.

I thought I should at least tell Momma my side of the fight and when I did, she said I shouldn't be angry. "Anton can't help how he acts. I understand he never goes to Sunday school or church so what can you expect from a boy who's father is in prison for killing his boss at the feed mill. You should pray for him not fight him.

Thank goodness, Mr. Paulsen, the school principle and football coach wasn't involved in the punishment. He would grab the offending student or students by the hair on the top of their heads and lift them off the ground and shake them like a dog shaking a rattlesnake. For that reason, most of the boys kept their hair cut very short. He use to lift students by their ears until the school board made him stop.

It seemed that the word was out that no one should talk to me and I thought I understood how a leper must feel. Even Miss Hawk didn't ask me any questions. I was, however, allowed to sit with Grampa Yo and listen to more of his stories.

Mostly he told me stories about trolls some of which I believed, most of which I couldn't. Then one night he asked me if I remembered the well at Uncle Ole's farm. I said I did and he continued, "Your Uncle Ole and Aunt Telinda is buried in that vell and the lid is nailed shut. They vas buried in the orchard but the Haugfolk done moved them to the vell because they was about to get found."

I asked him how he knew about this and he said he dreamed it. "The Haugfolk done put another dream in my head. It ver on a Sunday so I knowed it ver true."

This shocked me because, as far as I knew, no one except Momma, the sheriff and his deputies knew that the well lid had been nailed shut. Grampa Yo hadn't been to town for several months so he couldn't have heard it there. Maybe when Momma told Poppa, Grampa Yo heard them talking. I better tell Poppa about it but I doubt he'll believe me.

Sheriff Bjornburg arrested Malcolm Moore and charged him with the assault on Cousin Esther even though she said it wasn't him. I guess if you have ever done bad things to children you're suspected of every sex crime that comes along. It wasn't long until the sheriff released him because Malcolm had an alibi and Cousin Esther stuck with her story that it wasn't Malcolm that tried to rape her.

People in the community were divided about Uncle Ole. Some felt he had taken his family to another state to escape his debts. Poppa didn't agree and announced loudly that he had fallen victim to foul play. Few people agreed with him but I did and I knew for sure Uncle Ole wasn't the mountain man.

Sheriff Bjornburg came by one day last week and told Poppa the Texas Rangers had found Uncle Ole's furniture in a store in Dallas. They had gone to the store searching for furniture stolen from a mansion in Highland Park. They identified the furniture from a letter addressed to my brother they found in a bureau drawer and the buyer gave a description of the seller that sorta matched Uncle Ole."

The sheriff told Poppa he wanted to borrow a picture of his brother to take to Dallas and show it to the dealer. He also told Poppa that Judge Christenson has already issued a warrant for his brother's arrest charging him with arson. It made Poppa so mad he told the sheriff he wasn't gonna let him use a picture, said he'd do it himself.

After the sheriff left, Poppa gathered the family in the parlor and gave us the details. "We're going to Dallas next Saturday and prove that the sheriff's dead wrong. Also, I'm gonna talk to the judge about that warrant. The sheriff maintains that Uncle Ole must have moved all the furniture to the garage last July, then set fire to the house. Later, he must have returned to the farm, collected all the furniture and sold it to the used furniture store in Dallas. The sheriff showed the judge a bill of sale for the furniture that matches the list he obtained from me after the fire."

He stopped for a moment, then continued. "The sheriff said the seller insisted he be paid in cash and would not give an address, said he had lost his farm and was headed for California with his family. That was enough for the judge so he issued the warrant."

When he finished giving the report Poppa ask us to join him in prayer, a prayer for Uncle Ole and his family and a prayer for the sheriff and the judge that they may be guided in their persuit of the truth. And when we finished praying Poppa said, "I just can't believe my brother would do something like that."

"He didn't," I said

"How do you know, Son?"

"Because the mountain man did it."

"Do you have any proof? If you do, for goodness sakes, let us know."

"No sir. I just know he didn't do it."

"Son, I hope your right. Do you also know what happened to Baby Angel?

"I think the mountain man took Baby Angel and has her hidden somewhere so he can violate her."

Momma put her hands over her mouth, her face turned red and she said. "Jacob, how can you say things like that? What do you know about that subject?"

"One time Malcolm Moore tried to violate Cousin Esther and she told me about it. But she wouldn't tell me what he did. She just said he tried."

"Let's not talk any more about that," Poppa interrupted. "However there does seem to be somebody very interested in the farm, someone you call the mountain man. Would you describe him to us again."

And I did, as well as I could remember. I described his hair, his build, his clothes, his shoes and the sound of his voice. I even described the gun he carried, but I couldn't describe his face. There was something strange about it I couldn't describe. And the man we saw didn't have a mustache like Uncle Ole.

When I finished, Poppa said, "Well, that certainly doesn't sound like my brother. And it matches the description Cousin Esther gave of the man. There's got to be some big mistake, he would never do something like that."

None of us spoke for several minutes, then I asked, "Poppa, did Momma tell you about the lid on the well?"

"Yes she did, son. Why do you ask?"

"Because I thing the Mountain man killed Uncle Ole and Aunt Telinda and buried them in the orchard. When he thought they might be found, he dug up the bodies and put them in the well. Then he nailed the lid shut. I think they are in the well."

"My, my, Son, you have been busy. And what an imagination," Poppa said.

"But, Poppa, the holes in the orchard looked like graves. I saw them plainly. They could have been graves." I realized Poppa didn't like my theory so I added, "I think we oughta open the well and have a look."

"When did you dream up this story?" Poppa asked.

Tears filled my eyes as I answered, 'I didn't dream it up, Grampa Yo told me."

"And how did he know?"

"He dreamed it. He said the Haugfolk put the dream in his head."

"Who put it there?" Poppa asked.

"The Haugfolk. Grampa Yo says they can put dreams in your head and they are always true."

Poppa laughed so hard he had to sit down. The rest of the family laughed but not as hard as Poppa. I didn't see what was so funny about it. I thought it made good sense but I could see he didn't believe me and most likely wasn't going to ask anybody to open the well. If I ever get free from my bondage, I'm going to open it myself and prove I'm right.

"Where's Grampa Yo?" I asked. "Why don't you ask him about the dream?"

"He's at Uncle Andrew's house for a few days" Momma said. "He left this afternoon." That ended the discussion and we repeated our prayers and then went to finish the chores and Poppa lay down to take a nap.

That night, after supper, Poppa asked me a few more question about the mountain man, mostly about his appearance. He seemed a little more interested in my story and asked some more about the well. "Could you see what kind of screws, and what size nails had been used on the lid? And did you see the rope and the bucket and if you did, where were they?"

"Laying on the ground beside the well," I answered. "But I don't know about the nails and screws."

"Well, Son, maybe I'll go to town and see what the sheriff thinks about the story."

"Couldn't we maybe go to the well ourselves and try to open it?"

"Let me think about it," he answered which meant he didn't plan to do any thing, at least not now.

The next Saturday we went to the courthouse and Poppa hobbled to Judge Christensen's chambers. The judge was Momma's distant relative, third or fourth cousin she thought. That didn't surprise me because it seemed that everybody in Arendal was a relative of one kind or another, especially those living on the Flat. Even if he was a relative, Momma said Uncle Ole would get a fair trial if it ever came to that.

The visit with the judge went well. He assured Poppa that he had not formed an opinion about the case. He would let the facts speak for themselves. "I know he isn't perfect," the judge said. "However I also know he isn't the kind of person who would burn his house down. Unfortunately I couldn't ignore the evidence presented by Sheriff Bjornburg."

This seemed to satisfy Poppa so we got in the car and Brother Ben found the winding gravel road out of the Arendal valley and followed it east until we found the highway to Dallas. Several times Poppa yelled, "Slow down, son! You're going too fast!" When we arrived in Dallas, after asking directions twice, we found the used furniture store known as Honest Abe's Used Furniture Emporium.

Honest Abe seemed pleasant enough until Poppa told him the reason for our visit. He immediately said he didn't want any trouble. "If the furniture was in fact stolen I'll call the police, but I cain't give it back, at least not now." Poppa assured him that wasn't why we were here. "I just wanted you to tell me more about the man that sold you the furniture, that is, if you remember him."

"Sure I remember the man. Stock guy, about your size with farmer's hands like yours, kind of secretive."

"About my size?" Poppa asked.

"Maybe a little heavier but not much. Weathered skin, strong as an ox. He lifted the furniture out of the truck by himself."

"Son," Poppa said to me. "Go get the pictures out of the car." And I did.

Poppa showed him the picture of the Grandma Svendahl's family. The man studied it closely for several minutes, then pointed to Uncle Ole's picture and said, "That's him. He's the one sold me the furniture!"

"Are you sure?"

Pretty sure, about as sure as I can be. But it's been a few months and I might be wrong, but I doubt it."

I could tell by the look on Poppa's face that this upset him real bad. I really thought he was about to cry as he stood there, arms behind his back, gazing off into the distance but in a moment he turned to the man and said, "Did the man give you his name or give you an address?"

"Said his name was Jake and he demanded I pay him in cash. He said he had no current address and had lost his farm to the crooks at the local bank. Said he was moving to California with some of his relative to work in the peach orchards. I almost refused to buy the furniture but his asking price was so ridiculously low, I couldn't turn it down."

"Could I see the bill of sale?" Poppa asked.

"I don't have it. The Texas Ranger took it. He said he would return it but he hasn't. You say this furniture was stolen?"

"Maybe, we don't know for sure. Did he have anybody with him, maybe a woman and a baby?"

"No. He was alone."

"What kind of vehicle was he driving?"

"An old Model T Ford flat bed with high sideboards. Looked like a cotton truck to me."

"And he was alone?"

"That's right. He was alone."

"Could we look at the furniture?"

"Sure thing, I'll show you where it is." We followed him to the back of the warehouse filled with every conceivable type and style of furniture; old, new, plain, fancy, black, white, tables, chairs, beds, dressers, ice boxes, wood stoves, even commodes and thunder mugs. He seemed to have everything.

We found Uncle Ole's furniture bunched together against the back wall of the warehouse. Poppa took out the pictures he had made of the furniture in Uncle Ole's garage and it was immediately obvious the furniture in the warehouse was the same as in the picture.

"Son, go out to the truck and get my Kodak." I did and he took several pictures of the furniture. Then we went home.

Poppa didn't say a word until we got to Hillsboro and we stopped for gas.

"There's got to be a mistake! My brother would never do something like that." He said nothing else and soon we were home. He never said a word during the rest of the day but I heard him talking with Momma after we went to bed. I wanted to listen but I fell asleep.

The next morning I heard Poppa and Momma talking in the kitchen. "Guess I better go to town and tell the sheriff about the trip. Also, I guess I better tell my mother but she's gonna throw a fit. She's not gonna believe it and neither do I."

I don't know what happened during the visits. Brother Ben did the driving and I had stay home and clean the chicken house. I do know when they got back Poppa looked really worried and he and Momma went to their bedroom and talked. That evening we gathered in the parlor and Poppa told us the sheriff was convinced of his brother's guilt. It had now become a criminal case and the Texas Rangers were involved. The sheriff also told him that they might have caught the man who tried to rape Cousin Esther. "He said they found a man sleeping under the railroad bridge that kinda fitted the description Cousin Esther had given. At first, the man refused to give any identification but they found several sex magazines and a letter from his mother in his knapsack. From that they identified the man and obtained his record from the Waco police."

Poppa continued, "The file showed he had a rape conviction in his long record and had recently been released from Huntsville. Esther hasn't seen him and never will because when the other inmates found out he had maybe raped a ten-year-old girl, they beat him to death in the jailhouse. I guess there's honor among criminals and the inmates hated child molesters." With that, the sheriff closed the case and no charges were ever filed against the inmates.

"That's a blessing," Momma said. "It would have been real hard on her."

I wanted to talk with her about the incident and about the trip to Dallas, but I was still in solitary confinement.

A couple of days ago, Sheriff Bjornburg stopped by and told Poppa that the State Highway Department had definitely identified the Model T found in the Paluxy River as belonging to his brother. "Guess he must have driven it there, maybe on his way back from Dallas, then dumped it in the river to cover his guilt," the sheriff said. It made Poppa mad and he showed the sheriff to the door.

Chapter Twenty-Six
Out of Bondage

By now Poppa's leg had healed without the predicted complications and he could do just about anything. He could walk without crutches but still limped a little and had to take a pain powder every morning. And Uncle Ole and Aunt Telinda were still missing.

Poppa kept his promise not to plant cotton. Instead we planted range grass with the grain drill. It was already up and the cattle seemed to like it.

The calf crop was especially good. Seemed like half the cows in the area had twins and now we had twenty four on the bottle. Poppa bought more bottles and nipples and built a rack so we could feed six at a time and it only took about an hour to feed them all.

In May we lost Daisy, one of our cows, during delivery. The hind legs came first and after ten hours of fruitless labor Poppa tied a chain around the calf's hooves and pull it out with the tractor. The calf came out okay but the mother began to bleed and Poppa called the vet. But by the time he arrived the cow was dead. So, we added another calf to the bottle list.

I could tell Poppa was very upset. Daisy was one of his favorites and one of ours best producers. He had done this type of delivery before, several times, with good results. But such is life on a farm.

The school year went by without any further problems and in two weeks we'll be out for the summer. Cousin Esther came back to school two weeks after the injury and six weeks later they took off the cast off and she began to walk, limping at first, but now she walks normally.

Although I wasn't allowed to speak to her, she always winked when we passed in the hall. Yesterday she slipped me a note that said, "Could we maybe sit with each other on the bus? I really miss you."

"Of course we can if our parents don't find out. I'm still grounded."

"Jacob, I think it'll be okay with them," She wrote. "I'll tell you about in on the way home."

I turned around, nodded my head and winked.

One of the back row boys saw the wink and after some furious ill concealed whispers, someone yelled, "Jacob loves Esther " which prompted a trip by the entire back row to Mr. Roberts's office. Miss Hawk apparently wasn't going to put up with any more of their foolishness.

I got on the bus first and saved her a seat, and when she sat beside me, my heart began to pound and I knew she was something special to me. I held her hand and she whispered, "I know a secret I'm not supposed to tell."

"What?"

"Your Poppa's gonna release you Sunday and we're gonna have a party."

"You're sure?"

"Sure, I'm sure. Momma told me."

I was so happy I couldn't say anything else until we reached out gate. As I got off the bus, I said, "Well, bye. I gotta run," and I did and went straight to the barn and started with the chores feeling as if a heavy weight was about to be lifted from my shoulders.

Sure enough, on Sunday, when we got home from church, a special meal was waiting starting with Kjottboiler and ending with Sjokoladekake and ice cream. Cousin Esther, Grandma Svendahl, Aunt Helena, Cousin Joseph, Uncle Andrew, Cousin Gertrude and, of course, Pastor Pierson attended. After a long and tedious prayer by the pastor, Poppa announced that I had satisfactorily completed my punishment and was now released from all restrictions.

After the meal everyone left except Aunt Helena and Cousin Esther. We walked out to the pecan tree, hand in hand, and sat in the swing, then moved to our favorite place, the hayloft.

I could hardly keep my eyes off of her. She had on the prettiest white dress I had ever seen and I told her so.

"You look pretty good too," she said and squeezed my hand. "Jacob, I've really missed you. Have you missed me?"

"More than you'll ever know."

"Me too."

We lay down in the hay, our legs hanging over the edge and watched a huge rat scurry across a rafter followed by five babies. At the end of the rafter the rat stopped, looked at us, then disappeared into the hay. We talked for hours and I realized I was the happiest I had been since that disastrous day when someone tried to rape Cousin Esther.

At first she didn't want to talk about it and I didn't push. However after maybe an hour, she sat up, turned to me and asked, "Jacob, do you like me?"

I could see tears in her eyes and I answered, "Of course I do."

"Are you just saying that to make me feel better?"

"No, I'm not just saying that. I like you very much."

"My momma told me boys don't like girls who have relations before they are married."

"You didn't have relations. I heard Momma tell Poppa that the man tried to rape you but he didn't. Is that right?"

"No he didn't, but he tried." She paused, then continued, "If I had been raped would you still like me? Momma told me boys think if a girl is raped she probably asked for it." Now the tears really began to roll.

"That's stupid!" I answered. "That's the stupidest thing I ever heard." We both fell silent, absorbed in our own thoughts. After a few moments she turned to me and said, "Momma even asked me if we had ever had relations and I told her she was crazy."

"Well she is," I answered. We both lay back on the hay and she rolled on her side and kissed my cheek and my heart almost stopped.

Nothing happened for a few moments, then she turned on her back, looked at the corrugated tin roof and said, "If the man had raped me, I wouldn't be a virgin. Momma says boys won't marry girls unless they are virgins. Would you marry me if I wasn't a virgin?"

"Of course I would. I wouldn't care." She turned on her side and kissed my cheek again and this time I blushed and held her hand.

We lay in the hayloft until time for evening chores reliving all the recent events. We talked about Uncle Ole and the trip to Dallas. We talked about school and vacation plans. I told her about Grampa Yo's dream and Poppa's reaction. We even talked about next years school when we would be in the fifth grade.

We said nothing for a few minutes, each absorbed in private thoughts. Then Cousin Esther said. "You know what? I think Malcolm Moore is the mountain man. I know he doesn't look like the mountain man but the voice sounds like him. I know, I heard it for years. Why don't we sneak into his house some day when we know he's gone and look around. Maybe we can find something that will prove he's the mountain man.

After a moment's thought, I said, "Okay. When?"

"I happen to know he's going to be working for Momma all next week repairing the garage roof. That last hail storm tore it up pretty bad."

"Then why don't we go there after school on Monday? It's right on the way and we could walk home."

"Okay, it's a date," she answered, "But don't tell anybody."

"Okay."

When we climbed out of the hayloft and went to the house it was almost dark. Momma and Aunt Helena were both in the kitchen and looked at us suspiciously and I knew we had a problem. We both had straw on our clothes and Cousin Esther had straw in her hair. "What have you kids been up to?" Momma asked and I knew she was angry.

"Just talking," Cousin Esther said. "We haven't been together for months."

"You didn't do anything else did you?" Momma asked.

"No ma'am," I answered. "We just talked."

Both Momma and Aunt Helena looked at us for several minutes and I could tell they didn't believe us. In a minute, Aunt Helena added, "You're sure all you did was talk?"

"Yes ma'am," we both said in unison. Then I added, "We had a lot to talk about."

Then Aunt Helena said to me, "I hope you didn't talk about dragging my daughter up into the mountain again."

"No, ma'am. We just talked about stuff."

"Jacob," Momma asked, "Did you mess around with your cousin?"

"No ma'am. We just talked. We didn't mess around." I knew exactly what she meant by 'mess around'.

Pastor Pierson had recently discussed sexual relations in our Sunday school class. He said we were growing up and needed to understand the evil ways the Devil would use in an attempt to gain control of our souls. To gain that control he would tempt us with liquor, greed, arrogance and carnal pleasures we would find hard to resist. He told us extra-marital relations were the worst of the temptations and would lead to a life of sin and depravity from which we could never escape.

In a very stern voice he told us, "You must never ignore the commandment that states, *'Thou Shall Not Commit Adultery'*. An extra-marital relationship is an adulterous relationship and is a mortal sin against God and his Commandments." He said we were to remain chaste until we were joined in a union blessed by God and the church.

I believed these messages and mostly understood what he meant. And I knew that Cousin Esther and I would never break this Commandment or any of the other Commandments.

Poppa had discussed this same subject with me recently, but he used such oblique terms that I didn't fully understand. I think he was embarrassed. But when Pastor Pierson discussed it, I understood. You should never have relations with a woman before you get married.

The more I thought about Momma's suspicions the more it upset me.

After all, we were both only ten and not even in high school. I guess mothers just don't trust their sons and daughters even if they're only ten, actually ten and a half.

Aunt Helena collected the dishes she had brought and they left. Cousin Esther winked at me as she walked out the door. In my prayers that night, I thanked God for bringing Cousin Esther back into my life and promised never to have relations with her until we were married.

The next Monday it rained and we couldn't go to Malcolm Moore's house. Besides, because of the rain, he would probably be at home. The same was true on Tuesday. On Wednesday and Thursday, her mother picked her up from school. On Friday, school let out for the summer and Aunt Helena sent Cousin Esther to spend the summer with a friend in Waco.

Chapter Twenty-Seven
The Well Revisited

Sometime around the first of June Poppa persuaded the sheriff to check the well on Uncle Ole's farm. I don't know how he convinced him to do it because I had heard him say many times, "Ole Svendahl's guilty and I don't believe in trolls." I think Poppa probably nagged at the sheriff until he agreed to go to get Poppa to shut up, at least that's what Momma said. I also think he felt secretly this might a chance to clear his brother's name.

But when he went to the farm and tried, he couldn't get the lid open. The next weekend he brought heavier tools and tried again and when he did someone took a shot at him, missing him by inches. It made the sheriff furious and he announced loudly, many times, "I'm gonna get to the bottom of this mess if have to bring in the whole damn U.S.Army." He told several privately he thought Uncle Ole was the shooter, but he didn't tell Poppa.

By the next Saturday everybody in town knew about the plans and many said they might come along and watch. The sheriff let it be known that anybody who tagged along would be arrested. It was obvious to all he was plenty mad.

I asked Poppa if we could watch and he said he would check with the sheriff but admitted he would like to be present when they open the well. "He's my brother and I think maybe I should be there."

In his investigation concerning the missing furniture, the sheriff did find one neighbor who, on his way to town sometime in August or September of last year, saw two people loading furniture into a truck. He couldn't remember the exact day. He was pretty sure the truck was a Model T. The sheriff asked him if he recognized the people loading the truck. He said he couldn't, he was too far away. He said he assumed Poppa had sold the furniture and it wasn't any of his business so he didn't stop and ask questions. He also said he called Poppa a few days later to ask about the furniture but no one was at home. He didn't try again and had actually forgotten about it. So there remained many unanswered question regarding Uncle Ole and Aunt Telinda's disappearance and especially concerning Cousin Angel and the furniture.

Last Sunday, Sheriff Bjornburg gathered his troops; six deputies, four National Guardsmen, one Texas Ranger, and we followed him to Uncle Ole's farm. I wished Cousin Esther could have been with me to watch the excitement, but she's in Waco.

When we arrived at the farm, the Texas Ranger took charge and stationed the National Guardsmen in a circle around the well facing the hills with binoculars and rifles at the ready position and sent the two deputies up into the hill to look around and two to guard the periphery. Shortly, the Fire Chief and his crew arrived and parked near the well. There would be no ambush today.

The sheriff and two deputies took crowbars and sledgehammers but they couldn't get the lid open. So the sheriff backed his truck up to the well, strung a log chain around the base and hooked it to his trailer hitch. He gunned the motor, the truck lurched forward and the structure broke loose from its moorings and the pieces flew everywhere.

In a minute the sheriff and two of the deputies walked to the well and peered in the hole. The stench was so unbelievably bad that the sheriff covered his nose with a handkerchief, the deputies backed away and one vomited.

The sheriff went to is his truck and pulled out a grappling hook with a long rope attached and he and the deputies took turns repeatedly lowering it into the well and pulling it back up.

The first few tries yielded nothing. On the fifth try the hook struck something but broke loose when they got it to the surface of the water. "Looks like a log to me," the sheriff said.

After several more unsuccessful attempts the sheriff added, "It's a water soaked log. We're wasting our time so let's go up into the mountain and look around. Chief, you can take your crew and fire truck and head back to town. I'll see you there later."

"You ain't leaving and neither is the fire truck until you drain that well," I heard Poppa say. "There's something dead in that well, cain't you smell it?"

"Aw hell, Gunder, it probably ain't nothing but a log somebody threw in there years ago. They can smell pretty bad. Besides, it'll take hours to pump that well dry."

"So do it! What else you got to do except sit on your butt shuffling papers," Poppa replied. This kinda surprised me because Poppa rarely ever raised his voice to anyone and I could tell he was really angry.

"Now Gunder, don't go getting your tail over the dashboard, they ain't nothing in that well."

"I'm telling you I ain't leaving and neither are you till you get that well pumped dry, at least enough to see the bottom." Then Poppa added, "You got an election coming up next year and if you don't pump that well dry, I'll make sure the people of the county know you been shirking your duty."

"Okay, okay, Gunder, you win. Boys, get out the hoses and let's pump that sucker dry." And when they did they found two cotton sacks that obviously contained something and it wasn't cotton and it wasn't a log. They had to keep the pump going because, when they stopped, water seeped in and covered the sacks.

The sheriff stood there for a few moments apparently trying to decide what to do. Several more attempts under direct vision were unsuccessful. The hooks just wouldn't snag the sacks. Finally he got in his truck and drove back to town to find the County Coroner, Knute Olson, affectionately known as 'Digger', who owned the Arendal Funeral Home. When they returned, Digger borrowed some tools from the fire chief: a ladder, a gas mask, hip boots and heavy long sleeve gloves. He climbed into the well and determined that both sacks contained something. He tied a rope around each sack and in a few minutes, they lifted two wet cotton sacks out of the well. Digger carefully made a small slit in each sack and determined that each contained a body.

"Should we unwrap them?" the sheriff asked.

"I don't think so," Digger replied. "I think it's best we let the Waco Medical Examiner do the unwrapping." So he returned to Arendal, called Waco, and in about an hour, a truck from the pathologist's office arrived, loaded and hauled the sacks away. The excitement over, everybody packed up and left and we followed.

Just as we were crossing the cattle guard, I glanced up at the mountain and saw two men standing behind a cedar bush watching the activities and one had a gun. "POPPA, LOOK!" I shouted, pointing to the mountain. But before he could stop the car, the men had disappeared.

"Could you tell who they were?"

"No, but they kinda looked like brothers and one of them had a gun."

"Probably a couple of hunters. " For some reason I didn't tell Poppa the man with the gun kinda looked like the mountain man.

It took a week to establish their identities, but, in the end, there was no question that the bodies found in the well were that of Uncle Ole and Aunt Telinda based mostly on clothing and dental records. Like most older people in Arendal County, both had false teeth that were still in place when the bodies were retrieved. The pathologist said they died from blunt trauma to the head and had been dead for an unknown period of time.

By the next week, the well was half full of water and Poppa went back to the farm and covered the hole with boards.

Sheriff Bjornburg turned the case over to Conard Thorson, the Arendal County District Attorney who asked for help from the State Attorney General's office. I asked Poppa if they had found Cousin Angel's body in the well and he said they hadn't. So her disappearance remained a mystery but was now classified as a kidnapping.

The District Attorney theorized that unknown Person or Persons had killed Uncle Ole and Aunt Telinda, kidnapped Cousin Angel, moved all the furniture to the garage then set the house on fire to hopefully cover the crime. That Person or Persons buried the bodies in the orchard. Later the guilty Person or Persons loaded the furniture in a truck and sold it in Dallas then apparently disposed of the truck.

When the guilty party realized the sheriff was going to dig up the orchard, he or they removed the bodies and dumped them in the well and tried to secure the lid in such a way that it couldn't be opened. He or they apparently stood guard over the well and shot and wounded Gunder Svendahl and shot at Sheriff Bjornburg on two occasions. So, by the end of June, many of our questions had been answered. But we still didn't know what happened to Cousin Angel.

I know Poppa was sad about his brother's death but I think, deep inside, he was relieved. Now everybody knew his brother wasn't a criminal.

Sheriff Bjornburg came to the house night before last to apologize to Poppa. We were milking the cows when he came so he sat on a milking stool and talked.

"Gunder," he said, "I'm sorry about your brother and I'm sorry about his wife. I'm also sorry that I accused him unjustly. I thought I was doing the right thing but the furniture salesman led me astray. I should never have suspected your brother."

"You was just doing your job," Poppa said

The sheriff picked up a straw, stuck it in the corner of his mouth and continued, "You know, Gunder, if that man hadn't shot at me, they'd still be in the well maybe until somebody bought the farm. And this brings up another problem. Who the hell is the son of a bitch that was doing the shooting and of course where is the child, Angel?"

"I been wondering the same thing," Poppa said. "It's got to be somebody that looks like my brother. But they ain't anybody around these parts that looks like him. Maybe something will turn up one of these days."

"I sure hope so," the sheriff said. "Again, I'm sorry about your brother." He put on his hat and left and we finished milking.

Chapter Twenty-Eight
The Depression Continues

Summer is about over and the livestock market is down, so far down that Poppa worried he might not be able to sell the rest of his calves. The same is true of the hog market. The average price for pork on the hoof is now eight cents a pound or sixteen dollars for a two hundred pound pig.

According to the radio, unemployment is up to twenty five percent and pictures in the Arendal Record and in the Fort Worth Star Telegram show soup lines and food riots in the east. Momma said things are getting worse every day.

Poppa said President Roosevelt has been unable to rid Washington of the crooks responsible for the situation. "Why doesn't he just fire them?" I asked

"Son, that ain't the way the government works," he answered.

Well, no wonder they cain't get things straightened out, I thought. To me, that seemed like a dumb way to run a business.

Many families came through town headed west hopefully to find work. One family came through town heading east minus a husband and father who had been killed in an accident at the construction site for the Hoover Dam and the CCC boys were building a park along the Arendal River.

Two weeks before school let out for the summer, Olivia Nordstrom, a girl in our class, didn't show up for school. When we asked about it, our teacher said the family had moved out of town. When I told Momma about it, she said, "That ain't true. Her father, Otto Nordstrom, placed his four children in the Methodist Orphan's home in Waco. He couldn't feed them any more."

"Why couldn't he feed them?" I asked

"Because he fell off his tractor and broke his back, He ain't been able to work for four months."

I thought about that for a moment, then added, "The last couple of weeks when she was at school, Olivia was always begging for food. Every day she claimed she forgot her lunch sack at home. Nobody believed her but we always felt sorry for her and some of us shared our lunches with her."

"I really feel sorry for the children but I'm not so sure about Otto," Momma said. "The church gave him twenty-five dollars and the Ladies Aid Society collected food, mostly canned goods, and gave them to the family. But charity can only go so far and many of the church families are as bad off as the Nordstrom's but they haven't put their kids in the orphanage. Besides his back shoulda been well by now. Most people think he's just turned lazy."

"Where's their mother?" I asked. I couldn't recall having seen her in town or at church for a long time and had occasionally wondered why. But that wasn't on any of my worry lists, at least not yet.

"She's not right in the head," Momma replied. "Been that way since her fifth child died in childbirth. Stays in bed most of the time. We visited her about two months ago but she chased us off. She looked like a skeleton and I fear she ain't long for this world."

The story upset me a lot and that night I included the family in my prayers asking God to heal the father and mother and protect the children until the family could be reunited.

I couldn't tell for sure, but I think Poppa was in financial trouble. Several times, after I had gone to bed, I heard him talking with Momma but couldn't hear what they said. I thought of sneaking into the parlor to hear but decided it wasn't any of my business.

Brother Ben graduated from high school and went to work at the feed mill but they laid him off after the farmers finished their harvest. Poppa asked him to help with the farm work but said he couldn't pay him anything. He did promise to help him with his college tuition at Texas Tech.

Sister Sybil continued to work at the school library, but they could only pay her forty cents for four hours work. So she helped Momma with the canning and cooking. And Poppa still gave us twenty-five cents most Saturdays.

I guess Sister Selma was the luckiest of all my relatives. When she finished nursing school and got her RN degree, she went to work for Dr. Nygard making thirty dollars a month and he moved to a larger office in the old bank building. She gave Poppa fifteen dollars a month for room and board.

In April Cousin Matthew left home and found a job in the East Texas oil fields making five dollars a day. By the middle of June he bought a motorcycle and drove it home. He took us riding several times and I told everybody if I ever had a job like that I would also buy a motorcycle. However, on his way back to work, he crashed into a bus and was killed instantly. I suddenly lost my desire for a motorcycle and cried at his funeral. Now Cousin Joseph is Uncle Andrew's only son and his responsibilities have increased.

Grampa Yo died the first day of July. He had gone with Brother Ben up in the mountains to help him fix a fence Crazy Clem's goats had torn down. This involved cutting away some of the scrub cedar so they could get the wagon with the posts, the barbed wire and the tools to the top of the hill. Grampa Yo insisted on helping but cut his leg with an axe, a nasty gash just below the knee that went to the bone. He refused to go to the doctor with the comment "I knows how to treat it better than no damn doctor."

So, when they got home, he applied an ointment made out of tobacco juice, boiled prickley pear leaves and cane syrup. He applied the gooey mess to the wound and covered it with a handkerchief.

He redressed it every day and applied more of the ointment but it continued to bleed and began to stink. A week later, when his fever shot up to 104, Momma called Dr. Nygard who came to the house and, after examining the wound, advised hospitalization in Waco. He thought it might even require amputation, but Grampa Yo refused to go stating "I ain't gonna let no damn doctor cut off my leg." The leg got worse, his fever went higher, and two days later he lapsed into a coma. His last words were, "Don't send me to no damn hospital." The next day he died.

We buried him next to Grandma Yo in the cemetery behind the Buffalo Flat Church. Pastor Pierson conducted the service in Norwegian and the choir sang, "Hil Dig, Norge" and the soloist sang, "Vaaren." Then Pastor Pierson read the eulogy and the gospel lesson and the choir closed with Momma and Grampa Yo's favorite hymn, "Den Store, Hvide Flok."

After the service we all went to the cemetery and stood by the freshly dug grave. Pastor Pierson sprinkled three handfuls of dirt on the casket and intoned the Benediction. Momma placed a bouquet of wild flowers on the casket and the attendants lowered it into the grave. Then relatives, except the immediate family, picked up shovels and filled the grave. And when the task was completed we returned to the church in Arendal for a luncheon prepared and served by the Ladies Aid Society. The bell in the steeple of the old church began its mournful toll an hour before the services began, one bong every thirty seconds. It was silent during the services then resumed afterwards and continued for an hour. We could still faintly hear the bell when we returned to Arendal.

There was something creepy about the mournful sound of that old bell. I asked Momma about it and she said they rang it to announce Grampa Yo's passing to a better life. She also said it would wake up St. Peter so he would open the pearly gates to allow another saved soul to enter.

I asked Momma what would happen if the departed person's soul wasn't saved. She said that was for St. Peter to decide. He determined who went to heaven and who went to hell. I had always thought God made those decisions, but I guess He sometimes needs help.

I really wasn't too sad about Grampa Yo's death. I hated his pipe but had enjoyed his stories and would probably miss the telling, but I still couldn't believe most of them. I did wonder how he knew Uncle Ole's and Aunt Telinda's bodies were buried in the orchard? And how did he know they had been moved to the well? I guess I'll never know until I join him in Heaven. We moved his bed out of the parlor and sleeping arrangements returned to normal and, as far as know, I never talked in my sleep.

I now weigh eighty-five pounds and am five feet two inches tall. When Cousin Esther came back from Waco to start school, her mother took us to town and paid a penny each to check our height and weight. We discovered that I'm two inches taller than Cousin Esther and outweigh her by fifteen pounds and Momma said I'm gonna be as strong as a horse. It hurt my feelings when Poppa told me I couldn't drive the tractor because it was too dangerous.

About the only other excitement of the summer occurred in July. Second Cousin Gunnel Gilliam, who had joined the Army Air Force two years ago, flew his plane over the town, turned two flips, buzzed the water tower, then landed in Aunt Helena's pasture. I ran all the way to the plane but by the time I arrived, half the people in town were already there.

He told us it was an Army Air Force training plane he had borrowed for the day. It had two seats and two yellow wings with blue and white stars on the tips and a black body and a white tail with a blue and white star on each side. He took several people up for a ride but he didn't take me, said I was too young and it was too dangerous. A month later he died when his plane crashed during a training mission in Oklahoma.

The day Cousin Esther returned, I rode to her house and we sat in the swing and I held her hand as we reviewed the events of the summer. We talked about Malcolm Moore and wondered again if he could be the mountain man. "We never did get to search his house," Cousin Esther said. "Maybe we oughta do it real soon.

"Yeah, we should, but when."

"School starts next Monday, we could do it then," she answered.

"Okay, it's a deal," I answered and I went home.

Chapter Twenty-Nine
Coming of Age

Cousin Esther didn't come to school on Monday so we couldn't go to Malcolm Moore's house. I asked Sister Sybil if she knew what was wrong. "Cousin Esther's finally come of age," she answered which meant she was having her first menstrual period.

When she didn't show up, Anton Heidl claimed she was off somewhere having another abortion and accused me of being the father. That, of course precipitated another fight. Professor Roberts wasn't too happy that we were fighting on the first day of school and suspended us both for a day and reported it to our parents. When Poppa heard my side, he said the Heidl boy deserved it and for me to study all day and not turn on the radio. Well, that wasn't so bad, I had expected worse.

After supper I heard Momma ring Aunt Helena's number, two longs and two shorts. When she answered, I heard Momma say, "Well, I guess you don't have to worry any more about her being pregnant." I assumed she was talking about Cousin Esther.

That really hadn't occurred to me and wasn't on any of my worry lists. But it was true. Pregnancy out of wedlock could ruin a life. I didn't hear Aunt Helena's response but Momma replied, "I know that's a little young to start. But both Selma and Sybil started when they were eleven and Esther will be eleven in December. So, I wouldn't worry about it. Just be thankful she isn't pregnant."

On Wednesday she came back to school and seemed to have a slightly different look about her. Maybe she seemed more mature, maybe more sure of herself. And when we met at lunch, she said, "Well, are we going to Malcolm Moore's house this afternoon? Or did you chicken out?"

Actually, I had forgotten about our date on Monday but I quickly recovered saying, "Of course we are, if you feel okay."

"I feel fine, just fine!" she snapped back. "See you after school." She took her sack lunch and sat with the older girls at a table in the far corner of the lunchroom. This surprised me because we almost always ate together unless there was some good reason not to. Had I offended her? If so, what had I done? But in a minute she caught my eye and winked. Then I felt better. Maybe she just wanted to prove to me that she was now a woman and I noticed she was wearing a dress and shoes, most unusual, I thought.

Apparently our parents were no longer suspicious because her mother didn't pick her up after school. We didn't ride the bus so we could go to Macomb Moore's house. Swinging our schoolbooks bound together by leather straps, we set off up the road. Cousin Esther seemed the same as she was in June as she chattered on and on about this and that. I wanted to ask her about her period but felt maybe it wasn't appropriate and was something you never discussed with a girl. Soon we reached Malcolm's house situated on a tiny lot at the edge of the mountain. Standing at the broken gate we saw the tiny house with the faded green clapboard siding and an unpainted door. Weeds filled the yard and the one car garage was filled with all kinds of trash including many magazines. "What if his mother's at home?" I asked as we entered the yard and climbed the steps to the porch.

"Momma says she leaves almost every morning and doesn't get home until dark," Cousin Esther replied. "You know my mother knows everything about everybody in this part of town."

"Does she go to work?"

"I don't know and neither does Momma."

"What if Malcolm is home?"

"He's not," she answered. "He's working for Momma today castrating the pigs."

I knocked on the door but no one answered. "I guess she isn't here," Cousin Esther said and when she tried the doorknob, it turned in her hand. She pushed the door open and we waited a few moments.

"Hello, anybody home?" she called. Again no one answered so we went on in and looked around.

The living room contained an easy chair by the small window with magazines piled high on either side. A narrow bed filled one side of the room and the light from the window illuminated a magazine in the chair opened to a picture of a naked woman lying on a bed with her legs spread apart. A huge man holding a bullwhip stood over the woman and appeared about to strike. The woman had a cut on her face and we could see blood smeared on the bed and her hands and feet were tied to the bedposts. Speechless and motionless, we both studied the picture then looked at each other.

"This scares me!" Cousin Esther said. "Let's get out of here!" and we did. She slammed the door and we ran over the hill, across the flat until we reached our farm, hot sweaty and exhausted.

Momma fixed us a sausage sandwich and a glass of ice tea and we went to the back porch and sat in the swing. I wanted to go to the barn and sit in the hayloft but she said we better not because her mother might still be a little suspicious. "I think she still suspect we did something bad last spring."

"Well, we didn't."

"I know we didn't. I've told her so a dozen times. But should we tell our parents what we saw?"

"I don't think so. We shouldn't have even been there."

"Yeah, I guess you're right." We talked a little longer, then she went home and I went to the barn and started the chores. After supper I went to bed, exhausted. I didn't even want to listen to Amos and Andy.

Chapter Thirty
Anton Heidl

Anton Heidl got expelled from school for the rest of the year for injuring a fellow student in a fight. But that wasn't the end of his troubles.

The reasons for the fight were somewhat vague but seemed to revolve around Suzie Swisher who he considered his girl friend although everybody knew the feeing was not mutual.

Suzie told one of her classmates that she went with him to a movie once to shut him up and swore she would never go with him again. She said he tried to grope her body all through the movie until she slapped him and walked out.

Saturday before last, Suzie accidentally met Lester Daws, a high school freshman, at the drugstore. They shared a Coke, then went to the movie. Anton apparently heard about it and on the next Monday he cornered Suzie in the hall and snarled, "I hear you been cheatin on me."

"I'm not your girl friend so leave me along!" Suzie shouted, threw a book at him and stomped off down the hall. At lunch she told Lester about it and he and Anton had words that became so loud and threatening that they both ended up in the Mr. Roberts office. What happened there is unknown but he sent Anton home for the day.

Furious, Anton went home, armed himself with a baseball bat and waited in the bushes for Lester. When school let out, Lester started home and when he walked by, Anton jumped out and hit him on the head with the bat knocking him momentarily unconscious. Anton ran away but many students saw the attack and reported it to the school principal. He called the town constable who came, took a report and called the sheriff.

Lester seemed okay after about thirty minutes and went home. The sheriff picked up Anton and took him to the jailhouse until he could contact his mother. When she arrived the sheriff released the boy then called the school and talked to Mr. Roberts who talked to the School Board President who agreed they should expel Anton for the rest of the year.

Mr. Roberts then called Anton's mother and informed her of the suspension. According to Mr. Roberts she didn't seemed too surprised or upset. That seemed to end the matter until three days later when Lester passed out on the school playground and ended up in the hospital in Waco with a blood clot on his brain. One week later, he died.

Punishment for Anton by the Judicial System was swift and certain. There was no trial, just a hearing before a visiting juvenile judge who sent him to the Texas Youth Counsel in Gatesville there to remain until he reached twenty-one years of age. The county was anxious for a speedy solution mainly because they had no proper facilities to handle a juvenile, especially one only twelve years old.

The hearing lasted less than hour mostly because his court appointed lawyer offered no defense and his mother entered no objections to the sentence. Poppa said he thought she was relieved. Suzie's father withdrew her from school and enrolled her in a private girl's school in Dallas.

Chapter Thirty-One
Malcolm Moore Again

Last week Cousin Esther and I had our first real fight or maybe it was just a disagreement but it left me totally devastated. At lunch she sat with her girl friends as usual and I sat alone. Just as I started to eat my peanut butter and jelly sandwich, Sally Christianson sat down beside me, smiled sweetly and asked, "Can I join you?" I didn't ask her to join me, she just did it and Cousin Esther saw it.

"Sure," I replied and I think Cousin Esther heard it.

Well, she wouldn't speak to me for the rest of the day and wouldn't sit by me on the bus after school. And when the bus reached our house, she didn't get off with me and that's when I realized I had a serious problem.

That evening I called her on the phone but she hung up on me. I called again and Aunt Helena informed me that Cousin Esther did not wish to speak to me. "She also said for you to quit calling."

The next day I cornered her in the hall before the first class and asked her what was wrong. "You obviously prefer to eat with Sally instead of me. So you just go right ahead, I'll eat with the girls or maybe I'll eat with Jim Olson." That cut me deeply because I had often heard the girls discuss his good looks. I tried to explain why I ate with Sally but she would have none of it and we haven't spoken since.

Last Friday, when I got on the bus and tried to sit next to her, she got up and got off the bus and so did I. "I'm gonna walk with you," I said.

"I'm walking home by myself," she snarled as she started up the road.

"No you're not!" I yelled. I tried to catch up but the faster I walked, the faster she walked and soon we were running. As the incline grew steeper she slowed down and so did I. From then on I silently walked a respectful ten paces behind. After maybe fifteen minutes, as we approached the bridge over the creek where Malcolm Moore had shown me the picture of the naked lady, I heard Cousin Esther call, "Malcolm, what's the matter? Why are you running so fast?"

I ran to the bridge in time to see him start up the creek and heard him shout, "Don't tell anybody you seen me here!"

"Why," Cousin shouted back but got no answer and in a moment he disappeared. But in another minute a car came up the road, going fast, and skidded to a stop. Immediately the driver jumped out, gun drawn; and yelled, "You kids see that bastard Malcolm Moore go by here?" It was Sheriff Bjornburg.

Without a word, we both nodded our heads and pointed up the creek. The sheriff jumped off the edge and headed in that direction, gun still drawn.

Fascinated, we watched and in about ten minutes we saw Malcolm walking in our direction followed by the sheriff, gun pointed at his prisoner. When they climbed out of the creek bed, I heard the sheriff mutter, "I shoulda shot the perverted son-of-a-bitch." He shoved the prisoner in the car, locked the door and roared off in the direction of the jail.

I tried to discuss what we had seen with Cousin Esther but she wouldn't listen. When we got to our house, she stomped wordlessly up the road. I stood on the porch and watched and, although it was over a mile away, I thought I could here her slam the door.

After a glass of milk, I went to the barn and told Poppa what had happened. He immediately got in the car and went to town. In about an hour he returned and we all gathered in the kitchen so we could hear what happened.

"Malcolm exposed himself to Amie, Sheriff Bjornburg's eight year old daughter, on the way home from school. When she told her father what happened, he went berserk. I'm really surprised he didn't kill the man, he was so mad. The hearing for an indictment and for bail is scheduled for in the morning.

I tried to call Cousin Esther and tell her what happened but she snapped, "Don't bore me with old news" and hung up on me. When I called her back, her mother asked me not to call again. And I didn't.

Judge Christenson set bail at ten thousand dollars so he would remain in jail until Grand Jury Hearing and maybe until the trial. He said he didn't want the bastard exposing himself to any more children.

The sheriff obtained a warrant permitting him to search Malcolm Moore's house and that immediately presented a problem. Malcolm's mother refused to allow the deputies to enter and ordered them off the property at the point of a gun. They left and informed the sheriff of her actions. The sheriff called Pastor Pierson who accompanied him to her house. After lengthy negotiations, she allowed them in.

What they found shocked everyone, even the sheriff. They found hundreds of magazines with sexually explicit pictures and stories depicting violent sexual crimes. They even found one stack of magazines with pictures of small children being criminally molested by adults. The sheriff took some of the magazines to the District Attorney who logged them in as evidence for the Grand Jury.

Poppa said Malcolm was in a heap of trouble because he had a previous conviction for a similar offence. Malcolm couldn't post bail so he remained in jail which was a pretty good idea because the town folk felt he ought to be castrated or hanged or maybe both, the sooner the better.

Back at school I continued to fret about my relationship with Cousin Esther. She still avoided me and I avoided her. I ate lunch with Sally Christenson three days in a row and on the fourth day Cousin Esther stomped across the playground and threw a dried flower I had given her last Christmas at my feet hissing "You can give that to your precious Sally Christenson. I don't want it any more!" She stood with her hands on her hips for maybe a minute then began to cry, softly at first, then with body shaking sobs. I didn't quite know what to do so I took her in my arms and stroked her hair. Then she fell against my chest and threw her arms around my waist. I looked around the playground and saw several girls watching. In a minute they began to clap and several boys began to whistle. One of the girls yelled, "They made up. Esther and Jacob made up."

More clapping, then the bell rang and everyone returned to his or her respective classroom. And it wasn't long until the back row boys yelled in unison, "Esther Loves Jacob" and off to Mr. Roberts's office they went. The teacher didn't even have to tell them to go. Mr. Roberts accused them of deliberately provoking an incident to get out of class, applied the paddle to each clothed bottom then sent them back to the classroom.

We walked home together hand in hand each trying to outtalk the other and apologizing for our tacky behavior. I wanted to stop on the bridge and maybe take her in my arms again. But it wasn't to be.

When we got there a woman was waiting on the bridge. "You're the bitch that got my son put in jail, ain't you?" the woman shouted.

Surprised, I said, "Hello Mrs. Moore." but she didn't answer. Instead she drew a walking cane from behind her back and hit Cousin Esther over the head. It happened so fast neither of us had time to react and before I could get out of the way she hit me over the head then screamed, "I'm gonna kill both of you lying scum. Take that," and she tried to hit me again but this time I was ready. I grabbed the stick, jerked it out of her hands and threw it into the creek.

"Come on, let's run!" I yelled and we did. The crazy old woman didn't follow; instead she hurled profanities at us as we disappeared over the mountain.

We continued to run across the Flat until we reached my cousin's house and told her mother what happened. She immediately piled us in her car and took us to see Dr. Leonard who treated us both; stitches for Cousin Esther, iodine and a bandage for me. Then we went to the sheriff's office and when he heard our story, he sent two deputies to arrest her. Golly, how could such a wonderful day end up so bad?

When they arrested Mrs. Moore, it presented another problem; the jail had no accommodations for an elderly woman. They took her to Judge Christenson who accepted the charges and bound her over to the Grand Jury and set her free on her own cognizance. It would be up to the jury to determine if a trial was indicated.

Aunt Helena and Poppa urged both of us to stay away from the woman but she wouldn't stay away from us. The next day she was waiting in the schoolyard and when school let out she approached Cousin Esther and screamed, "I'll get you, you lyin bitch." I immediately grabbed Cousin Esther's hand and we ran and jumped in the bus. The woman stood outside, screaming obscenities until the bus left the area.

Two days later she was again waiting for us when school let out. This time she had a gun, a black powder muzzleloader that she immediately fired in our direction. An earsplitting sound filled the schoolyard and thick black smoke surrounded the old lady. Students in the area either ran or fell to the ground, but neither Cousin Esther nor me sustained any injuries. Either her aim was bad or she had forgotten to insert a rifle ball in the gun.

She tried to reload but dropped both the gun and the powder. Two senior boys grabbed her and threw her to the ground and restrained her until the deputies arrived. This time they found a place for her in the Waco jail.

When she appeared before the Grand Jury she claimed she had not meant to injure either of us. She had just lost her temper over the treatment of her son. She also claimed she had not intended to shoot Cousin Esther. She had purposely failed to insert a rifle ball in the barrel of the gun, which seemed to be true. She just wanted to scare us because of the lies we told the sheriff. "Malcolm would never expose himself to anyone, especially a young girl." I never was quite sure why Cousin Esther got the blame for Malcolm's arrest.

The Grand Jury no-bill her for the assault, mostly because of her age and the extenuating circumstances. Judge Christenson administered a stern warning, fined her one hundred dollars for reckless discharge of a firearm and, when she paid the fine, the sheriff set her free. She promised to leave us alone and agreed to cooperate in the trial of her son.

163

It was from his mother that the prosecuting attorney and the court appointed defense attorney learned about Malcolm Moore. At first she wouldn't talk continuing to maintain that Malcolm had done nothing wrong, it was all a bunch of lies. Judge Christenson called her in and told her she HAD to answer questions about her son or he would hold her in contempt and lock her up again. Then he explained that the District Attorney needed to know details about his background so they would know how to handle the case and the Defense Attorney needed information about his background so he could plan a defense. That seemed to change her mind and she agreed to an interview with both attorneys to be recorded by a court reporter.

The sheriff showed Poppa his report to the judge and that night he read it to us.

"At first she seemed reluctant to talk to either attorney but finally she seemed more willing. And after a few questions she appeared eager to get her story out.

"From the onset, it was obvious hers had been a hard life filled with anger, abuse, disappointments and strife. He husband, Malcolm's father was an alcoholic with violent alcohol induced fits of rage. They had been married only one month when he beat her senseless after she scolded him about his drinking. Three months in the county jail failed to curb his anger and craving for alcohol. However, on the night of his release from jail he remained sober long enough to conceive a son they called Malcolm.

"The pregnancy apparently curbed his anger and he remained mostly sober until the delivery in July of 1900. Then, when Malcolm was three months old, someone killed his father in a bar room brawl. With no money and no resources, Malcolm and his mother moved to Waco to live with her mother and stepfather, a fifty-year-old itinerant preacher who had lost his last two congregations because of sexual improprieties involving young boys.

"The arrangement worked well. She found work as a saleswoman in a dry goods store on Austin Ave. Her mother worked as a hairdresser in the beauty shop one block down the street and her stepfather cared for the baby while they worked. But when Malcolm was three the man began to sexually molest him, occasionally at first, then almost daily. Malcolm's mother suspected these activities but felt she could do nothing about it. In the interview, she refused to describe exactly what he did but she said it was terrible and the attorneys didn't press her for details. That would probably come out at the trial.

"When Malcolm started school the problem came to a head when he tried

164

to imitate his step grandfather's actions with a classmate. An alert teacher observed the event and notified the school principal who called County Social Services office. The investigation uncovered the stepfather's actions with Malcolm and at his trial the Jury sentenced him to life in prison.

"Malcolm was devastated by this turn of events. The man was the only father figure he had even known and he felt the man's actions were an expression of his love for the child. A Psychologist examined the child and recommended extended therapy for a year in a controlled setting such as the Orphans Home in Waco and that's where the court sent him.

"Malcolm's mother made no effort to regain custody of her child and moved to Arendal. There she gained employment in a downtown dry goods store and became involved in the church.

"A year at the orphanage apparently helped Malcolm because there were apparently no further deviate actions, at least none that were observed. He came home, enrolled in school and seemed okay until the principal caught him peeking into the girl's bathroom through a broken window. He claimed he didn't know it was the girl's bathroom and that he didn't see anything, so it went no further.

"On another occasion he hid under the teacher's desk apparently in an attempt to look up her dress. The laughter of the students alerted the teacher who sent him to the principal's office who sent him home for a day. On several other occasions his teacher caught him lifting the back of girl's dresses and popping the elastic on their bloomers. Also he seemed to spend an inordinate amount of time in the boy's bathroom.

"At this point, Mrs. Moore stopped talking so the next part of our report came from our investigations. When he was ten his actions got so bad and there were so many complaints from families with children in school that the School Board suspended him for the rest of the school year. There was talk of taking him from his mother and sending him to the TYC in Gatesville. However dismissal from school apparently solved the problem, at least it solved the problems at school.

"Somehow he acquired a magazine filled with sexually explicit pictures. He studied it day and night, especially the pictures and the advertisements with addresses from which a person could order other magazines covering all the various forms of deviate sexual behavior. To get money for these subscriptions he began to look for a paying job.

"At that time in his young life jobs were plentiful even for a ten year old. His first job was as a stocker at the grocery store. He had only worked there for a month when they fired him for hiding under the produce shelf so he could look up the patron's dresses.

"Then he went to work at the blacksmith shop running the forge. He held that job until school started and he enrolled in his previous class, which made him a year older than his classmates. His schooling ended after a month when he cornered a girl in the school library, slipped his hand up her leg and tried to fondle her crotch. Her screams brought the librarian and a teacher to the rescue. This time he ended up in the TYC.

"His mother claimed she knew nothing about his activities at the TYC. She never visited him or wrote to him and he never contacted her. She continued to work at the dry goods store and increased her activities at the church.

"The next part of the summary comes primarily from his mother. On a hot sunny day in the summer of 1921 Malcolm appeared at her front door. He said he had been released from TYC three months ago but had been unable to find employment and asked to stay with her until he could find a decent job. He said he had spent the last five years at TYC working on their farm so his only skills were in farming. He felt surely someone in the community needed a strong young man to help with the backbreaking farm work. Of course she let him stay and he still lived with her.

"There were several farmers at that time whose sons did not returned from the war so Malcolm had no trouble finding work until the depression. He saved little money mostly using what he made for subscriptions to the sexually explicit magazines that he never threw away.

"His mother said she knew about the magazines but considered them harmless. When jobs became scarce she supported him and gave him money. Sometimes he would leave for a few days but he always came back. Once when he was twenty-five he stayed gone for three years. 'Yes, I worried about him,' she said. 'But he's a grown man and has his own life to live.' She said she didn't know he was in prison those three years. 'They said he molested a little child, but I know he didn't. It was a frame up just like the frame up that's going on now.' And that was the end of her statement."

Chapter Thirty-Two
A Trial

It didn't take the Grand Jury long to indict Malcolm Moore for exposing himself to a child. Judge Christianson set bail at ten thousand dollars, the highest anyone could remember other than in a murder case. Feelings ran high in the town of Arendal and Poppa said the Defense Attorney moved for a change of Venue. In the appeal he claimed he could never impanel an unbiased jury in this hostile atmosphere but Judge Christenson denied the appeal. "The town wants its revenge," Poppa said.

Some of the townsmen questioned Sheriff Bjornburg about whether Malcolm might have been responsible for the deaths of Uncle Ole and Aunt Telinda and the disappearance of Baby Angel. He told them he was investigating the deaths with that possibility in mind but so far he hadn't been able to make a connection.

The trial started on the first Monday in January 1936 and was over by the end of the second day. I wasn't allowed to attend, I had to stay in school but Poppa never missed a moment and told us that night that the jury found him guilty and sentenced him to twenty-five years in the State Pen. He said they put Amie on the stand but all she could do was cry.

That night, after we finished milking and before Amos and Andy, I went with Poppa to the front porch. We sat in the swing and he asked, "Did Malcolm Moore ever expose himself to you?"

"No sir," I answered. I didn't want Poppa mad at me because I hadn't told him what happened under the bridge two years ago. Besides nothing else ever happened so why bring it up.

That night I prayed for Amie and again asked God to forgive Malcolm for his grievous sins. And I asked God to forgive me for telling another lie.

In December Cousin Esther and I had our eleventh birthday. Momma and Aunt Helena gave us a birthday party and Momma baked Blotkake, a very tasty Norwegian layer cake with whipped cream on the top along with chocolate store bought ice cream from the Corner Drug. I ate so much I almost got sick and so did Cousin Esther. There were no birthday presents. I knew they would come later.

I got a new winter coat for Christmas. The sleeves of my old coat barely covered my elbows. Besides it was worn out and Sister Sybil said I looked awful, and Momma agreed. I had grown four more inches and gained twenty pounds and now my Sunday suit fit real good and I looked forward to wearing it every Sunday. Cousin Esther was still two inches and twenty pounds behind me and was still my best friend.

Chapter Thirty-Two
Look What We Found

After the trial, the Prosecuting Attorney continued the investigation of Uncle Ole and Aunt Telinda's deaths and the disappearance of Baby Angel. A child was missing and since Malcolm Moore was a twice-convicted child molester, he had to be a suspect.

The sheriff went to Dallas and showed Malcolm's mug shot to Honest Abe, the furniture salesman who had bought Uncle Ole's furniture. He studied it closely and said, "This might have been the guy that sold me the furniture. I can't be sure, it's been so long." He studied the picture some more, then continued, "I do remember the seller had a bushy mustache just like the man in the picture. But I can't testify conclusively that he's the one that did it." He stopped, scratched his head and repeated, "It' just been too long."

The deputies searched the area around Uncle Ole's farm again, and found nothing except a spot where someone had dropped numerous Lucky Strike cigarette butts. This didn't implicate Malcolm Moore because he didn't smoke, never had.

There were no fingerprints on Uncle Ole's furniture probably because the furniture dealer had cleaned and polished all the pieces and some of the pieces had already been sold. So the sheriff dismissed Malcolm Moore as a suspect in the deaths for now.

In an attempt to identify the probable murderer, Sheriff Bjornburg brought both Cousin Esther and me to the courthouse to look at pictures of all persons prosecuted in the county in the last five years for any offence. However, none of the pictures looked like the mountain man. The sheriff even took us to the Waco police station so we could look at their collection of mug shots.

"That's him!" Cousin Esther said pointing to a really nasty looking fellow.

"Is that the mountain man as you call him," the sheriff asked.

"No, no, that's the man that tried to rape me!"

"Well, I'll be darned! That's the man we suspected did it, you know, the one the prisoners killed in the jailhouse. I'll have to tell the judge. He'll be pleased to know we didn't make a mistake picking him up."

We kept looking at the mug shots for an hour and when we finished we told the sheriff we hadn't seen anyone that looked like the mountain but there certainly were a lot of pictures of people who, to me, looked like criminals and I guess they were or their pictures would not be on file. So, for the time being, the identity of the killer or killers of Uncle Ole and Aunt Telinda and the disappearance of Cousin Angel remained a mystery. I still felt the mountain man was the killer, but who is he and what did he do with Cousin Angel?

With no leads to follow, the sheriff put the case on the back burner and said he would wait until something else turned up. All of this was common knowledge mostly passed around the square in Arendal on Saturdays, after church on Sundays, and at various meetings during the week. I knew Poppa wasn't pleased but there didn't seem to be anything he could do.

Cousin Esther and I discussed it many times, mostly on the way to and from school on the bus. Then, last Saturday, Poppa went to town and we went with him. We found Cousin Joseph in the drugstore and shared a double Dr Pepper float, Then we went to the theatre and studied the marquee but saw nothing interesting so we went to the Popcorn Man in front of the Corner Drug and gave him a nickel for a large sack with melted butter and a lotta salt on the top. We walked back to the City Drug, sat on the bench and shared the popcorn while we discussed the case.

"What do you think we oughta do?" I asked

After a moments thought, Cousin Esther replied, "I think we oughta go back out there and scour the mountains around Uncle Ole's farm. They may have missed something."

"Yeah, that's what we oughta do," Cousin Joseph agreed. "But when?"

Without any hesitation, Cousin Esther said, "Next Saturday."

"Will our parents agree?" I asked.

"We'll tell them we're going swimming," Cousin Esther suggested.

"It's too cold to swim now," I answered.

"Well, let's just tell them we're going to Uncle Ole's place and look at the orchard. There shouldn't be any danger in that. Malcolm Moore's in jail."

"But we don't know if he's the mountain man or not. Maybe the mountain man is somebody else and is still there. We might get shot."

"Well, if it isn't Malcolm Moore, then whoever it is has nothing to hid and is probably gone," I answered. "Let's just tell our parents we're going for a ride and plan to visit the grave yard at the Old Buffalo Flat Church."

"Okay," Cousin Esther answered. "We can tell them we went to look at the headstones of relatives for a school project."

We continued to discuss other possible excuses and the possible consequences of our lies but finally agreed to my plan. We would meet early next Saturday at Uncle Ole's farm and go from there. So we spent the next six Saturdays searching in and around Uncle Ole's farm.

The first Saturday it started to rain shortly after we arrived, so Cousin Ester and me rode home and Cousin Joseph started down the river road toward his house. When we got to Cousin Esther's house, her mother fixed us a big cup of hot Ovaltine and we played dominoes for the rest of the day.

The next Saturday we were able to start the search. We concentrated on the area at the top of the mountain across from Uncle Ole's farm but found nothing of interest. However, we saw a county maintenance truck unloading gravel into the water well on Uncle Ole's farm. We walked down to the well and asked the driver of the truck what he was doing. He said the county was going to fill the well so no one would fall in. "Your father requested it and the county's gonna pay for it. It's gonna make it hard to sell the land without a water well, but that ain't my problem."

The third Saturday we concentrated on the area where Cousin Esther had been assaulted. We found the exact spot where the assault occurred and worked out from there. Usually we made a lot of noise when we were exploring, mostly to cover our anxieties. It was a little scary out in this isolated area with no adults to protect us. But today we proceeded with caution and hardly made a sound. Again we found nothing and debated about abandoning the search but finally agreed to give it at least one more try.

The fourth Saturday produced no results and we again debated abandoning the search. But by the time we left, we decided to give it one more try. The fifth Saturday also produced no results until time to go home. When we met back at the assault site about an hour before sundown, Cousin Esther said she had found something about a mile to the west she wanted us to see. We followed her until we stood at the base of a rocky cliff about twenty feet tall and Cousin Esther pointed to a hole about half way up the side, maybe ten feet below the top.

"Doesn't that look like a cave?" she asked.

"Yeah, it does. Might be a snake den," I replied remembering the snake den on our farm.

"You think we oughta explore it?" she continued.

"How we gonna get up there?" Cousin Joseph asked.

We stood back and surveyed the scene for a few minutes, then Cousin Esther pointing to the side of the cliff and said, "Is that a trail? It looks like a trail coming down from the top of the mountain. Let's go look."

Looking at the setting sun, I said, "We don't have time. We can come back next Saturday and spend all day." After further discussion, we agreed.

It was almost dark when I got home and found Poppa and Brother Ben in the barn milking the cows. "Where you scalawags been?" Brother Ben asked. He had come home from Texas Tech yesterday for spring break. "Did y'all have a gangbang?"

"Benjamin!" Poppa yelled and Brother Ben answered, "Sorry."

I didn't know what he was talking about so I ignored him. Maybe I'd ask my cousins what he meant by 'gangbang' the next time we met. Thank goodness he'll be going back to college in about ten days.

The next Saturday, our sixth attempt, we each packed a lunch, peanut butter and jelly sandwiches, and met at the base of the cliff and began our search. Arendal County contained many similar rock formations along the edges of the prairie. The largest is known as the Bee Rock because of the many beehives clinging to its face. It is said that the Comanche, when they ruled the area, threw their enemies to their deaths from the top. Also, there is the story of a farmer who caught his wife committing adultery so he punished her by throwing her off the cliff but she survived to bear him ten children. There is also the story about a young couple, perhaps imitating Romeo and Juliet, who plunged to their deaths in despair over wedding plans blocked by their parents.

I don't know if any of these stories are true but I know one that is because I saw it with my own eyes. It involved the honeycombs on the face of the cliff.

A group of students from Arendal Junior College, as part of Freshman Initiation, lowered one of their new classmates down the cliff with orders to collect a bucket of honey. The bees became angry, as bees will do, and attacked him. He apparently was allergic to the bee stings and died hanging from the rope. When they tried to bring him up, the bees followed and everybody ran away and left him hanging for two days.

Half the people of Arendal, including our family, drove to the base of the cliff to view the body. They finally cut the rope and allowed his body to plunge to the bottom of the cliff. The school and the county passed many new rules aimed at preventing a repeat of the accident. The sheriff did not file any charges.

When we were in her grade Miss Hawk had explained how these structures had formed. Millions of years ago, the Arendal River ate away the limestone rock layer over the prairie to form the Arendal valley leaving exposed cliffs along the edges. In my mind, this immediately created a problem because Pastor Pierson had told us that God created the world in six days and on the seventh day he rested and that the world was only four thousand four years old based on Chapter One of the Gospel of St. Matthew.

When I asked Poppa about it, he explained, "Son, a day in God's eyes might be a million years so we really can't say when the world was created. But following the creation, humans have only been on this earth for four thousand four years."

I knew this to be absolute Lutheran Doctrine straight from Holy Scriptures and if you didn't believe it you're an atheist and will surely burn in Hell. I wasn't sure I understood but I didn't doubt God's word. And I certainly didn't want to burn in Hell.

Once Cousin Esther and me met at Cousin Joseph and rode our bicycles up the river road to the Bee Rock and tried to climb to the top. Half way, up we became so terrified that we climbed down and raced back.

The cliff we approached wasn't as high or frightening as the Bee Rock but we realized if you slipped and fell serious injury could occur. So we approached the opening with great care.

Soon we found the trail, a rocky footpath, steep and narrow, barely wide enough for one person and it had been traveled frequently and recently. The trail seemed to start at a clearing on top of the cliff where someone had obviously parked a car many times judging by the oil stains on the ground. Car tracks led off across the prairie probably connecting to the road to Hamilton. There was enough room on the ledge in front of the opening for the three of us to kneel and look in the cave but the interior was so dark, we couldn't see a thing.

"Do you want me to crawl in?" Cousin Esther asked.

"One of us has to, and you're the smallest," I replied. "Go ahead and I'll follow. Joseph, you stay out here."

I had some concern about rattlesnakes but they normally didn't climb cliffs to find a den. Usually their dens were at ground level. I also had concerns about mountain lions that were occasionally seen in the area. We threw some rocks into the cave and when nothing came out we decided it was safe to crawl in. I thought it might be best if I went first and use the matches to light the way.

I put a few in my pocket then crawled into the cave. The opening was about two feet square but inside it was much bigger, maybe twenty feet to the back, four feet to the ceiling and ten feet wide. We both had to crawl on our bellies to get in and when we did, we couldn't stand up. It had a musty smell and there was evidence of habitation, probably rats or bats but, thank goodness, at the moment, it was empty.

I still couldn't see a thing so I struck a match and held it above my head. Then I saw it, an oilskin bundle about four feet long lying against the back wall partially covered with brush.

"Look," I said to Cousin Esther. "What's that?"

"I don't know. Should we try to open it?"

"I don't know," I replied and I didn't. "It might be a body. Let's talk to Cousin Joseph about it." So we crawled back out and sat on the ledge and tried to figure out what to do. It also seemed like a good time to eat lunch so we did.

After we finished eating, Cousin Joseph said, "I want take a look" but he couldn't get through the whole, so Cousin Esther and me crawled in and dragged the bundle out to the ledge. "I think we oughta open it and see what's in it," Cousin Joseph said.

"Yeah!" Cousin Esther said, then added, "it might be a treasure, might be gold, it might even be diamonds. It could even be stuff the Comanche left here."

"Okay, let's do it," I replied and began to unwrap it. It was a big piece of oilskin and I almost fell off the ledge trying to get it open. Finally it lay before us and we began to examine the contents.

The biggest item was a 30-30 Winchester rifle along with two boxes of shells. We also found a pair of 1934 license plates and a heavy jacket. Wrapped in the jacket we found two rubber masks, a football, several filthy sex magazines and two packs of Lucky Strike cigarettes.

"That's the mountain man's rifle," I said. "And that's probably Brother Ben's football."

"And that's the mountain man's face," Cousin Esther gasped pointing at the rubber masks. "Now I know why he looked so peculiar, he had on a mask. What are we gonna do?"

"I don't know. Let's think about it," I answered.

After ten minutes of discussion we decided that Cousin Joseph should ride to town and bring the Sheriff. Cousin Esther and I would stay here and guard the evidence. We rolled up the bundle, dragged it back in the cave and covered it with brush. Then we crawled out, sat on the edge of the ledge and waited.

Cousin Esther still had a slice of bread in the sack so we smeared it with peanut butter and shared it and my stomach felt better. Then we realized we could see Uncle Ole's entire farm in the distance. "This must be where the mountain man sat and watched," Cousin Esther whispered. Then pointing to the bottom of the cliff, she added, "And there's a trail that leads to Uncle Ole's farm. It probably also leads to where he fired the rifle."

Cousin Joseph had been gone about thirty minutes when we heard a car approaching and seemed to stop at the edge of the cliff above us. Soon we heard a door slam and someone coming down the trail. "Do you think it's the sheriff?" I whispered.

"Must be, but it hasn't been long enough," she answered and we fell silent.

In a moment we saw a pair of legs wearing work pants and dirty well-worn work shoes, coming down the trail and we froze. "That ain't the sheriff," I whispered and in a moment we knew.

"What the HELL are you kids doing here?" the voice boomed and we both immediately knew who it was. It was Malcolm Moore's mother and she was obviously surprised and very angry. "Is SHE the mountain man?" I whispered.

We were both so terrified we couldn't answer so she repeated the question.

Finally, Cousin Esther stammered, "H-hunting."

"You fools been in that cave?" she asked pointing to the opening.

"No Ma'am. We were scared to go in because there might be rattlesnakes in there."

"Like hell you didn't! Young kids like you couldn't resist crawling in a cave. Might contain some treasures. I'm gonna crawl in and take a look."

"Should we run away?" I whispered. When Cousin Esther didn't answer, I answered myself. "Somebody's gotta stay here and guard the evidence." I knew if we ran away, she's liable to take the bundle and hide it somewhere else or throw it in the river. But if we stayed and she realized we know about the bundle, she'd probably kill us. She'd march us to the top of the hill and throw us off the cliff or she might take us to the Bee Rock and push us off. But I didn't think she could overpower both of us.

We watched her get down on her hands and knees and crawl into the cave. Neither of us said a word as we listened for her reaction that was not long coming. She stuck her head out the hole and snarled "What the hell are them burnt matches doing in the cave?" and I knew that she knew we had been in the cave and probably had seen the bundle.

She seemed to be having a little trouble crawling out of the cave and, out of the corner of my eye, I saw Cousin Esther quietly sneaked up the trail. I figured she was trying to run away and I didn't blame her, but I couldn't make myself follow. I had to somehow protect the evidence.

Finally the old lady made it out of the cave dragging the rifle behind. Then she stood up and pointed the rifle at my chest and shouted, "You lied to me! You been in that cave and I betcha you looked in that bundle!" Before I could object, she added, "Now I gotta kill you." Looking around she asked, "Where's that Johansson bitch? I gotta kill her too."

Suddenly, a body came flying from above and landed on her back knocking her flat on her stomach with her chest and head hanging off the ledge and her arms flailing the air. When she hit the ground the gun exploded, flew out of her hand and tumbled to the bottom of the ravine. It took me a moment to realize what had happened, then I saw Cousin Esther sitting on her butt and I grabbed the old woman's feet and tried to pull her back.

"My God, Esther, are you okay? You coulda gotten killed. You coulda fallen off the edge."

"Jacob, I didn't want her to shoot you so I jumped."

"Well, I'm glad you did."

When the old woman came to her senses and realized what had happened and where she was, she screamed, "Don't let me fall! Please don't let me fall!"

'Stop wiggling, Mrs. Moore, or you WILL fall!" Cousin Esther shouted.

Continuing to wiggle, the old lady screamed, "Get off my ass, you damn whore!"

"Mrs. Moore, BE STILL!!" But she continued to wiggle. As they got closer to the edge, Cousin Esther slid back to the woman's thighs and I pulled harder on the woman's feet and now most of her body hung over the edge.

"Mrs. Moore," Cousin Esther hissed, "If you don't stop wiggling, I'm gonna get off and let you fall."

"If I fall, you bastards are going with me!" the old woman screamed as she reached around and grabbed the bottom of Cousin Esther's dress. Instantly, I sat on her feet and put my arms around Cousin Esther's waist and pulled back with all my strength. In a few moments, the woman stopped pulling and began to scream at the top of her lungs, "RAPE! RAPE!"

I guess that was the longest thirty minutes of my life as we sat on the edge of the cliff listening to the woman scream while trying to keep her from falling. In spite of my fears it seemed a good time to ask a few questions.

"Why did you shoot my father?" When she didn't answer, I continued,

"What did you do with Baby Angel?" but she didn't answer that either.

"Why did you kill Uncle Ole and Aunt Telinda?"

"I don't know what the hell you're talking about, I ain't kilt nobody."

"What were those masks doing in the bag?" Cousin Esther asked.

"You lying bitch, I thought you told me you hadn't seen the bag."

"We seen plenty, Mrs. Moore," I said. "Did you know that's the mask your son wore when he shot my father?"

"He didn't shot your father!"

"How did that football get in that pouch?"

"I don't know nuthin about no football!"

This went on for maybe fifteen minutes, questions and denials, more questions, more denials then she quit talking and I was beginning to wonder how long we could last in this perilous position. Finally I heard a car door slam near the top of the ledge and in a few minutes, Cousin Joseph, Sheriff Bjornburg and Brother Ben came down the trail. When the sheriff stepped onto the ledge and Mrs. Moore realized who it was, she yelled, "Sheriff, get these damn monsters off of me, they're trying to kill me!"

"They killed Uncle Ole and Aunt Telinda!" I hollered.

"Who's they?" the sheriff asked.

"This woman and her son, Malcolm Moore."

"How do you know?"

"Just look in the cave, you'll understand," I answered

"We best get you three out of the predicament you got yourselves in. Then maybe we can straighten out this mess."

The sheriff held onto Mrs. Moore's legs, we got off and he pulled her back on the ledge and helped her to her feet. Immediately all three of us, me and Cousin Esther and Mrs. Moore, began talking at the same time and the sheriff told us to shut up. "We'll sort this out at my office."

"But we gotta get that stuff out of the cave," I protested. "That's the evidence that proves they killed our aunt and uncle. And the gun she tried kill us with is down there."

"Okay, Ben, you get the gun and Jacob, you get the stuff out of the cave you think implicates this lady and her son." So I crawled in the cave and retrieved the bundle, then helped the sheriff carry it to his car. By the time we got to the car, Brother Ben returned with the gun and the sheriff unrolled the bundle. The first thing the sheriff found was the jacket. Inside the collar he found Malcolm Moore's name and TYC stenciled in white. That's when Brother Ben saw the football.

"Hay, let me see that," he said as he picked it up and turned it over and over in his hands. "That's my football. See that mark? I put it there when I first got it so my idiot brother couldn't claim it was his." He turned it over again and then asked, "Where did it come from?"

"It was in the cave," I answered.

I could see his anger building as he asked our prisoner, "How did it get in the cave? Did Malcolm steal it?"

"No he didn't steal your damn football. I found it in the well," Mrs. Moore muttered. "It was in the bucket when I brought it up to get a drink."

"How in the name of Jesus did it get in the well?" Brother Ben asked. I think he already had a suspicion that I was somehow involved. He hadn't yet figured it out but, in a moment, my involvement became obvious.

"Your scum of a brother put it there. He kicked it in the air and it landed in the well."

"How do you know?" Brother Ben asked.

"I seen him do it. He was there with your father and he kicked the football and it bounced into the well. I was settin right here and seen it all."

Brother Ben turned to me, his face livid with anger, and I knew what was coming. "You lied to me!" he snarled. "You told me a bald faced lie and I believed you!" He paused to catch his breath, then continued, "What other lies have you told me? Your father is certainly going to hear about this. I doubt you'll ever get off the farm again. And I don't think you'll ever see Cousin Esther again. I hope he sends you to an Orphans Home in another state."

"Poppa already knows about it."

"What!!" he yelled. "There you go. You lied again. Sonny Boy you're in big, big trouble!"

I knew better than to say anything else when he was this mad. I guess I had it coming but we HAD solved the case except for Cousin Angel. Wouldn't that count for something? I realized I better let Poppa settle it. I also realized Mrs. Moore, in her anger, had confessed to knowing about the cave and its contents With that, the sheriff placed her in handcuffs and we returned to Arendal. He took our statements and when we finished, he put Mrs. Moore in jail. "I think I got enough evidence to file charges on both Mrs. Moore and her son," he said.

And, thank goodness, in a few days, Brother Ben went back to school. If he hadn't, he mighta killed me he was so mad.

Chapter Thirty-Four
End of Another Summer

When Brother Ben came home for the summer he was still mad. His anger about the football never abated even though Poppa took my side in the dispute.

What apparently hurt him most was that Poppa and I had kept the football a secret. He tried to get Momma involved but she referred him to Pastor Pierson who was an expert in settling family disputes. After a few days he got a job at a feed mill in Waco and moved out.

Sister Selma is still working for Dr. Nygard and now makes forty-five dollars a month. That seemed like a lot of money to me but I guess he can afford it. He now charges seventy-five cents for office visits and dollar for house calls. Again, there was some grumbling among Arendal residents because he now charges fifteen dollars for delivering a baby and the doctors in Waco only charge ten but Sister Selma told everybody he was worth it.

On the Monday after we found the cave, Sheriff Bjornburg brought Mrs. Moore before Judge Christenson for arraignment. After the hearing he bound both Malcolm Moore and his Mother over to the Grand Jury on two counts of Capitol Murder and one charge of Arson and one charge of Kidnapping. He set bail for Mrs. Moore at one hundred thousand dollars, the highest bail ever set in Arendal County. He would let the Grand Jury decide who was the murderer and who was the accomplice in this bizarre case.

Investigators found that her name was Ada Mae Moore, age sixty-three, and that she had one other child conceived and born out of wedlock. She refused to give his name or his address stating she hadn't seen or heard from him for twenty years and didn't know where he was. "Might be dead for all I know."

The Grand Jury met two weeks later and after a two-day hearing indicted Malcolm Moore on all charges except for Kidnapping. Since there wasn't a body, they felt that charge would not stand up at a trial. They indicted his mother as an accomplice to all charges and bound them both to the courts for separate jury trials. Malcolm's trial would be first and was set for the third week in September.

The Prosecuting Attorney hoped Malcolm's mother would assist in his prosecution in exchange for leniency. I knew all this because Second Cousin

Selmer who was on the Grand Jury told Poppa who told us. There were few secrets in Arendal.

In August, my parents took my cousins and me to the Texas Centennial in Dallas celebrating the birth of the Republic of Texas. Sister Sybil went along but Brother Ben didn't. He claimed he couldn't stand being in the car with me for that long and planned to take his girl friend next week if Poppa would let him use the car. If not, they would ride the bus. His Model T had died and he didn't have enough money to get it fixed. Poppa said he wasn't gonna pay for it because he had forgotten to change the oil and had burned up the bearings racing on the highway. Although it didn't have a speedometer, Brother Ben claimed it would go forty miles an hour with the wind providing you were going down hill.

We enjoyed the trip and the many activities and exhibits, especially the section where you could win prizes. I had a two dollar allowance and blew it all in the first hour on a hot dog and a soda and trying to win a stuffed doll for Cousin Esther by knocking over a bottle with a baseball. After four attempts I was broke and had to borrow money from Cousin Joseph.

We rode the Ferris wheel, the roller coaster, and the swing that looked like an airplane and I got sick and vomited. By then we were all broke so we spent the rest of the day walking around and looking at everything. By mid afternoon, my new shoes had rubbed blisters on my feet to I took them off, hung them around my neck, and went barefooted. As instructed, we all met at the entrance at four, found the car and went home exhausted but happy. Cousin Esther said she had heard the marching band was scheduled to visit the fair in September to participate in a contest. Maybe we could come along.

My cousins and I were now in the sixth grade and our teacher was Miss Peddis, a dour no nonsense sixty year old spinster whose expertise was Language and History but taught all subjects. It only took her a week to convince us, especially the back row boys, who would be the boss in her class. If you misbehaved she didn't send you to the principal or Mr. Roberts. A ruler applied to an open hand on your desk quickly established her authority.

But there was no question about her abilities. She was a very good teacher and if you behaved you could learn a lot, especially about History.

Thank goodness I didn't have to pick cotton this year. For the last two years Poppa had kept his promise not to plant cotton and that was okay by me. So when school let out for cotton picking maybe I could make some money helping Uncle Andrew. And for the first time in my life, during the summer, I drove the tractor on the road.

I had grown about four more inches since last year and now weighed a hundred thirty pounds and I could crank the tractor almost as good as Brother Ben. Momma said when I grew up I was going to be as big as Uncle Andrew, maybe bigger but she didn't think I would be as fat.

Cousin Esther was also growing bigger and taller and it made me a little angry when older boys showed an interest in her. However she didn't pay them any attention and continued to be my closest friend. She said she knew what they were after and she wasn't interested. She wouldn't tell me what she thought they were after but I was certain I knew and I loved her even more.

Poppa told us Malcolm's mother so far had refused to testify against her son and continued to maintain it was all a setup. She denied placing the bundle in the cave and denied having any knowledge about the murders. However her fingerprints as well as Malcolm's were on the rifle and the handwriting expert identified the letter left in Uncle Ole's mailbox as having been written by her. And after the first night in jail, she asked for a cigarette, a Lucky Strike please.

The jacket found in the cave definitely belonged to Malcolm They had been unable to trace the gun but the license plates were from Uncle Ole's truck and had his fingerprints so the DA felt he had an airtight case. They were just trying to decide which of the two actually committed the murders and why.

He didn't think the murders were done for money because there wasn't that much involved. The furniture only brought fifty dollars and Uncle Ole had nothing of value in his house.

"Maybe Baby Angel is at the bottom of the whole mess," Sheriff Bjornburg suggested to Poppa a couple of week ago. "Maybe he killed your brother and sister-in-law to get the baby. Maybe he molested the child and they caught him. Maybe to cover his crime he killed them then burned the house down. Because of his past history, he knew he would go to prison forever if he got caught."

The sheriff continued, "But why didn't he just leave the bodies in the house when he set it on fire? The deaths must have occurred several days before the fire to give him time to remove the furniture. I guess he thought if the bodies were not found in the fire, everyone would think Uncle Ole had taken his family and traveled to another state."

Scratching his almost bald head, he continued, "Yep, that's it. Baby Angel is the key to this case so the murderer has to be Malcolm. He has a history of molesting little children and I think he couldn't resist Baby Angel. She was such a beautiful child." This all seemed logical to me. But where IS Baby Angel?

There was one problem with the case. The Defense Attorney received a call from Gus McDougal, a farmer from out on the prairie east of Arendal who claimed that Malcolm Moore was working for him the day Poppa got shot. He was sure of the date and said he could prove it and would testify at the trial for twenty-five dollars. The Defense Attorney agreed to call him as a witness.

Malcolm Moore's trial would start the second week in September. They transferred him from Huntsville on the Saturday before the trial and put him in a cell in the Arendal County jail. They transferred Mrs. Moore from the Waco jail to a cell near him but not close enough for them to talk.

Chapter Thirty-Five
Second Trial

I don't ordinarily listen when Poppa talks with someone after church. It's usually about something I didn't understand. But that day, two weeks before Malcolm Moore's trial I listened because it concerned the trial.

So after Rev. Pierson dismissed the congregation I followed Poppa as he walked across the churchyard and found Conard Thorson, the District Attorney. They shook hands then the District Attorney began, "Howdy, Gunder, how are things on the farm?"

"'Bout like always, dry and windy. Cain't get a decent price for nothing," Poppa answered.

"Same thing in the lawyering business. Got a nasty case to prosecute in a couple of weeks and I don't know where the money's coming from for the expert witnesses."

"That's what I wanted to talk to you about." Poppa kicked a rock with his shoe, then continued. " Is it true that old Judge Collins is gonna hear the case?"

"That's true."

"I thought he retired."

"Yes he did, but he's on the panel of judges available for emergencies such as this one. As I'm sure you know, Judge Christenson suffered a heart attack two weeks ago and the state sent old Judge Collins to handle the trial."

"Ain't he a drunkard? I hear he gets drunk almost every day, especially during trials."

"Oh, that ain't exactly true. I know for a fact he drinks every day but usually doesn't get too drunk to function. Every morning, about ten thirty, he calls a recess so he can go to his office and 'answer phone calls'. In about thirty minutes he returns reeking of rye whiskey. Same thing about three in the afternoon and sometimes the bailiff has to lead him back the bench. When he's like that, he gets downright cranky and the lawyers know to be on their best behavior or face the wrath of his acid tongue."

"But you think he's a pretty good judge even with his problem?"

"Oh yeah. He usually goes to sleep after the afternoon nip but the bailiff wakes him if a decision is required. Sometimes he begins to snore, and if he does, the Defense Attorney will ask for an adjournment to 'confer with his client' and the Prosecution won't object. This is agreed upon before every trial because he's actually a very good judge and they don't want to get him any trouble."

"Well, I hope you're right because I'm gonna be there every day" With that, the men shook hands and we went home.

It took three days to impanel a jury. The Defense Attorney exhausted the jury pool with Challenges and Judge Collins had to bring in more prospective jurors. Finally they completed the selection and the Defense Attorney challenged the jury array based on bias. The judge denied the challenge and denied another motion for a change of Venue.

Because we would be witnesses Cousin Esther and I could not attend. We both went to school every day and on the fourth day they called us to appear. I went first.

Mr. Thorson asked me a bunch of questions that took a couple of hours, then the Defense Attorney asked me a bunch of silly question. My answers apparently made him mad because the judge kept calling him to the bunch so he could fuss at him. He kept asking how come we knew about the cave. "Did you steal the football and hide it in the cave." Did you steal Mr. Moore's coat and hide it in the cave. And I betcha you stole the gun and kept it hidden in the cave."

"Where would I have gotten Malcolm Moore's coat," I answered. "And where would I get a rifle and why did Mrs. Moore come to the cave?"

Obviously furious, he snarled, "I ask the questions, son, you supply the answers."

"Objection!" Mr. Thorson yelled.

The judge sustained Mr. Thorson's objection and the questions continued.

"Isn't it a fact that you know about the cave because you and your cousin go there to have sex?"

"Sir, we've never gone there to have sex. In fact we've never had sex anywhere anytime. It's against the Commandments and a sin against God. I believe in God and so does my cousin."

"And you expect the jury to believe that crap?" When Mr. Thorson objected the judge called both attorneys to his office. When they returned the Defense Attorney apologized to me and dismissed me as a witness and I left.

Cousin Esther came next and after her testimony that took the rest of the afternoon, the judge declared a recess until the next morning.

That night I walked to her house and we sat in the swing on the front porch and I could tell she was upset. "The Defense Attorney kept hammering at me about my relations with Malcolm Moore," she began. "He suggested that I had begged him for sex and when he rejected me I swore to get even with him. He accused me of a lot of other things and said he knew why we knew about the cave. It was because we had gone there many times to have sex. And when he said that I began to cry."

Suddenly Cousin Esther began to sob, angry sobs that shook her body and I gathered her in my arms. The crying continued until held her closer and brushed away the tears. Then, slowly, hesitantly, our lips met, a soft lingering kiss that surprised us both and sent my heart racing and caused her to blush. I think the exchange scared us both so we went in the house and shared a piece of cake. Then I went home.

The next morning the Prosecuting Attorney questioned Cousin Joseph briefly but the Defense Attorney declined. He said, "I don't want to expose the jury to any more lies." This caused another trip to the judge's chambers and another apology to the jury. At that point the prosecution rested and everybody went to lunch.

That night Poppa told us about the afternoon. The Defense only called two witnesses, Gus McDougal and Malcolm's mother. "Mr. McDougal went first and swore Malcolm was working for him on the day I got shot. Nobody believed him because he's a known liar who would deceive his own mother for twenty-five dollars. Mr. Thorson didn't even cross-examine him.

Poppa continued, "When Malcolm's mother testified, she recited the many detail of his background omitting the previous convictions for child molestation. She vehemently denied having anything to do with the murders and was sure her son was innocent of the charges."

"The Prosecuting Attorney spent two hours tearing her testimony apart repeatedly asking her why she went to the cave if she knew nothing about its contents. He asked how her fingerprints got on the gun and who fired the shot that injured Poppa. Finally, folding her arms across her chest she snarled, "I ain't gonna talk to you no more" and she didn't. The judge woke up, conferred with the bailiff and held her in contempt and ordered her held in the county jail until she agreed to talk.

Poppa never missed a day of the ten-day trial, an uncommonly long time for a trial in Arendal County. And in the end the jury found Malcolm guilty on two counts of Capital Murder and one count of Robbery and sentenced him to die in the electric chair. They acquitted him on the Arson charge for lack of evidence that he had actually started the fire.

There was some grumbling about the sentence because he hadn't been charged with kidnapping but the sheriff explained about the lack of evidence. He thought they might get more information about Baby Angel when Malcolm's mother went on trial. And, much to the lawyers surprise and the spectator's disappointment, the judge remained reasonably sober and only fell asleep once during the trial. Poppa said he thought more people came to the courthouse to watch the judge than to watch the trial.

So Malcolm Moore went to Huntsville to await his appointment with 'Old Sparkey' as the electric chair was called. His mother stayed in jail on the contempt charge. Three times the judge gave her a chance to talk and each time she refused.

And we still didn't know what happened to Baby Angel.

Chapter Thirty-Six
Trial Number Three

Cousin Esther and me are now twelve years old and half way through the sixth grade, a grade considerably harder than the fifth. So many things to remember, so many tests to pass and my sister says next year will be worse. But, I'll worry about that later.

Brother Ben still hasn't forgiven me concerning the football. But at least he isn't here harassing me day and night. It got so bad before he returned to college that Poppa threatened to whip him if he didn't shut up. "If you think you gotta be mad at somebody, be mad at me!" Poppa said.

The football team lost all but one of its games and there was talk of firing the coach or dropping football as a sport. All the good players had graduated and the previous coach transferred to a larger school in Dallas and nobody, including most members of the School Board, liked the new coach.

The basketball teams were doing better than last year, especially the girls who won second place at an Invitational Tournament in Waco. Sister Sybil, now in her second year of high school, was on the team as a substitute. She thought next year she would probably be a starter. Mrs. Moore's trial was scheduled for the second Monday in December 1936. She still refused to talk to the judge and during the first week in December her court appointed Attorney pled for a continuance and examination by a psychiatrist. Judge Christenson (who was back on the bench) denied it at first then changed his mind and arranged for her transfer to the State Hospital for the Insane in Austin. She returned on Christmas Eve with her sanity established and a new trial date for the second Monday in January 1937.

When Brother Ben came home for Christmas he was still mad. "If you think I'm gonna give you a Christmas present, you better think again," he announced when he came in the door, then added, "On second thought, maybe I'll give you a box full of cow manure."

"Stop that, Benjamin!" Mamma said. "If you're gonna act like that, you can get on the bus and go back to school." From behind Momma's back I stuck out my tongue and made a face at him. He never said another word to me all the time he was home and when he left, I stuck out my tongue at him again.

Poppa saw me do it and he said, "Jacob, you oughta be ashamed of yourself."

My Christmas present was the same as last year, a new winter coat because I had outgrown my old one. Sister Sybil got a basketball and a hoop that Poppa nailed to the garage. We were still not speaking so I don't know what Brother Ben got for Christmas. I asked Momma but she said it wasn't any of my business. I think maybe it was money for college because the package was small.

Christmas came and went with the usual festivities at home, at church and at Grandma Svendahl's house. About the only difference was the Christmas Pageant at the church and the meal at Grandma Svendahl's house. When I practiced for my annual solo my voice broke so many times they cancelled my performance. Momma said it was because I was growing up. Cousin Esther thought it was very funny and teased me about it.

Grandma Svendahl had been unable to obtain lutefisk and that didn't bother me at all. Now I didn't have to pretend that I liked it. She was also unable to get pearl tapioca for the Sotsuppe. That disappointed me because I had been looking forward to that dish for a year. Instead I loaded up on Julekake and Cousin Esther, Cousin Joseph and I were put on the list for the first table.

Another difference this year was Grandma Svendahl's gift to the grandchildren. Each got a crisp new five-dollar bill. She said that, in spite of the depression, she had had a good year and wished to share her good fortune with her family. I knew she gave her children, including Poppa, a gift of money but he never told us how much.

After the meal the men went to the upstairs parlor and played a new board game called Monopoly. We were allowed to go upstairs to watch.

The game had just been invented and everybody wanted to play. It was very complicated with each player buying and selling property depending on the throw of the dice and went on all afternoon. Brother Ben lost all his property and his play money after an hour and had to drop out. I wanted to take his place but they said I was too young and wouldn't understand the game. Cousin Esther said she got the same game for Christmas so we could practice it until we understood the game. "Maybe next Christmas, we can join the game.

Ana Mae Moore's trial began as scheduled but only lasted three days. She refused to talk to either Attorney and refused to testify. Mr. Thorson presented the evidence and my cousins and I testified. The defense Attorney asked about the same questions as he did in Malcolm's trial and we gave the same answers. On the third day the jury found her guilty of being an accessory to the crimes. Mr. Thorson asked for extended prison time for the defendant and the jury sentenced her to twenty-five years. Poppa said that meant she would probably spend the rest of her life in prison.

Shortly after the trial Cousin Esther and I cut each other's hair using Poppa's electric sheep shearer. At the time Cousin Esther wore her hair in pigtails that hung down almost to her butt. She washed it every week and her mother spent two hours brushing it and braiding it into two long pigtails, one on each side of her head. Everybody complemented her on her hair because it was so soft and silky. She said several times she hated the attention because the boys were forever yanking one of the braids even if she asked them to stop.

My hair was still about the same color as Cousin Esther's, soft and straw colored. Momma usually cut my hair by placing a mixing bowl on my head and cutting off anything that hung below the edge. This was how most boys had their hair cut so we all pretty much all looked alike. Before special occasions, like at Christmas, Poppa usually took me to the barbershop and paid the barber twenty-five cents to cut my hair. He always cut it too short but Momma said I looked nice with short hair.

Cousin Esther cut mine as close to the scalp as she could, leaving a narrow strip down the middle, front to back. Several of the boys in school had similar cuts they called a Mohawk. I cut Cousin Esther's hair about even with the bottom of her ears. Cousin Joseph decided he didn't want his hair cut. "Poppa's liable to whip my butt if I do," he said so we didn't.

Esther's mother about had a stroke when she got home and saw what we had done. The next day she took her to a beauty shop in Waco and when she came back she looked really cute. Cousin Esther said it cost a whole dollar.

Momma took one look at my head and said, "You ain't going to school looking like an Indian." So she sheared off the Mohawk strip and I never got to show it off. All the girls called me baldy so I took to wearing my work hat to school. I don't think Cousin Esther's mother ever forgave us our foolishness as she called it. And I guess I kinda missed the pigtail that had taken her twelve years to grow.

And we still didn't know what had happened to Baby Angel.

Chapter Thirty-Seven
Conformation

August 1937

In May, my cousins and me were confirmed. There were twelve in our class, the boys in new suits and the girls in new white dresses standing before the entire congregation reciting the Lord's Prayer, the Apostolic Creed and the Ten Commandments and answering Pastor Pierson's questions about each item, especially the Ten Commandments. We had to repeat passages from the Bible and demonstrate our knowledge of Lutheran Doctrine. It was just like an oral quiz at school. Following the questions we were accepted as full-fledged members of the Lutheran Church and received our first Communion.

We listened as Pastor Pierson consecrate the items on the alter: wafers on a silver platter and a tray of small glasses the size of a thimble filled with red wine. The congregation repeated the Lord's Prayer then Pastor Pierson stood in the pulpit and began the ceremony.

"We do not presume to come to Thy table, O merciful Lord, trusting in our own righteousness, but in Thy manifold and great mercies. We are not worthy so much as to gather the crumbs under Thy table. Grant us therefore, Oh Lord, to eat Thy Flesh and drink Thy Blood that we may evermore dwell in Thee and Thee in us. Amen."

"Amen." The entire congregation murmured then we kneeled at the communicant's rail and waited until Pastor Pierson stood before us.

He walked down the line and offered each communicant a small white wafer that tasted like dry cardboard stating, *"This is my Body which was given for you. Take, Eat, in remembrance of Me."* Then he set the platter aside, picked up the tray of tiny glasses, offered each communicant a glass containing something that tasted like sour grape juice and said, *"This is My Blood which was shed for you. Drink this in remembrance of Me."*

I ate and drank both and so did the rest of my class.

I remembered what he had told us in Conformation classes. "These objects do not REPRESENT the body and the blood of Christ, they ARE the consecrated Body and Blood of our Lord and Savior who gave His Life for us on the cross." Pastor Pierson was very specific about that point. I really didn't understand but I accepted it as true.

Our parents honored us with a traditional Norwegian dinner at Grandma Svendahl's house. We were allowed to sit at the first table and after we ate we were allowed to participate in the Monopoly game. Cousin Esther ended up with all the money and the property including the money and property of the grown men. I think it embarrassed the men but they said they had let her win because it was a special occasion. I knew this wasn't true, she just whipped them good and they couldn't admit being beaten by a twelve-year-old girl. They didn't know we had been practicing the game since last Christmas. Before we left, Grandma Svendahl gave each of us a ten-dollar bill and new leather bound Bible with our names in gold on the cover.

There was a new program on the radio that came on every week called the Mystery Theater. I heard the first episode sorta by accident. I was hunting for another program and caught it just as it started and heard the deep scary voice rumble, *"Who knows what evil thoughts lurk in the heart of man. The Shadow knows!"* It nearly scared the life out of me and I had bad dreams for a week. They closed the program with *"The Weeds of Crime Bare Bitter Fruit, Crime Does Not Pay!"* When I tried to tell Cousin Esther the story she got mad because I hadn't called her so she could listen. I told her I was too scared to call and that ended the discussion. I could tell she was still mad but she got over it in a day or two.

In June the Brown Bomber, Joe Louis, knocked out Jim Braddock to regain the world heavy weight championship. 'The Life Of Emile Zola' won the Academy Award but we hadn't seen it yet.

Several months ago, Poppa had begun bottling our milk and selling it to the grocery store. He had allowed several of our female calves to grow up and become producers and now we milked ten cows twice a day which meant we had to get up at five to get it done before the school bus arrived. At night we had to hurry so we could listen to the radio. Poppa sold the milk for eight cents a quart and I think he really appreciated the extra money.

Then, a couple of weeks ago and man from the State Health Department came to the farm and wanted to see the vaccination records for the milk cows. When Poppa said we didn't have any, he shut us down. Poppa said he thought the Adolph Brothers, who have a diary across the river, turned him in. So he took all but three of the cows to market and stopped selling milk. And I was glad we didn't have to milk so many cows. Now maybe I can catch my favorite afternoon programs, like Jack Armstrong, the All American Boy and The Lone Ranger.

In spite of the loss of income, Poppa seemed kinda optimistic about the future. We now had twenty sows and two boars and over fifty shoats ready to be sold. Poppa still got up every morning at five, made coffee and listened to the livestock market report. When that was over he let me listen to the Light Crust Doughboys who came on at six thirty, singing their songs and advertised for the Burrus mills.

Over the past few months Pappy Lee O'Daniel came on during the program extolling the virtues of the products made by the Burrus Mills and his plans for the state when he became Governor. "He's a slick fast talking salesman and I ain't gonna vote for him, he's a fool and an idiot," Poppa said then added, "But he's a Democrat so I reckon he'll be elected." When they signed off, the announcer rang a cowbell indicating they were changing stations.

One morning I asked Poppa if he liked the Light Crust Doughboys.

"Sure, I like them, they're good," he replied then continued, "Heck, they oughta be good. Each one of them gets seven dollars and fifty cents a week and don't have to do a lick of work."

The sheep shearers came in June and sheared all the sheep. Some of the older sheep shearers used traditional hand clippers but the younger ones preferred electric shears, the kind Cousin Esther and me used to cut our hair.

We had a good lamb crop this year. Almost every ewe had a baby and several had twins and no deaths occurred during birthing. Shortly after the lambs were born we cut off their tails and castrated the males. Soon there would be a load of lambs ready for market.

We plowed up the potatoes two weeks ago. The crop was excellent this year and filled twenty sacks that we stored in the smokehouse. So, all in all, life seemed good and we appeared to be secure for the time being if the market didn't collapse before we sold all the animals.

I know times were hard in other parts of the country and even in Arendal. Many people still couldn't find work and the papers continued to show pictures of soup lines and food riots and people standing in long lines for jobs. The AAA was still trying to raise the price of livestock and farm products by controlling production. But they hadn't come around again to kill any more animals. I knew the grain elevator down by the railroad track was full of grain the government had purchased, but I also knew they wouldn't sell any of it to anyone. This didn't make any sense because the paper claimed people all over the country were starving. When I asked Poppa about it he said he thought the government didn't know what the heck they were doing.

The CCC still hired young men and paid them thirty dollars a month to work in the forests planting trees, digging ditches, building reservoirs and fighting fires. They were required to send two thirds of the money to their families.

Then there was the WPA (Works Progress Administration) that hired eight million unemployed men nationwide to build roads, bridges and parks. And there was something called the NRA (National Recovery Administration), another government program to help business recover from the depression. They put up posters in store windows with pictures of a blue eagle.

Sometimes Poppa complained about the amount of money the government was spending trying to build up the economy. "Someone's gonna have to pay for it and I expect it'll be the common folk, like us, who have managed to stay solvent.

Several of my classmates moved with their parents to California where jobs were said to be plentiful. One family returned after two months telling everybody that things were worse there than they were here and the Mexicans and the Chinese got most of the jobs and you actually had to bribe a Union man before you could get a job.

Apparently bad things were happening in Europe. Poppa usually listened to the news every morning, noon and every night and I could tell some of the things he heard upset him a lot. He said there was some crazy man in Germany trying to take over the country and that the people in Washington feared we would have another war.

We always listening to President Roosevelt's Fireside Chats and often listened to the crazy man in Germany scream his speeches. I really didn't know why we listened; none of us understood German but Poppa said we should listen because history was being made.

Ada Mae and Malcolm Moore still refused to give any information about Cousin Angel. They still professed that they had not killed Uncle Ole or Aunt Telinda so they couldn't possibly give any information about the baby. Both still maintained they had been framed and appeals of their sentences were in progress. But I think, and Poppa agreed, that they were both guilty and someday maybe one of them would confess. Then we would know.

Most people in Arendal felt Malcolm had molested Cousin Angel then killed her and buried the body somewhere in the county. The sheriff arranged to have the orchard plowed up but they found nothing. Hunters were always on the lookout for a possible gravesite and me and my cousins spent several Saturdays searching the area around Uncle Ole's farm and along the river looking for a grave but found nothing.

Sheriff Bjornburg assigned one of his deputies to search the Moore house looking for clues to Cousin Angel's disappearance. All he found was stacks and stacks of filthy magazines. The county collected all the magazines and burned them in the square.

Brother Ben came home for the summer in June but couldn't find any work so he helped Poppa run the farm. Counting Aunt Helena's farm that Poppa had leased for a year we had over three hundred acres in cultivation and Poppa was worried that we wouldn't get it all plowed before Brother Ben returned to college. So, Poppa installed lights on the tractor and we plowed day and night from the middle of July until he left for school. Poppa plowed during the day and Brother Ben plowed at night and it appeared, if the weather held, we would finish in time.

I offered to help with the plowing but Poppa said I wasn't old enough and didn't have the experience required to run the tractor, especially at night. So my job was to bring food and water to the tractor drivers and haul ten-gallon cans of kerosene to the field in my red Radio Flyer wagon so they wouldn't have to stop plowing. The only time they stopped was to eat a meal sitting on the tractor seat, fill the tank with kerosene and grease the tractor and the plow. Also we stopped for thirty minutes every third day to change the oil in the oil pan.

At first Bother Ben couldn't sleep during the day but finally he got so tired he could and this was, I think, the time he decided he would never be a farmer. And I was beginning to have the same thoughts as I pulled the wagon to and from the field during the day and by the light of a kerosene lantern at night. I never dreamed, when I wished for the wagon for Christmas when I was six, that I would ever use it to haul kerosene.

I knew Brother Ben was still mad at me but he no longer yelled at me and we pretty much stayed out of each other's way. Sometimes, when I brought his food during the night, he would remain silent or snarl, "Kiss my grits, Knucklehead" and I would stick out my tongue.

We worked seven days a week during the plowing and we didn't go to town on Saturday and we skipped church on Sunday. Pastor Pierson told Poppa we should not consider it a sin because we were doing God's work. I wasn't sure I understood but didn't worry very much about it. And I never got a quarter during this time because we never went to town.

On Sundays, if she could, Cousin Esther would accompany me on my trips to the field and we would talk. Sometimes we talked about Malcolm Moore, sometimes we talked about his mother but usually we just walked together and she helped me pull the wagon resting her hand on mine. Several times, when no one was around, I gave her a little peck on the cheek and she blushed but she didn't object.

I hadn't seen Cousin Joseph since school let out. He was helping his father run their farm. I was a little bit jealous because Poppa wouldn't let me drive our tractor but it really didn't bother me. My main concern was how soon would we finish the plowing so I could get a decent night's sleep.

Chapter Thirty-Eight
A Successful Football Season and Other Concerns

November 1941

It has now been seven years since Cousin Angel disappeared and four years since Malcolm Moore and his mother went to prison for killing my aunt and uncle and we still have no idea what happened to my beautiful baby cousin.

In 1939, Poppa visited Malcolm Moore's mother in the prison hospital shortly before her death from lung cancer. She maintained until her last breath that she and her son were innocent of the charges therefore how could she possibly know anything about Cousin Angel. Poppa came home from the visit very depressed and we gathered in the parlor and join him in prayer.

Having exhausted all his appeals, Malcolm's execution is scheduled for next spring and that seemed our last chance to gain any information. Like his mother, he continued to maintain his innocence in the deaths and had no idea what happened to Cousin Angel. But the evidence was so strong nobody believed them.

Many things have happened since August 1937. Brother Ben dropped out of college before his senior year. Momma said Poppa didn't have enough money to pay his tuition but Sister Sybil said it was because he broke up with his girl friend. Whatever the reasons, he said he planned to get a job and return to school when he had saved enough money.

Grandma Svendahl died in July 1941. She apparently slipped while getting out of her bathtub and became lodged between the bathtub and the commode. She apparently lay there for twelve hours before Uncle Helmer found her. They put her in the Arendal hospital but she died two weeks later, from kidney failure, Dr. Nygard said.

We buried her beside Grampa Svendahl in the Arendal cemetery. There must have been a thousand people at the funeral. The church was packed and the grounds around the church were filled and Poppa said they were mostly relatives. Very few made it to the gravesite and the Arendal Lutheran Church couldn't handle the massive crowd returning for the after funeral meal and many were turned away.

I can't remember the pastor's name. They said he was a Doctor of Theology connected to Luther College who happened to be visiting the area doing research on the Lutheran Church. In the sermon he told us that, when he was a child, he and his father had stayed at Grandma Svendahl's house and had never forgotten the kind treatment and the water well in the kitchen so he felt honored to have the privilege of conduct the services. And a great service it was, it said so in the Arendal Record.

I'm now sixteen and so is Cousin Esther. We're seniors in high school and we'll be seventeen in December. I made the football team in my sophomore year as a guard mostly because of my size and weight. And this year, at six feet and one hundred ninety pounds, the other players elected me Captain of the team that earned me a star to go with the three stripes on my letter sweater.

In September Joe Louis defeated Lou Nova for his eighteenth consecutive win. Most people felt he could never be beaten. He would have to retire before we would have a new champion. In November of 1940, Roosevelt was elected to his third term as President. Poppa let me use the car and Cousin Esther and me went to Waco to see the Academy Award winner, 'How Green Was My Valley'. Cousin Esther cried but I didn't.

Last year, the city built a small hospital and Dr. Nygard brought in a partner, a surgeon, and now they rarely sent patients to Waco. Sister Selma still works for Dr. Nygard making sixty dollars a month. She has her own car, a Model A Ford Roadster with a rumble seat in the back where Cousin Esther and me usually rode. It cost four hundred seventy five dollars and she won't let anyone else drive it, not even Poppa or me. She makes all the house calls and charges a dollar-fifty. She also does all the home deliveries if the doctors are tied up. Again there is some grumbling about charges because office visits are now a dollar and the hospital charges five dollars a day. Dr. Nygard now charges twenty-five dollars for a home delivery even if he isn't present and Sister Selma actually does the delivery. More women now have their babies in the hospital, the total charge being seventy-five dollars for the delivery and a three-day stay.

Sister Sybil is a senior at Luther College in Iowa and plans to go to Norway next summer. Cousin Joseph quit school after his junior year in high school to help his father run the farm.

There are serious troubles in Europe because of the man in Germany who seemed set on taking over the entire continent and maybe the entire world. He made himself Chancellor of Germany in 1937 and annexed part of Czechoslovakia in 1938 then stole the rest of the country in March of 1939.

In October 1939 he attacked Poland. When the Russians joined in the attack, the Polish Government surrendered. Russia invaded Finland in

November 1939 but had great difficulty conquering them and finally signed an agreement with them to stop fighting if Finland would declare its neutrality. Denmark surrendered before being invaded and Norway and Sweden declared neutrality. In spite of Norway's declaration of neutrality, the Germans attacked them because they needed Norwegian resources and deep harbors.

England and France had sworn to defend Poland and sent forces to Belgium to help, but they never had a chance because of the speed of the German attack. As soon as Poland surrendered Hitler attacked Belgium on his way to conquer France and drove the British out of France through the port of Dunkerque.

France surrendered to the Germans on June 25, 1940 and formed the Vichy puppet government friendly to the Nazi. Winston Churchill became prime minister of Britton and the Battle of Britton began.

The war spread to Africa in 1940 and to Yugoslavia in an attack on April 10, 1941. The Battle of Briton spread to the oceans as Germany's submarines blockaded the sea-lanes used by ships to bring food to Britton; and the air war continued.

Growing more worried, the U.S. enacted the Lend Lease program in March 1941 designed to help Briton and its allies. In September 1940 the United States Congress enacted the Selective Training and Service Act and began to draft young men for duty in the Armed Services. In August of this year they extended the draft for another year.

In spite of a treaty between the two, Germany invaded USSR on June 22, 1941 and hoped to take Moscow before cold weather set in. However winter arrived early and now they seemed bogged down around Moscow.

There was also trouble with Japan. They invaded Asia several years ago and now controlled all if Korea and most of China. Because of these warlike actions we stopped supplying them with oil and discontinued shipping them scrap iron in June of this year. In an attempt to regain those resources, they tried to arrange a treaty with the United States but President Roosevelt turned them down. Now there are two of their statesmen in Washington trying to negotiate a settlement.

I knew all of this because our teachers insists we follow the events closely and frequently gave us tests on the subject. Like Poppa, I listened to the radio every day and sometimes glanced at the front page of the Fort Worth Star Telegram. But I was more interested in the comics, especially the Katzenjammer Kids and Mutt & Jeff. I realized I should be worried about all these warlike actions but I had other worries that to me were more important than any war like how to win Cousin Esther back. We broke up just before school started this year and I was devastated because it was my fault and this was when I knew I loved her more than anything else in the world. And I was certain she felt the same way about me.

In July she went to live with relatives in Waco because Aunt Helena had to have cancer surgery. I wanted her to stay with us and so did she and so did Momma but her mother wanted her in Waco. Apparently she felt temptation might overcome us.

I didn't see her for two months and one Saturday, two weeks before school started, I took Thora Pierson, Pastor Pierson's daughter, to the movie followed by a visit to the Corner Drug Store for Coke float. I don't know why I did it; I liked her but not nearly as much as I liked Cousin Esther. I guess I was just lonely.

Cousin Esther somehow found out about it and wrote me a scathing letter stating she never wanted to see me again and to give back the picture she had given me for Christmas. I tried to call her on the telephone but she wouldn't speak to me.

I felt when she came home and we started to school we would make up. Apparently her anger was more than I realized and when she started dating Jim Olson, I knew I had a serious problem. If she would just talk to me maybe we could patch things up. And I was certain she would be interested in someone with three stripes and a star on his letter sweater, but she wasn't.

When school started in September my spirits sank when she left my last year's football letter sweater on my desk. They sank even further when she returned the necklace I had given her on her last birthday. And I thought I would cry the first time I saw her wearing Jim's letter sweater. Although it was too big for her somehow she made it fit.

I refused to go to town on Saturdays for fear of seeing them together in the drug store or in the movie house holding hands and maybe smooching. I quit going to Luther League for the same reasons and dropped out of my Sunday school class but I continued to sing with the Choral Group. For some reason both Cousin Esther and Jim quit coming to church and I envisioned them somewhere together enjoying each other's company and doing things I didn't want to think about.

My heart skipped a beat every time I saw her at school. She wouldn't acknowledge my presence when we passed in the hall and refused to accept my notes passed to her between classes.

She was so beautiful with long blond hair falling around her shoulders and at five ten she was the tallest girl in our class. It made me mad when I heard one of my classmates describe her as, 'well put together.' And Momma called her our Norwegian Princess. If I could just hold her and put my arms around her and feel her cheek against mine, I'd be the happiest man in the world.

When I found out she would be Jim's date to the football banquet I felt my life had come to an end. I couldn't bring myself to ask another girl so I went alone. And when I saw her enter the hall on his arm and saw her sitting by his side at another table laughing at his stupid jokes, I realized how much I loved her and how much I missed her. At that moment I pledged to get her back no matter the cost. She was mine. She belonged to me.

Anton Heidl escaped from the TYC and showed up in Arendal the first weekend in July. But when Sheriff Bjornburg tried to find him he was gone. Some said he joined the Arney, others said he went to Galveston to find work on a ship. Most people felt he would eventually come to no good and would probably end up in prison.

I finished my 4H project in February of this year when I took my calf to the Fat Stock Show in Fort Worth. I didn't win anything but sold the calf for almost two hundred dollars. When I squared accounts with Poppa I had cleared about seventy-five dollars. I put the money in a savings account at the bank earning one percent interest and received an A+ on my Ag report.

It seemed to me that the depression was about over and now there was actually a shortage of farm workers. That made it more difficult for farmers to make a living although they now could produce as much as they pleased. The government bought the surplus at a fair price and sent it oversea, but this didn't help the farmers. There weren't enough workers to handle the increased production and the workers who were available demanded more money, at least four dollars a day and Poppa wondered how he could possibly make a living.

Roosevelt claimed credit for the improvement in the economy and Poppa agreed, but it seemed to me that the war in Europe was what made the difference. Now there are jobs everywhere and the Hobo Jungle is empty.

Chapter Thirty-Nine
So Now It's War

December 8, 1941

It was Sunday, December 7, 1941 when it happened. Our little Choral Group had been asked to sing at the Lutheran church in Waco. We were to sing at both services, the one at nine and the one at eleven so I left the house shortly after seven to pick up the rest of the quartet. Poppa said he needed to stay home and take care of Momma because she felt another headache coming on so he let me take the car.

We had formed our little group at the first of the school year and were often invited to sing at various functions in the Arendal area. About a month ago we sang at the local Baptist Church and I took Communion. When I told Momma about it, she became extremely upset because I had taken Communion in that heathen place. She called Pastor Pierson who told her the Body and Blood of Christ was the same everywhere, even in the Baptist church. I never told her about our visit to the Catholic Church. She would have had a stroke or at least a sick headache that would probably have lasted a month.

I had never attended a Catholic service before and was surprised how similar it was to ours and I wondered why Momma was so against them. If Cousin Esther and I ever made up, I'll ask her and she can ask her mother who knows everything.

When we got home, Momma was waiting at the back gate waving her arms and screaming, "The Japs bombed Pearl Harbor! The Japs bombed Pearl Harbor!" Poppa immediately came out of the house and tried to calm her down.

I had no idea why she was so upset. I had never heard of Pearl Harbor and I assumed it was some remote fishing village somewhere in the Pacific. Poppa seemed about as upset as Momma, but why? The Japs were always stirring up trouble somewhere. But when he said Pearl Harbor was in Hawaii it finally sunk in. The Japs had attacked the United States of America!

"Does it mean war?" I asked Poppa and he answered, "Probably."

Together, we sat in front of the radio until time to do the chores. Several times I heard Poppa mutter, "We're gonna wipe them slant-eyed idiots off the face of the earth. They won't get by with attacking Hawaii."

During the evening it sounded to me like things weren't going well, not like we thought they should go. Our warships docked at Pearl Harbor had apparently been sunk but the radio announcer said that our aircraft carriers were somewhere at sea and were apparently safe. He also said that the Japs had invaded the Philippians and were trying to invade Hawaii. And by the time we finally went to bed it was midnight, Momma was crying and Poppa didn't look much better.

The next day we got nothing done at school. The teachers in every class wanted to talk about the situation and what might happen. Some said Japan had already invaded California and one teacher said the Jap bombers were headed for Texas and we practiced hiding under our desks if an air raid occurred.

Professor Roberts summoned all the students to the Auditorium after lunch so we could hear President Roosevelt address congress. He tuned the radio, increased the volume, the room fell silent and we heard, *"Yesterday, December 7, 1941, a day that will live in infamy, the United States was suddenly and deliberately attacked by naval and air forces of the Empire of Japan."* After thunderous applause from congress, he made a few more remarks, then concluded with, *"I ask that congress declare that since the unprovoked and dastardly attack by Japan on Sunday, December 7th, a state of war has existed between the United Stats and the Japanese Empire."*

There wasn't a sound in the room until Professor Roberts requested that we join him in prayer and we did. I could tell he was quite upset.

After the meeting I looked for Cousin Esther and when out eyes met she threw herself in my arms and I smothered her with kisses and told her how much I loved her and she kissed me back and told me how much she loved me.

I knew I should be worried about the war. But how could I, I had Cousin Esther back. I didn't have to worry about anything. She put on my football letter sweater and we walked back to our room arm in arm. We met Jim Olson in the hall and when he saw us together he spread his arms and Cousin Esther told him to get lost. She told him she would return his sweater in the morning. I hardly slept that might because of the joy of having Cousin Esther back. And the war was the last thing on my mind.

Chapter Forty
Confession

April 1942

Things changed rapidly after the beginning of hostilities. Although we had declared war on both Germany and Japan, all efforts seemed to be directed toward the war in Europe. Japan would come later our teachers said.

A week after December 7th, Brother Ben volunteered for the Navy but they turned him down because of his weight. He went on a severe diet, lost thirty pounds and three months later they accepted him. When he came home on leave after boot camp, he had lost another thirty pounds and looked great in his bellbottoms with the funny flap on the front and the sailor hat cocked jauntily on the back of his head. When he left he said he had orders to report to a ship but wouldn't tell us what ship or where they were going. "Loose lips sink ships," he said.

The Draft Board started calling up men and sending them off to training camps. Two of my classmates, who were now eighteen years old, quit school and joined the Marines. Cousin Joseph, over his father's strong objections, left home and joined the Army. B.J. Dahlen tried to enlist but the Army turned him down because of his asthma and the Draft Board classified him 4F.

By March of 1942 rationing and coupons became a way of life. Because of the war, jobs were available almost everywhere. Many who worked on the farms had been drafted into the service. Others left town to work in the factories near Fort Worth making aircraft or in the automobile factory in Dallas making trucks for the Army.

Almost anything you purchased, if it was available, required a coupon of one sort or another. Tags obtained from the local rationing board and pasted on your car windshield indicated your priority in obtaining gasoline. A, B, & C tags entitled you to buy three gallons a week; a T tag got you ten gallons a week and an X tag got you unlimited supply but was only available to important persons like Congressmen and Senators. Farmers had the highest priority for fuel oil and could get almost unlimited supply for their trucks, cars and tractors. Ordinary citizens had the lowest priority and that effectively prevented unnecessary travel. New cars were not available. The automobile factories used all their resources to make trucks and tanks and airplanes so everyone kept their cars in running condition as long as possible.

Coupon books issued monthly were necessary to buy almost anything including meat, butter, eggs, clothing and shoes. Candy, soft drinks, alcoholic beverages and chocolate were not rationed but were scarce. The adage USE IT UP, WEAR IT OUT, MAKE IT DO, OR DO WITHOUT, ruled the day. The war effort and our troops came first.

Tires were only available from the rationing board to essential individuals like policemen, city officials and firemen. Many wives of men who had gone into the service left the area to work in the defense factories. It seemed like everyone now had a job and money was available but there was little you could buy so people bought War Bonds.

I was only seventeen so I didn't have to worry about the draft until next year. Poppa said he might go to the daft board and ask for a deferment stating he needed me in the production of products essential to the war effort.

I wasn't too happy about it because he didn't even ask for my opinion, but I knew he couldn't run the farm alone and the things we produced were essential so I did not object, at least not then and not to him.

It upset Cousin Ester when I mentioned my desire to join the Navy like Brother Ben. With tears in her eyes, she murmured, "Jacob, please don't go."

"But Esther, so many of our classmates have either been drafted or volunteered, it makes me feel like I'm shirking my patriotic duty."

"I know," she replied and grabbed my hand. She didn't let go until the bell summoned us to our next class.

Two weeks ago, Malcolm Moore, who had a date with the electric chair, wrote a letter asking Poppa to visit him in prison. He had exhausted all appeals and his execution date had been set for May 1st. In the letter he said he was trying to get straight with the Lord before he died and that he had something important to get off his chest. We assumed it concerned Uncle Ole and Aunt Telinda and maybe Baby Angel.

Not wishing to waste gasoline Poppa took the train to Huntsville and met with the man. The visit took all afternoon and Poppa missed the return train and slept on a bench in the train station until the next morning. Momma was very worried when he didn't come home and called Sheriff Bjornburg who assured her he was okay because nowadays trains were always hours behind schedule. The next day he returned and late in the afternoon he invited all members of the family including Uncles and Aunts and a few cousins who were still around to meet with him in the church. He asked Pastor Pierson to attend because he felt serious praying would be in order.

He began by telling us he had talked with Malcolm Moore and he believed most of the man's story was true. He felt Malcolm was truly repentant and had come to know the Lord and wished to cleanse his soul and seek forgiveness for his many sins before he left this world.

"Back in 1934 before their house burned down, Malcolm told me he was working for Uncle Ole cleaning out his orchard. One day Baby Angel came to visit him in the orchard and he was so taken by her beauty that he picked her up and held her to his body. His passions became inflamed and he took her to the barn and molested her. He told me what he did but I can't repeat it, not now and maybe never."

"When Uncle Ole heard the child screaming, he went to the barn to see what was wrong. When he opened the door and saw what Malcolm was doing, he grabbed the screaming child and said, "You bastard, I'm gonna call the sheriff and get you locked up for the rest of your life." Malcolm begged him not to go to the sheriff saying he would work for him for a year for nothing if only he would forget about the incident. When Uncle Ole refused, Malcolm grabbed a crowbar and crushed his skull. Malcolm then picked up the baby, went to the house and killed Aunt Telinda. Suddenly realizing what he had done, he took the baby and went home."

"He said his mother had quizzed him for hours about the baby and finally he admitted what he had done. Together they returned to the farm and buried Uncle Ole and Aunt Telinda in the orchard. They took the baby and went home but the next day they went back and piled tree limbs on the graves. His mother suggested they burn the house and make it look like Uncle Ole had left town with his family She wrote the note found in the mailbox and they prepared to set the fire. Then she suggested that they move all the furniture to the garage and maybe they could sell it later after the investigation was completed."

"After moving all the furniture, which took several hours, they hid Uncle Ole's truck in a ravine about a mile away, then started the fire and left when they heard the fire truck in the distance. They still had the baby who continued to cry most of the time. Malcolm said he did not try to molest her again. He wanted to but his mother forbid it."

"Malcolm's mother searched the area, found the cave and stored the gun and the bullets. When winter came they added the coat and when he removed the license plates from my brother's car, he took them to the cave."

Sitting on the ledge in front of the cave, they discovered they could see the entire area without being seen. Mrs. Moore quit her job and every day one of them went to the cave and watched the farm. He said if he had work to do, she would go. If he didn't have a job, he would go."

"I asked him who shot me and he said his mother did. He said he was working for Gus McDougal at the time and she told him when he got home. I asked him about the masks and he said that was his mother's idea. They bought them in Waco and wore them when they thought they might be seen."

"When they realized the sheriff was going to dig up the graves, they moved the bodies by the light of a full moon and dropped them in the well and secured the lid."

"He said they were both there when we found the bodies. He said his mother wanted to shoot the sheriff and all the rest but there were too many armed officers."

"He said he disposed of the truck after they sold the furniture by pushing it into the Paluxy River hoping it would never be found. He said he wanted to throw the gun in the river but his mother felt it could eventually be sold just like the furniture, so they left it and the other items in the cave. He felt if they had disposed of everything, they would never have been caught and I agreed."

"What about the football?" I asked.

"He said they found it when they pulled the bucket out of the well."

"And how about Cousin Angel?" Cousin Esther asked.

"I'm getting to that," Poppa replied, "but I'm not sure I believe his story. He said his mother took the baby to the Hobo Jungle and gave her to a barren couple on their way to California. He didn't know what happened to her after that. His did say the couple's name was 'Arrensen', a Swedish family who she felt would take good care of the baby."

Cousin Esther raised her hand and asked, "Uncle Gunder, did Malcolm see who tried to assault me?"

"Yes he did," Poppa answered. "He said it was the man the sheriff arrested sleeping under the bridge, the one the inmates killed in the jailhouse. He said he saw the attack, but when the man saw him, he ran away. Seems to me like Malcolm Moore saved you from a heap of trouble."

We sat in the church sanctuary and discussed the news for an hour. Then we joined hands and Pastor Pierson prayed a very emotional prayer. *"Almighty God, we beg Thee to guard Baby Angel under Thy protective wing and if it be Thy will, return her to her rightful family. But God, if in Your Infinite Judgment, she is safe and happy with her present family, leave her there and guide her through life in Thy footsteps that she may stand by Thy side on that glorious Judgment Day reborn in Thy blessed image. Thy will be done, Amen."*

"Amen," we all responded.

Everyone cried, then they all left except Aunt Helena and Cousin Esther who were crying so hard they couldn't leave. I held her and whispered in her ear until she stopped, then they left.

The war apparently was not going well. The Japs had invaded the Philippians and occupied Guam, Wake and Midway islands. They had invaded Indonesia and were moving toward Hong Kong. They had occupied Malaysia, Burma, Borneo, Singapore, East Indies and New Guinea and they were poised to invade Australia. Bataan fell on April 9th and the brave souls on Corregidor were in a pitched battle for their lives.

I still wasn't too worried about the war but I tried to keep track by listening to the radio, especially H.V.Kaltenborn and Edward R. Marrow who came on every night and summarized events of the day. There would be a quiz in the Current Events class at the end of the term and I wanted to do well on the test.

Cousin Esther and I were inseparable during these trying times. We talked about my deferment when I reached eighteen and my unspoken desire to go in the service. We even discussed marriage but made no definite plans. When Momma got wind of my desire to enter the service she threw a fit. "Poppa can't get along without you," she wailed. "Besides, I don't want you to go off to some strange place and get killed. I already got one son in danger. Stay here where it's safe."

And when she found out we were considering marriage she threw a bigger fit.

"You can't marry your cousin," she cried. "Your father and I will be disgraced and so would Aunt Helena. Pastor Pierson would refuse to marry you and you would be fools enough to run off to some heathen establishment and be married by some infidel. Your children might be born dead or so abnormal you'd have to put them away in some institution."

"But, Momma, President Roosevelt married his cousin and their children are okay," I replied.

"Only rich people are that lucky," she answered. That ended the argument and shortly she came down with one of her sick headaches that lasted almost two weeks.

That night, a new idea seized my mind. We would wait until after the war, get married but not have any children. We would leave Arendal, hunt for Baby Angel and adopt her as our own. She would be about thirteen or fourteen by then depending on how long the war lasted.

The next day I told Cousin Esther about my plan and she was thrilled.

"Let's start as soon as we're eighteen," she suggested. "We can get a marriage license in Arkansas. Or in Mexico." We discussed the suggestion for an hour until we both realized it wouldn't work. If I left the farm my deferment would be cancelled and I would be drafted immediately. And if I didn't report for induction I would be classified as a draft dodger and put in prison.

Neither of us had much money and no transportation. The chance for getting money from our parents was slim to nil. So we decided it would be best to wait until the war was over. In the meantime we would save our money and try to get more information about the people who took the child. But how do you find a missing person who probably lived in California? At that point we didn't have a clue about how or where to start. Maybe Sheriff Bjornburg could give us advice. But if we went to him, he would tell our parents. So, in the end we did nothing. We both decided we needed to concentrate on final exams and graduation that was set for May 29th.

Chapter Forty-One
Another Death

I was sitting in the study hall that day, May 20, 1942, waiting to take my last test of the year. It would be an easy test covering current events, mostly about the war. I hadn't even studied for it because I kept up with the news very closely.

It was a little difficult to tell who was winning the war at this point. We were now sending supplies, planes and ships to Europe and Russia and there was talk of invading Africa. The Philippians had fallen, France was now a puppet state under the Vichy government and the Germans were bombing England every night. The Japs had seemingly stopped their invasions after they lost most of their fleet in the Battle of Midway and later in the battle of Coral Sea and Leyte Gulf.

Now everybody had a job and those who didn't enter the service worked in essential industry. We were getting use to rationing and continued to buy war bonds and collect anything that was scarce like iron, tin foil, even gum wrappers. Farmers planted as many crops as they could handle and older men replaced the boys on the farms. Silk stockings were unavailable because silk was used to make parachutes. So, women went barelegged and painted a stripe down the back of their legs to simulate the seams.

Rubber tires were unavailable so everyone became proficient in patching the ones they had. Tires made of synthetic rubber were available but no one would buy them because they were expensive and wore out in a few months and were forever going flat. To save gasoline, the speed limit was reduced to thirty-five miles an hour.

Cousin Esther and I were anxiously looking forward to graduation. She was the Salutatorian of the class and I wasn't far behind. Suzie Swisher, who had returned to the Arendal School two years ago, was the Valedictorian and Beauty Queen at the Junior Senior prom. Jim Olson, her escort, was voted the Most Popular Boy. They had become an item last winter. We elected J. B. Dahlen the class president even though he spent most of his time on the schoolhouse steps smoking the medicinal cigarettes he used to treat his asthma. I don't know what they were called but they stunk almost as bad as the prickly pear leaf and no one could stay around him when he smoked.

We voted not to have a Senior Annual because film was scarce and no one said they would buy one if we did. However we did have the Junior Senior Prom last weekend at the town auditorium. Like always there was no dancing even though we had voted to allow it. The School Board overturned our decision because they felt it was evil and would surely lead to lascivious behavior.

My date for the prom was, of course, Cousin Esther. Poppa allowed me to use the car and after the prom we went to Lake Waco, sat in the moonlight and talked about everything and anything, mostly about the war, until three in the morning. And when I got home Poppa gave me my last whipping. Momma, as usual, cried about our actions certain we had committed carnal sin as she called it. She didn't believe me when I tried to explain we had done nothing wrong. I didn't know until later that she had called Pastor Pierson who assured her we were good kids. I think he maybe settled both she and Poppa down and the next morning, they acted as if nothing had happened. I think Poppa was maybe a little ashamed of himself.

When Professor Roberts came to my desk and said I was needed at home and for me to leave immediately, I didn't know quite what to think. The only time that had happened before was when Grampa Yo died.

Anxiety building, I told Cousin Esther where I was going, then hurriedly left the building. I had inherited Brother Ben's old car and usually drove it to school, when it would run. I was trying to teach Cousin Esther to drive it but she hadn't yet mastered the three pedals.

The car, as usual, proved difficult to start. After adjusting the throttle and the spark lever it required eight or ten turns of the crank to get it going. And when it started, it struggled over the hill, then sailed down the other side and across the Flat headed toward our farm. Just before I got to our gate, I met the funeral home hearse headed toward Arendal. I crossed the cattle guard and skidded to a stop in the back yard between Uncle Andrew's truck and Dr. Nygard's car. I jumped out of the car, dashed to the back porch, threw open the kitchen door and found Momma in hysterics. Dr. Nygard followed me into the kitchen, put his arm around my shoulder and said, "Jacob, your father is dead."

"What!!" I screamed.

"Apparently he was trying to change the tire on his tractor and somehow it slipped off the block and crushed his chest killing him instantly. Your mother saw it happen and called her brother. When he got here, he used a block and tackle to lift the tractor, but it was too late.

At first I couldn't comprehend what he was saying. Nothing made any sense. Then I remembered that he had asked me yesterday to change the tire and I forgot; my mind filled with final exams and Cousin Esther. As that sunk in, I began to cry almost as hard as Momma.

Dr. Nygard offered both Momma and me a sedative. Momma took hers but I refused. I could handle my guilt and grief without resorting to drugs.

In a few minutes Sister Selma arrived and took charge of everything. Dr. Nygard had called her from the hospital and told her what had happened. She took Momma to the bedroom and made her lie down and finally got her calmed down and Dr. Nygard went back to the hospital to attend a delivery.

It wasn't long until Aunt Helena and Cousin Esther arrived. Sister Selma had called her from the hospital and she immediately went to the school and pulled Cousin Esther out of class. When they arrived I fell into her arms and continued to cry and she patted my back and rubbed my shoulders until I calmed down. We went out on the back porch and I confessed my sins of yesterday and again began to cry. "It wasn't your fault," she kept repeating until the crying again stopped. Then we went to our favorite place, the hayloft, and sat there until suppertime. By then the yard was full of cars, some I recognized, many I didn't.

There was something comforting about sitting by her side. When I cried, she cried, when I stopped she stopped and I knew I loved her more than anything in this world. In spite of my grief, I knew I could take her in any way that I wanted and she would not resist, we were that much in love. But nothing happened. I think the realization of our longing for each other scared us both and we backed away from the precipice of mortal sin. But god I wanted her as a woman and I know she wanted me as a man.

We went in the house and looked at the food friends and relatives had brought. I ate a drumstick and a small bowl of chocolate pudding. I could eat nothing else.

Digger Olson said it was the biggest funeral he had ever supervised. Flowers filled the church sanctuary, all the seats were full and people stood out in the yard. Cousin Esther sat by my side and held my hand. The choir sang Poppa's favorite song, 'Abide With Me' and I cried. Then Pastor Pierson preached the most eloquent sermon I had ever heard extolling Poppa's virtues and good deeds and that his family, the church, and the community would sorely miss him. Then he asked God's blessings on the family, the choir sang another song and the bell in the steeple began its mournful chime. The family stood beside the casket and Momma placed a rose bud on Poppa's chest and kissed him goodbye. Then Digger Olson closed the lid and the pallbearers moved the casket to the hearse.

The two-mile funeral procession stretched from the church to the cemetery and filled all the gravel roads between the graves. Many people parked on the highway and walked to the open gravesite, some from as far as a mile.

Poppa had grown up in Arendal and I guess he knew everybody and everybody knew him. In a way it made me feel better and it certainly made me proud of my father. I did feel sorry for Brother Ben. The Red Cross had been unable to locate him and we didn't know if he even knew about the death. Maybe that was best because we were told they would not have allowed him to come home, even for his father's death.

After everyone arrived at the gravesite and Digger seated the immediate family, he slowly lowered the casket into the grave. Pastor Pierson shoveled three scoops of dirt on the coffin, then intoned, *"Almighty God, Creator of Heaven and Earth, we commend to Thee the soul of our dearly departed brother, Gunder Svendahl and we commit his body to the ground. Earth to earth, ashes to ashes, dust to dust in sure and certain hope of the resurrection to eternal life. Guard him under Thy protective wing until that glorious day when we shall all stand by Your side."*

He paused and then continued, *"I am the Resurrection and the Life. Whosoever believeth in me, though he be dead, yet shall he live. And whosoever believeth in me shall never die. I am the Alpha and the Omega, the Beginning and the End. God have mercy on us and forgive us our many sins that we may join Gunder on that glorious day when we shall all stand together, reborn in Thy Holy Image."* He raised his arms to the sky then said, *"May the Lord bless you and keep you. May the Lord Make His Face to shine upon you and be gracious unto you. May the Lord lift up his countenance upon you and grant you everlasting peace this day and evermore."* He paused again, then said, *"In the name of the Father, and of the Son, and of the Holy Ghost, Amen."*

"Amen," we repeated and then departed.

We returned to the church for the traditional post-funeral feast repaired by the Ladies Aid Society. In spite of my grief, I found that I was famished and must have sampled every dish on the long serving table. Cousin Esther and I sat on the steps on the side of the church and talked about the day and our future.

I knew there were many decisions the family had to make while we were all together. What would happen to the farm? Who would take care of

Momma? Who would tend to the livestock and see that they were taken to market at the proper time? Who would harvest the current crops? Should the farm be sold or leased out to somebody? What about all the farm implements, the truck, the tractor, the combine, the various plows?

I could do the daily chores but could I run the farm? Would the family let me take over? I doubted it. To them I was a spoiled brat of a brother who could not and would not assume that much responsibility.

Certainly Momma couldn't run things. Her negative outlook about everything and her frequent illnesses would prevent it. I knew Brother Ben couldn't run the farm, maybe after the war, but not now.

Sister Selma would probably marry a farmer from another county she was dating. But he had expressed no interest in abandoning his farm and taking over ours. Sister Sybil had absolutely no interest in farming and would probably go into teaching or maybe music when she graduated from college. So what were we to do?

Aunt Helena inquired about the possibility of buying the farm but we knew she could never swing it with the bank. Uncle Andrew showed no interest. "With my sons gone, I got more than I can handle now," he replied. So he was out of the picture. Maybe we could solve the dilemma at the family meeting scheduled for next Sunday.

I asked Cousin Esther for her opinion. Her only comment was that it would be a nice farm for us to run after we get married and I agreed. But who would run it until then?

The family meeting was an absolute disaster. All the old grievances spilled out like pus from a putrid boil. Everybody blamed everybody else for past injustices, real or imagined. Sister Selma blamed me for Poppa's death. Even though he wasn't there Sister Sybil said Brother Ben's education almost bankrupted Poppa. Then Sister Selma told Sister Sybil her education did bankrupt Poppa and he had to borrow a bunch of money from the bank so she could finish.

I wanted to give the farm to momma but other members of the family did not agree stating their fears that some land shark might fleece Momma out of her inheritance. Aunt Helena blamed Momma for spoiling her child. Uncle Andrew expressed some grievance I didn't understand concerning a promise Poppa made and never kept many years ago. It made my sisters mad and they began to scream at him and he screamed back. Soon everybody was shouting at everybody else and I was afraid a fight might erupt. That's when Momma called Pastor Pierson and asked him to come to the house. She had been crying for the last hour and said she felt one of her headaches coming on.

Pastor Pierson arrived in about fifteen minutes and asked us to hold hands while he prayed. He stayed for two hours while we slowly carefully negotiated a settlement. Then, after another prayer, he left.

The final decision was as follows: we would sell the farm after the crops were all in. We would sell the cattle, the sheep, the chickens and the pigs for the best price we could get. Momma would move to the Lutheran Retirement Center after the farm sold.

I would continue to run the farm for now. I was to arrange for the sale of the animals, harvest and sell the wheat, oats, barley and the corn to the feed mill. I would receive five dollars a day from the proceeds of the sales and would deposit all monies collected into a special account in her name at the bank. Poppa had died without a will so a lawyer had to be contacted to handle probate. It was also decided that the lawyer should handle the estate and look after Momma's finances and make periodic reports to Sister Selma.

All in all, I was satisfied with the arrangement, but when Sister Selma asked how I stood with the draft board, I realized I had a problem. As long as we had the farm and I was responsible for running it my deferred status wouldn't change. But after the sale I was sure I would be reclassified 1-A and would be drafted almost immediately. So what should I do?

Chapter Forty-Two
Wedding Plans

Things went reasonably well with the plan. I graduated from High School in May 1942, a week after Poppa's funeral and began the serious business of running the farm. I hauled all the cattle and the young pigs to the auction barn in Arendal. I could have gotten a little better price in Fort Worth but I was afraid the car wouldn't make it that far. The truck had quit running several months ago and the mechanic at the repair shop said he couldn't get any parts to fix it so it sat on blocks in the garage most likely until the end of the war.

It took several months to do it but I finally sold all the chickens. The laying hens went to a colored family who lived across the river. I sold all the fryers to a restaurant in Waco. A hog farmer in the next county bought all the sows and both boars and Sister Selma's boyfriend bought all the sheep at a special price that she negotiated.

I harvested all the oats, wheat and barley and sold it to the feed mill down by the railroad track. I ended up plowing up the corn because it was doing poorly due to the dry weather. Now Momma had over a thousand dollars in the bank after paying off the loan Poppa had made at the bank several years ago.

We had no offers for the farm so in the fall I began to plow and later planted wheat and oats. I knew I wasn't expected to do it but it seemed a shame to let good farmland lay fallow. In my spare time I enrolled as a freshman in Arendal Junior College arranging my courses to allow time to run the farm.

Cousin Esther also enrolled in college but dropped out after one week. She couldn't fit it into her schedule as the head salesperson and cashier at the Dry Goods store. Also, she didn't feel the courses they offered would be of any value to her. Instead, she wanted to enroll in the business school in Waco or Dallas as soon as she saved enough money.

Finally, in May of this year we sold the farm. The sale would close on August 1, 1943 giving me time to finish harvesting the grain. Momma said she planned to move to the retirement home right away, but when the time came to move, she refused. She said she just couldn't abandon the hopes and dreams of thirty-five years of toil. So, she stayed on the farm and I watched after her and I guess she watched after me. But we both knew she would have to move once the sale was final.

I had little chance to spend time with Cousin Esther. We rarely saw each other during the week. I was too busy with farm work and college and she worked six days a week at the dry goods store. But, every Sunday we attended church together and usually went to Waco to eat and see the afternoon movie.

Those were such happy days. We saw 'Gone With The Wind' and I fell in love with Vivian Leigh and Cousin Esther fell in love with Clark Gable. I'm only kidding; we loved each other too much to fall for make believe celluloid fantasies.

One Sunday we saw a rerun of 'Wizard of Oz' and talked about it all the way home. I told Cousin Esther that 'Dorothy' reminded me of her, she was so pretty, cheerful and wholesome.

While we were in Waco, we usually ate at the downtown Elite Café or the one at the Circle. We remembered both from high school trips and liked the food. You could get a t-bone steak with potatoes and gravy and a piece of apple pie for a dollar forty-nine or a hamburger, French Fries, and a soft drink for ninety-nine cents. And on the way home we always talked about the future.

We were now eighteen and Cousin Esther worried constantly about my going into the service after the farm sold and I lost my deferment. One day she blurted out, "Why don't we get married? Then you wouldn't get drafted." I thought about it for a minute then said, "They may not be drafting married men now but if the war continues, everybody is going to get drafted, married or not."

"You just don't want to marry me, you want to marry Thora Pierson!" she teased.

"That's not true. I want to marry you but don't you remember, we agreed to wait until after the war."

"Don't you want to make love to me?"

"Certainly I do, but not until we're married."

"Then let's get married and we can make love every day and every night." She leaned over and kissed me full on the lips and it took all my manpower to resist her charms right there on the road from Waco. I knew she was teasing me but I also knew she wasn't kidding. We kissed for many minutes until the passions faded, then we drove home.

Over the next few days I thought about her suggestion. Maybe it would work. Maybe if we married I wouldn't get drafted. I could work at one of the defense plants; heck we could both work at the same place. They were crying for workers, both men and women. By the next weekend I had reached a decision and I proposed to her and she accepted. Now all we had to do was get our parent's consent.

I knew both Momma and Aunt Helena would throw a wall-eyed fit about it. I could hear them now. "You're too young," Aunt Helena would say. "Neither of you are old enough to know what your doing. You're both just kids."

Then Cousin Esther would say, "But momma, you were eighteen when you got married." And her mother would answer, "When I was eighteen, I was much more mature than you are."

I knew Momma was eighteen and Poppa was twenty-one when they married. But when I mentioned that, she replied, "Poppa needed me so we got married. You don't need each other; you're both independent and self-sufficient. Besides cousins should not marry."

I had already told her President Roosevelt married his cousin. But when I told her if we got married I wouldn't be drafted and sent to fight the Germans or the Japs and wouldn't be killed she seemed to listen. I reminded her that Arendal already had two casualties in the Pacific, young men my age who had gone down when their ship was sunk by a Jap torpedo. I think maybe that's what did it. Fearing I might die, she grudgingly gave her consent.

It took a little longer to get Aunt Helena's approval. Nothing we said seemed to make a difference. But when we said we were going to run away and get married in Mexico, she relented and we set the date for June 30, 1943, a month before the sale of the farm would be final and I would loose my exemption from the draft.

Both Momma and Aunt Helena complained bitterly that the time was too short to properly prepare for a marriage. Invitations had to be mailed out, wedding dresses had to be made for the bride and the bridesmaids, The three mandatory sessions with Pastor Pierson to discuss all the pitfalls of wedded life had to be arranged.

"Maybe he would shorten the sessions to one or maybe two at the most," I suggested. "After all, these are unusual times."

It took three days to iron out the details. It would be a very informal wedding on July 20th with only the immediate friends and family. Cousin Esther would wear her mother's wedding gown that fit her perfectly and there would be only one maid of honor, Aunt Helena. And Uncle Andrew agreed to be my best man.

Cousin Esther wanted to have the wedding at our house but so many classmates and relatives wanted to attend, we moved it to the church.

I went to the draft board and told them I was getting married. "What's the matter, son? You knock up your girlfriend?" the head of the draft board, a crusty retired judge who lived in a small town in another part of the county, asked.

"No sir," I replied. "We just want to get married."

"If you think that'll kept you out of the draft I got bad news for you. We expect orders by the end of the year to start calling young married men if they ain't got no children so you better get her pregnant right away if you ain't already." I decided not to tell either Cousin Esther or Momma or Aunt Helena about the conversation at the draft board, it would only make them mad and Aunt Helena would go down there and raise heck him and probably cuss him out.

We celebrated our coming wedding by going to Waco to see a movie but I don't think either of us knew what we saw. We spent the time kissing and hugging and touching and on the way home we stopped at the city park and continued to neck and I knew I could take her and she wouldn't resist. But I also knew if I did, she would hate me in the morning and that I couldn't stand. I knew that was no way to start a marriage. So, in the end we drove home and I took her to the front door and kissed her goodnight.

Chapter Forty-Three
Brother Ben

The telegram arrived on the Monday before our wedding. Uncle Andrew and I were almost through harvesting when I saw a car pull into our drive and stop in front of our house. Curious as to the nature of the visit, I stopped the tractor and watched but nobody got out. In a moment the car headed toward the field and stopped at the gate. And when the man got of the car and started in our direction, my heart stopped beating. It was the man from the telegraph office.

"Howdy Jacob, howdy Andrew. I got bad news and I reckon y'all better be with your mother when I deliver it."

"What does the telegram say?" I asked knowing it was probably something bad. Several local families had received the dreaded yellow envelope and now I guess it was our turn.

"Cain't tell you, I gotta deliver it to your Mother."

So I turned off the motor and ran to the house arriving just as the man mounted the front steps.

Momma opened the door before he knocked and when she saw the yellow envelope, she screamed, "OH NO! JESUS NO! NOT BENJAMIN!!" Hand shaking she took the envelope, then handed it to me saying, "Jacob, you read it."

Though my eyes were swimming with tears, I opened it and read:

WESTERN UNION----JULY 10, 1943 (7:30 am)

Dear Mss. Svendahl,

The Navy Department regrets to inform you that your son, Seaman First Class Benjamin Svendahl is missing in action while in the service of his country. The department appreciates your great anxiety but details are not now available and delay in receipt thereof must of necessity be expected. To prevent possible aid to our enemies, please do not divulge the name his ship or station.

Signed,
Vice Admiral Ralph Armstrong, Deputy Chief of Navy Personnel

I expected hysterics but she didn't cry and she didn't say a word. Finally she said, "I knew it this morning when I got up. I just knew it!" She stopped for a moment, then added, "Andrew, we gotta have a memorial. Will you arrange it?"

"Sure, when?"

"After I the wedding."

"Momma, we can't have a wedding after something like this. We'll put it off. That's what Cousin Esther would want."

"No, everything is all arranged. We'll have a wedding. That's what Benjamin would want. That's what the community will expect."

"Let's talk to Aunt Helena before we make a decision."

"The decision is already made. There <u>will</u> be a wedding this Saturday. Also y'all need to finish combining." She wiped away one tear, then said, "Jacob, let me see that telegram."

She studied it for several minutes, and then said, "He ain't dead. It don't say he's dead, it just says he's missing."

"That's right Momma."

Momma continued to examine the message, then said, "Jacob, after the wedding, I want you to find me a little two bedroom house I can buy with the money from the farm. I'll need a bedroom for me and a for Benjamin when he comes home. And I want to move to the Retirement Home tomorrow. I'll stay there until you find me a house."

Momma's strength surprised both Uncle Andrew and me. Usually she bawls and squalls at every loss, great or small, but here, in the face of great personal tragedy, she didn't shed a tear. I think she must have been expecting it. When I called Aunt Helena, she went to the store, picked up Cousin Esther and they came to the house with Pastor Pierson close behind.

"Who called you?" she said when the pastor came in the door.

There was considerably more argument but Momma wouldn't budge. The wedding would occur as scheduled and the memorial would wait until the Navy confirmed Benjamin's death. And the next morning we continued the combining.

Chapter Forty-Four
Cousin Esther

After we finished at our farm we moved the tractor and the combine to Uncle Andrew's farm. Then we moved Momma to the Retirement Center. It was a sad day because of Brother Ben and leaving the farm but she said she did not want to be around newlyweds. Cousin Esther and I would live on the farm until the closing of the sale then we would move to town. I had already found a small house in Arendal that we could rent for fifteen dollars a month. We would furnish it with the furniture from the farmhouse Momma had given us as a wedding present. It wasn't a mansion but it would be our first home. I didn't think I would have any trouble getting work on someone's farm and Cousin Esther planned to continue working at the dry goods store.

Momma still hadn't budged from her plans so on Thursday we began harvesting Uncle Andrew's field of oats and finished about noon on Friday I started home shortly after lunch pulling the combine behind the tractor. It shouldn't take very long and I needed to get Cousin Esther a wedding present, a black nightgown we had seen at Monnig's in Waco. She had commented about it on one of our trips and thought it might be nice to wear on our wedding night and I agreed.

When I turned the last corner about a mile from our gate, I saw a bank of ominous black thunderclouds boiling over the western horizon that seemed to be rolling this way and I knew we would probably have a severe thunderstorm.

Watching it approach, I stopped the tractor and could hear the thunder rumbling in the distance and I could tell it was approaching rapidly over the Flat. Should I try to make it home before the rain or should I stop and hide under the combine? Watching the clouds, it only took a minute to decide so I jumped off the seat and scrambled to safety. And in another few minutes, it hit.

Lightning split the sky and thunder shook the earth and I saw one bolt hit the power line beside our barn. But in about thirty minutes, the rain stopped and in another thirty minutes a brilliant sun appeared so I cranked the tractor and headed home. When I got there I parked the tractor and the combine in the implement shed and turned off the motor satisfied there would be no more fieldwork for several days and tomorrow was our wedding day.

When I got to the house I heard the phone ringing, two longs and a short, a shrill sound that, for some reason, filled me with a premonition of disaster. I don't know why I felt that way; the phone had never affected me before when it rang. Usually I just ignored it unless I was expecting a call.

Thinking it might be Cousin Esther I picked up the earpiece and said 'Hello' expecting her to answer. She knew I had been working in the field all day at Uncle Andrew's and she was probably worried about me because of the storm. But it wasn't Cousin Esther; it was Aunt Helena who screamed, "Esther's dead!" My heart stopped, my head began to whirl, and I dropped the earpiece and sank to the floor.

In a moment, Aunt Helena repeated, "Jacob, did you hear me? I said Esther is dead! She was outside trying to finish mowing the yard before the rain started and a bolt of lightning struck and killed her instantly."

I couldn't answer because my chest hurt, my throat closed and I still couldn't breathe. "Jacob, Jacob, did you hear me?" she asked again and I still couldn't answer. I just sat there, motionless, with my head in a spin and the earpiece swinging against the wall. When Uncle Andrew arrived thirty minutes later, I was still sitting there numb and speechless.

I remember very little of the next few days. I couldn't eat, couldn't sleep. I went to the funeral home and asked to see her but they said I shouldn't, it wasn't a pretty sight.

I didn't go to the funeral because I couldn't stand to see the closed coffin knowing she was in it and I couldn't stand to hear the mournful sound of the church bell. When I heard the first faint bong, in the distance I immediately got in the car, drove to Waco, joined the Navy and asked to be inducted immediately. They sent me next door to the induction station, gave me a physical, pronounced me fit for duty and said I would be called within a week.

On the way home I stopped at a liquor store on the highway and bought the only thing available, a bottle of Wild Turkey. I drove to Cameron Park and for the first time in my entire life, I got drunk. But instead of passing out, I puked all over the car seat and the picnic table and thought I was going to die and wished that I could.

I couldn't drive until noon the next day. Famished, I stopped at a local cafe and ate a greasy hamburger and soggy French-fries, then promptly vomited all over the parking lot and finally managed to drive home. When I arrived, I fell in the bed and did not get up until noon the next day.

I went to the draft board and told them what I had done. Then I called the lawyer handling Poppa's estate and told him I had joined the Navy. If he had questions he should consult with Sister Selma. All that was left was to tell Momma. I guess I dreaded that the most of all.

But, she didn't even cry. She thought I had done the right thing and that I needed to get out of Arendal. "Don't worry about it, Benjamin can find me a house when he comes home."

Gosh, I hadn't even though about him since Cousin Esther's death. I guess it's okay for Momma to have her delusions and if Brother Benjamin didn't come home, Sister Selma can handle things so I felt free to leave Arendal and hopefully leave the pain behind.

Three days later I received orders to report for duty so I caught the bus to Hillsboro, boarded the Interurban to Dallas, found the induction station and, after being sworn in, boarded a train headed for boot camp in San Diego.

The train was packed with soldiers and sailors and I couldn't find a place to sit so I stood, swaying back and forth while hanging to the leather strap attached to the ceiling.

Bodies covered the floor between the seats, in the isles and in the space between cars. I finally found a seat when a soldier fell asleep and slid to the floor landing on top of two other passengers who didn't move. But, I couldn't sleep; thoughts of Cousin Esther filled my mind and fueled my anger.

How could He possibly allow such a tragic thing to befall her? She was pure and chaste. We had not committed carnal sin and had always obeyed all the Commandments.

The next morning, as the train pulled out of El Paso, I wondered if there really is a God. Maybe everything I had been taught as a child is untrue; a fairy tale, just like the troll stories.

Pastor Pierson visited the day before the funeral and explained that we cannot hope to understand God's plan. We must accept without question what He gives us and pray that our Faith will sustain us in this time of travail. I thanked him but already had my doubts.

Now, it seemed obvious to me that there is no God, and if there is, He is not the compassionate forgiving God of my childhood. Rather He is a spiteful unforgiving Master who has no compassion for His children and heartlessly allowed the catastrophic events of the past week. Exhausted, I slid off the bench, found a place on the floor and sank into a fitful sleep filled with dreams of Cousin Esther. And when we reached San Diego that night I became totally convinced there can be no God.

Chapter Forty-Five
Looking Back

July 1996

It is now fifty-three years since I left Arendal with a shattered dream and a broken heart. I struggled through WWII without any injuries. The enemy didn't sink my ship; in fact we never saw a Japanese vessel of any kind and were in dry-dock at Pearl Harbor undergoing routine repairs when the war ended.

As Momma had suspected, Brother Ben had not been killed. A Japanese torpedo sunk his ship near a remote island east of the Philippians. He floated for two days in a Kapok life jacket until a native fishing vessel picked him up. He ended up at the naval hospital in Hawaii, then at the naval hospital in San Diego for treatment of extensive burns.

The Navy never informed Momma that he had been found. The first letter she received was from a Navy Chaplin in San Diego who told her where he was and described his injuries and told her he was getting better. There was much rejoicing and many prayers of thanks in Arendal and his gold star in the church sanctuary was turned back to blue. He didn't make it home until a year after the war ended and Momma never got her house. Like me, he didn't want to stay in Arendal so he went back to college, obtained his degree in economics and went to work for the Agriculture Department and Momma stayed in the Retirement Center until she died.

After the war Momma wrote me several times but I never responded. My grief was still too great and I didn't wish to aggravate old wounds that, for some reason, refused to heal. After about a year, she stopped writing.

I used the GI Bill to enter SMU although I wasn't sure what I wanted to do with my life. I took various courses until I found something that interested me, Creative Writing. After graduation, with a degree in Journalism, I went to work for the Dallas Times Herald as a sports reporter and worked for them until they closed their doors and I retired. I did not wish to work for anyone else.

I guess I never recovered from Cousin Esther's death. For years, I had great difficulty sleeping and when I did, her familiar face and sweet smile and our unfulfilled passions filled my dreams. Finally the sleepless nights took their toll and in 1955 I had a complete emotional breakdown leading to a feeble suicide attempt. My grief was so great, I felt ending my life was the only answer.

The shrinks suggested EST but I declined. After a month in a mental institution, they released me and enrolled me in an outpatient program. Three month later, improved but far from cured, the psychiatrist suggested that I do a little traveling, maybe to Europe.

Instead of foreign trips, I spent several months in California unsuccessfully searching for Cousin Angel. At least it took my mind away from Cousin Esther except at night when she would appear in my dreams and I would awake with a start thinking she was by my side. When the money ran out, I returned home and went back to work, improved but still far from cured. I still couldn't accept God as an omnipotent compassionate Deity who somehow controlled our lives. So I abandoned all religious activities, beliefs, and affiliations and again submerged myself in my work.

Momma died of heart failure in 1962. Sister Selma called me from the hospital a week before she died to tell me Momma had asked, "When Is Jacob coming to see me?" But I couldn't, it would dredge up too many old memories. When she died I didn't go to the funeral for fear of seeing Cousin Esther's grave. Later, in a scathing letter, Sister Selma criticized my actions. The letter should have made me angry but it didn't because she was right.

In 1963, like everyone else in the country, I grieved over President Kennedy's death. Tears filled my eyes when I saw little John John standing on the sidewalk saluting his dead father's casket. I wept shamelessly as the Caisson bearing the flag draped coffin slowly wound its way to the National Cemetery to the mournful cadence of the muffled drums. My grief was so great I could not watch the actual burial or the lighting of the Eternal Flame.

I sympathized with the blacks in their struggle for equality and justice and participated in several of their marches. I attended the rally where Martin Luther King gave his famous 'I Have A Dream' speech and wept when he was assassinated. And I marveled at our ability to place a man on the moon and safely bring him back.

During the seventies, I worried about our involvement in Vietnam and understood the aims and hopes of the protestors but did not join in the protests. I felt sorry for the Veterans when they came home in shame to an angry country. I criticized the government for its arrogance and deceit. I voted for Nixon in '68 but not in '72 and rejoiced when he resigned.

For what I felt were legitimate reasons, I never married. I wasn't anti-social and I certainly wasn't gay. I had many female friends but when the relationship heated up, I backed away. Somehow I felt I was cursed and that my betrothed would die before we could be married and I could not handle the grief. So I remained single and childless.

Along the way, hoping to hang on to my sanity, I began to write; magazine articles at first, then novels. The first two were deemed unsuitable and were never published. The third was a murder mystery based on a story about a Highland Park woman who had been murdered, probably by her estranged husband. I became acquainted with the detective who investigated the case and after several interviews I began to write. A year later a publisher accepted the manuscript and after another year I had a new satisfying career.

A year after starting this story I quit writing. I still felt empty and unfilled and realized something was still missing from my life and writing about it had not solved my dilemma. I had no plans to have it published feeling no sane person could possibly be interested in the musings of an unsettled mind struggling with unresolved grief. Maybe I'll finish it later but I doubt it, it's just too personal and painful.

But what should I do with my time? Should I go to work for the Dallas Morning News? They had offered a job when the Times Herald closed but I turned it down. I guess I could flip pancakes at the Waffle Shop or play dominos at the city park with other retirees. Maybe I should rethink my marital status. An answer eluded me for weeks and I could feel the depression again taking over. What was wrong with me anyway? Why couldn't I rid myself of the grief? What had I done to earn this punishment?

After my first suicidal attempt, the psychiatrist suggested Cousin Esther's death wasn't the cause of my troubles. "Grief over a loss like that should only last a year or two, so there has to be something deeper, probably from your childhood."

That's a bunch of crap I thought at the time. That quack doesn't know what he's talking about. But, I guess, unconsciously, that's the main reason I started this manuscript. I was searching for answers, but I didn't find any. It only made things worse. And now they tell me I have cancer. I had ignored the cough for several months until I coughed up bright red blood. The bronchoscopy detected an Adeno-carcinoma and the CT Scan showed enlarged nodes in the mediastinum, in other words, inoperable.

I started smoking in 1943 while I was in Boot Camp when a little packet of five cigarettes appeared on my plate before every meal, put there by the Gray Ladies. At first I traded them for candy bars, but finally I acquired the habit, because everyone else smoked and it seemed the sociable thing to do.

"Oh, we can probably cure it," the oncologist, a young arrogant flippant egotist said. "A little chemo, a few cobalt treatments and you'll be as good as new."

What kind of a fool does he think I am? A good friend died last year of the same disease. At that time, I had researched it in the Internet and knew my chances of a cure were slim to nil. With my luck, I'm sure the treatments would fail and I would have subjected myself to weeks and weeks of torture only to die a miserable lingering death. What else can go wrong? What did I have to live for? NOTHING!

The night after receiving the report, I sat in my recliner taking stock of my situation. I knew my miserable life would soon end so why not end it now and avoid the pain and misery of months and months of useless treatments?

But, how should I do it? I didn't own a gun. I had a few sedatives on hand, but not enough to successfully end my misery. I had no idea where to insert the knife to commit seppuku. I'd probably botch it up and end up in the Psychiatric Hospital again with the same problems that put me there before. Also I was certain it would be quite painful and I hated pain and my kitchen knives were probably too dull to pierce the skin.

Maybe I should wait until morning, then climb the tallest building in Dallas and fling myself off the top. But that would never work. My terror of heights would prevent me from going near the edge.

I searched my bathroom but could find nothing lethal, not even a razor blade. I searched the pantry and kitchen but the only poison I could find was Cockroach bait, but I felt that would probably just make me vomit.

Maybe suicide isn't the answer.

I had been taught since childhood that suicide is a mortal sin that would condemn a person to an eternity in Hell. Many years ago I had convinced myself there is no God, therefore there can be no Hell. Now I wasn't so sure. Maybe I should just try to get some sleep and talk to a psychiatrist on Monday, but what could he offer?

About four the next morning, still unable to sleep, I turned on my television, cruised the channels, and came upon an early morning Evangelical program. Usually I just turned them off feeling that most television Evangelists aren't interested in saving souls. They're only interested in self-aggrandizement and accumulation of wealth. They usually have a Rolls Royce in front of their mansion, a condo in California, a yacht in Florida and a mistress in each, but something about this man seemed different.

He didn't come prancing across the flower filled stage of a multi-million dollar facility wearing a thousand dollar Armani suit to be greeted by hundreds of upturned shining faces seeking instant salvation. He sat on a plain unpainted bar stool on an empty stage clad in blue jeans and a khaki shirt and spoke in soft halting words that somehow riveted my attention.

I continued to listen as he recounted his trials and tribulations during his five years as a Vietnam prisoner of war. And when he described his anger and grief on learning his wife had died during his confinement, I felt he was talking directly to me. I listened, mesmerized, as he described how he had struggled through crippling depression and suicidal attempts until he returned to his roots and found God.

When he closed with a prayer and did not ask for donations, I knew the man was sincere. I still wasn't convinced there is a God but at least I abandoned the suicidal thoughts.

Chapter Forty-Six
Finis

November 2001

It's now time to finish the story while I still have the ability to sit and the strength to depress the keys on my laptop computer. Also, there is so little time left, I must somehow resolve my struggle with God.

Much to my surprise the treatments put the malignancy in remission but now it has returned with a vengeance. After the seizure, a brain scan revealed the presence of a tumor and the Neurologist suggested surgery using a Gamma knife. Further evaluation revealed recurrences in the lung and metastatic lesions in the liver. I knew surgery would do nothing for the other tumors so why subject myself to more pain and waste the government's money. Instead, they put me on anti-seizure medicine and transferred me to a Hospice facility.

I have made arrangements for the disposition of my body; I will no longer need it, but what about ME? What happens to all my memories, my ambitions, my skills, my hopes, and my dreams? Does God, if there is a God, have a gigantic hard-drive where all these memories are stored? Will the memories be returned to me when the world ends and life as we know it has disappeared? And what happens then? Is there really a Day of Judgment? What happens if I fail the test? Will He press the delete button and wipe away all traces of my existence. Is that what Hell is all about, total obliteration of everything related to *ME?*

Several months ago, before the seizures, I drove to Arendal and visited with Rev. Odie Olson, Digger Olson's son. seeking answers to my dilemma. His address at the high school class reunion had impressed me and I wondered if he could help. When I finished telling him my dilemma, his response was, "We do not have the ability or the knowledge to understand God's plan. However, I believe with all my heart that someday we will be reborn in His image and will stand before Him to be judged; it says so in the Bible. That's what Faith is about, absolute trust in the Almighty God and His Son, Jesus Christ who died for our sins that we may be saved." Unsatisfied, I scheduled another visit.

At the end of the second visit, he put his hand on my shoulder and said, "Jacob, you have wrapped yourself in a cloak of anger and self-pity. You have pulled up the religious roots so carefully planted and tended by your parents and now stand unprepared for and unprotected from the vicissitudes of life. To save your mortal soul you must shed that garment and stand before God, naked and unafraid, renounce your sins and accept him as your Savior. That's the only way you will solve you're dilemma." Perhaps what he said was true, but I wasn't ready to remove my cloak. It had become so much a part of me, like my skin, I felt I could not live without it.

That night, as I sat reviewing what he had said, slowly, like the light at daybreak, like the passing of a sudden summer storm, I began to realize Cousin Esther's death *wasn't* the cause of my problems. He's right. I have pulled up my religious roots, abandoned the blind Faith of my youth and fell prey to the raging storm of Esther's death. But IS there a God?

Many years ago I had accepted the premise that there must be a Supreme Being somewhere in the universe, or beyond, who controls the Earth and its inhabitants. I could never fully accept the evolutionary theory that we are the result of random chance over millions of years and that survival of the fittest controlled the path. Life and the creatures in it are just too complex to have been the result of accidental selection. There must be a force somewhere that guided us down the winding path to what we are today, a fantastically complex accumulation of atoms, molecules, genes, chromosomes, hopes and dreams. But does this Force control our daily lives?

It has worried me that my brother and both my sisters died of cancer. And now I have it in its most malignant form. Is this a genetic flaw? Does my family possess some familial trait that could be passed down from generation to generation?

Maybe this Force does control our daily lives and knew Esther and me should not marry for fear of passing on this genetic defect to our children. Perhaps knowing no one could prevent us from marrying, It chose the only available path. Maybe we were just not meant to marry. And could this Force be what Christians refer to as God?

Practically every society in the world, from the most primitive to the most advanced, practices some form of religion and worships some Deity. These religions go so far back their origins are often lost in antiquity. Does this mean religion is essential to our societies, essential to our development? Does this mean there must be a God, whatever we may call Him? Try as I might, I could not come up with an answer to any of my questions. During my final visit, Rev. Olson again replied, "We cannot fathom God's plan. Just trust in His judgment."

While the cancer was in remission, I spent over a year in California hunting for Cousin Angel, but I never found her. I also failed to find any record of the Arrensen Family and now suspected Malcolm Moore's story was untrue. I think he killed her and disposed of the body. Maybe I'll ask her when I see her in Heaven.

Is that what Faith is all about, the hope that we will someday gather in some wonderful place to be reunited with our love ones? I just know in my heart that someday soon I'll be reunited with Cousin Esther. To believe that, and I truly do, I must also believe in the Resurrection and believe there is a God.

Now I must quit, take another dose of morphine and get some rest.

Addendum
Arthur G. Nelson

February 2002

As Executor of J.K. Svendahl's Estate, especially after reading this manuscript, I feel compelled to finish the story. He died in December 2001, five days before his seventy-seventh birthday.

The last time I visited him in the Hospice facility in Dallas, I found him so short of breath he could hardly speak. He was able squeeze my hand and whisper, "The cloak has been removed." He reached to his bedside table, handed me his Will and this manuscript, then closed his eyes and fell asleep. I held his hand for a few moments, said a prayer for him and then left. That night he died.

In his Will he gave everything he owned to the Arendal Lutheran Church and requested that he be cremated and that his ashes be sprinkled on Esther Johansson's grave. He also requested that a monument be erected next to hers with the inscription:

Esther And Jacob
Together In Heaven
With God

Last week I drove to Dallas and retrieved his ashes. Yesterday, I sprinkled them on Esther's grave. Today I mailed the manuscript to his agent.

Author's Comments

This work is purely fictional and is strictly the product of my imagination. The names I have used are common to a Norwegian Community and refer to no specific person. Don't search your Texas map for Arendal; it exists only in my mind. The same is true for Buffalo Flat.

My main purpose in writing this document is to convey my impressions of life and times in a Norwegian Lutheran community during and after the depression and to explore Jacob's struggle with his Faith when Faith was central to our lives.

The information about trolls came from stories told by my grandfather who lived with us for ten years. Information about Norwegian foods came from memory and my mother's cookbook.

The historical facts are mostly from personal recollections and newspaper reviews. Information about Hobo Jungles came from the classrooms of my formative years. Information about electricity and radio came from personal recollections when radio was our main entertainment. Liturgy passages came from memory and the 'Common Prayer" book. Biblical passages, of course, came from the Holy Bible. I remembered the Norwegian Table Prayer from childhood, but a luncheon napkin given to me by a niece refreshed my memory.

I suspect my main motive in writing this book was to uncover my roots for my progeny. But whatever my reasons, I hope you enjoyed reading it as much as I enjoyed writing it.